Ann Granger has lived in cities all over the world, since for many years she worked for the Foreign Office and received postings to British embassies as far apart as Munich and Lusaka. She is married, with two sons, and she and her husband, who also worked for the Foreign Office, are now permanently based in Oxfordshire.

Ann Granger is the author of three hugely popular crime series: the Mitchell and Markby novels; the Fran Varady series and the Victorian mysteries featuring Scotland Yard's Inspector Benjamin Ross and lady's companion Lizzie Martin. MUD, MUCK AND DEAD THINGS heralds the start of a brand new Cotswold crime series.

Ann Granger's previous novels have all been highly praised:

'A good feel for understated humour, a nice ear for dialogue'
The Times

'This engrossing story looks like the start of a highly enjoyable series'
Scotsman

'An intriguing tale, with period detail interwoven in a satisfying way'
Oxford Times

'Enjoyable crime featuring credible characters in a recognisably real world'
Belfast Telegraph

ANN GRANGER

MUD, MUCK and DEAD THINGS

headline
review

First published in 2009 by
HEADLINE PUBLISHING GROUP

First published in paperback in 2009 by
HEADLINE PUBLISHING GROUP

1

Cataloguing in Publication Data is available from the British Library

ISBN 978 0 7553 2053 0 (B Format)
ISBN 978 0 7553 4924 1 (A Format)

Typeset in AGaramond by Palimpsest Book Production Limited,
Grangemouth, Stirlingshire

Printed and bound in Great Britain by
Clays Ltd, Elcograf S.p.A.

Headline's policy is to use papers that are natural, renewable and
recyclable products and made from wood grown in sustainable
forests. The logging and manufacturing processes are expected
to conform to the environmental regulations of the country of origin.

HEADLINE PUBLISHING GROUP
An Hachette UK Company
338 Euston Road
London NW1 3BH

www.headline.co.uk
www.hachette.co.uk

Readers of the Mitchell and Markby stories will perhaps recognise Jess Campbell, who appears in the last book of that series, *That Way Murder Lies*. With this new book, I have now launched Jess on her own career, also in the Cotswolds. I hope readers will enjoy her sleuthing as much as so many have kindly told me they did the earlier series.

Chapter 1

'Mud, Muck and dead things,' muttered Lucas Burton. 'I hate the country.'

The words burst from his lips although no one was there to hear him except the crows he'd scattered in a flurry of black wings from the road kill by the entrance. An unpleasant squelching noise beneath his foot had led him to look down and see thick slime rising inexorably round his once highly polished shoes. The crows flapped down to resume their feast. They hopped about jostling for position in an unruly scrum, chortling harshly. Their sharp eyes gleamed with joyful wickedness. It was hard to believe these ruffians of the bird world weren't laughing at him.

Lucas pulled his foot free. There was an ominous sucking noise and the imprint of his custom-made brogue began at once to fill with water. He hobbled to a nearby stack of rotting wooden pallets and attempted vainly to scrape the gunge off the soles. Whatever the components of this particular muck were – and Lucas didn't like to think too much about that – the stuff stuck like glue. With a sigh of resignation he gave up and put his feet back squarely into the mire. He was marooned now and, whether he carried on or turned back, he was going to get filthy.

The appointed rendezvous was a neglected, apparently abandoned, farmyard at the side of a B road where it crested a hill. The view from up here was spectacular, but Lucas was in no mood to appreciate it. On three sides stretched rolling greenery. On the fourth, going downhill, a copse of tangled native woodland provided a thick screen against whatever lay at the bottom of the steep slope.

'Miles from anywhere!' Lucas mumbled again, finding even the sound of his own voice obscurely comforting. But that was the whole point of being here, wasn't it? Why this desolate venue had been chosen as a meeting place. It was both remote yet accessible by road and there was little chance they'd be disturbed, except by wildlife. He'd thought the suggestion brilliant at the time. Now he wondered uneasily whether the person he was due to meet here had a quirky and unattractive sense of humour; in fact just like those damn crows out there.

It had at least been as easy to find as he'd been assured. 'It used to be called Cricket Farm,' his informant had told him. 'Don't ask me why. We don't have crickets in this country, do we? I suppose it might refer to the game.'

'You're certain the damn farm isn't in use?' Lucas had demanded. 'You know what it's like in these places. Not a soul to be seen, like the bloody *Marie Celeste*, and then, before you know it, you're surrounded by cows.'

'Relax, no one's farmed there for years. The buildings are all deserted and the house is derelict and boarded up. Trust me,' the speaker had concluded.

That was what Lucas didn't quite do. Their acquaintance had fairly recently been renewed after a gap of some years. Back then it had been productive; and Lucas had high hopes of it being so again. Up to this moment he'd had no doubts. But, standing in this forsaken spot, he was uneasily aware how little he really knew about the other. Generally he trusted his own judgement but basically he was a gambler; and any gambler knows that, sooner or later, you get it wrong.

He should have brought gumboots. No, correct that. He should have picked the place for their meeting himself. Lucas looked about him with increasing misgiving.

'The Merc will be out of sight of the road!' he'd been promised.

He wasn't at all sure about that. Abandoned barns and outbuildings lined two sides of the yard, sinking into ruin beneath the leaden sky. On the third side stood the former farmhouse, windows and door boarded up. The barricading was weathered to a pale grey. Years had passed, he decided, since the house had been a family home. Now only a pile of junk heaped in one corner of the yard suggested anyone ever came here. The heap attracted his attention to the extent that he spent a couple of minutes studying it. It appeared a curious mix of old washing machines, cookers and sundry metal items. All was rusting gently away and he wondered where on earth it had come from. Perhaps some fly-tipper had surreptitiously dumped a load of scrap before speeding off. Yet there was money in scrap, metal scrap, thought Lucas, pursing his lips. Not enough in this instance to be worth his bothering about, however.

There was a sizeable gap where the yard met the road. A pair of corroded posts leaned at drunken angles to the ground. But the heavy five-barred gate that had once hung between them had disappeared, probably, thought Lucas, gone for scrap like the stuff over there. Yet the posts still composed an entrance of sorts and led the eye of any observer towards his cherished Mercedes in its undignified surroundings. Better get it under cover. But where?

The obvious shelter was the open-fronted cowshed ahead of him, roofed with corrugated-iron sheets. They were coming loose, creaking and quivering in the stiff breeze sweeping over the hilltop. He squelched over to it and peered in. Little could be made out. It was dark and still smelled faintly of its former occupants, or rather, their bodily functions. He took a few cautious steps inside. No point in driving in and risking a tyre being ripped to pieces by some discarded piece of metal junk such has he'd seen outside.

His eyes were adjusting to the gloom. He could make out stalls. Ancient scraps of straw mouldered underfoot. Despite himself, Lucas became curious about the fate of this once-busy place, reduced to such misery. What was more, disused farming land, if it were for sale and if he could get planning permission, would be worth acquiring at the right price. Now, that was an idea worth serious consideration. Nowadays it'd be a project much more to his taste than a small heap of discarded scrap, something big and profitable. You could get six cottage-style homes around this yard alone, eight if you squeezed them up a bit. People, townies with a romantic yearning for country living, liked that sort of thing. They wouldn't think of buying a home that small in the city. But they'd shell out good money for a rabbit hutch with a reproduction inglenook fireplace and 'a view'.

He saw these desirable dwellings in his imagination: Cotswold stone (not the real thing, but a cheaper fake version), pointed wooden hoods above the front doors, and a residents' parking area. Individual garages added to building costs and took up valuable space. Reluctantly he thrust this vision of a shining investment from his mind. He hadn't come here to look for building land, but Lucas prided himself that he had an eye for an opportunity. Some of the best bits of business he'd ever done had begun like this: a chance encounter and a quick decision. See a gap and go for it.

He walked deeper into the shed. Behind him the silver-grey car was framed in the open square of light and, glancing back at it, it seemed to Lucas the Mercedes belonged to a different world from the one he now stood in: an 'out-there' world where things were unpleasant but normal. He'd entered an 'in-here' world where different rules applied and he wasn't sure what they were. He had a brief, irrational sensation of not being able to return, cut off the moment he took an irrevocable step under the rattling roof, its gaps letting in daylight and rain. In here it wasn't just a different place, but a different time belonging to a vanished culture. He'd stepped through the looking-glass. He felt a flicker of something he hadn't felt in years – panic – and turned back towards the daylight and the familiar universe he'd so rashly quitted.

He'd almost reached the doorway and (as his mind insisted on seeing it) safety, when he noticed the huddled form on the floor to his left. He must have passed within inches of it on entering but because his eyes hadn't then been accustomed to the darkness, he'd not made it out. He paused. The panic sensation was growing like a lump in the pit of his stomach. He felt nauseous.

'Don't be a bloody fool!' he admonished himself. 'Just a pile of rubbish like all the rest.'

But it drew him closer as if it exerted some magnetic force. He had to investigate if only, he told himself, to prove it was nothing important, to dispel the fears. It now lay at his feet. Yes, just an old jacket. *What's the matter with you, Lucas?* he admonished himself. *Seeing spooks?* This was just an old pink jacket: no more, no less. A woman's garment, probably, if the colour was anything to go by. For a moment his fears faded and then returned. It wasn't so very old actually, and come to think of it, not very dirty. Not nearly tattered and dirty enough to have been chucked away like this. It didn't belong here. A piece of torn sacking lying right nearby did very much belong in this setting. But why had quite an expensive-looking jacket been tossed down alongside it?

His shoes were now so muddy he no longer worried about dirtying them further. He put out a foot and prodded the coat. There was something solid beneath it which – another prod – continued beneath the sacking. Someone had wanted to conceal something: a large object that had taken both sacking and jacket to do the job.

Mud, Muck and Dead Things

Lucas flinched and took a step back. But he couldn't turn and run, much as he wanted to. A powerful urge to investigate the shrouded heap conflicted with an almost equal reluctance to touch it. The whole idea of physical contact, putting his naked palm against it, repelled him. He looked round and saw an old pitchfork leaning against one stall. Lucas retrieved it and stretched it out to hook the sacking with the bent tines and gingerly lift it free of what lay beneath.

A pervasive sweet odour was released and flooded over him, eliminating the lingering odour of cattle. A pair of legs in denim jeans, feet in trainers, sprawled on the dirt at his feet.

'No, no, no . . .' whispered Lucas. 'That's not what it is. It can't be.' His hand was shaking. 'Go on, you wimp!' he ordered himself. He lunged at the jacket in turn, and tossed it aside to reveal the rest of the thing on the ground. A roaring noise filled his ears. The walls of the cowshed receded and then rushed in. He had experienced the mud and the muck and now he had found the dead thing.

Not a fox like that thing torn to shreds in the road outside, but a human being, staring up with clouded bloodshot gaze that seemed to accuse him. A girl, a young girl. Rictus had drawn back her jaw to show even white teeth. Her bluish tongue protruded slightly and her lower lip was bloody as if she'd bitten it badly.

Lucas retched and hurled aside the pitchfork. He staggered away and blundered out of the cowshed across to the Mercedes. He scrambled inside heedless of the filth his shoes

7

spread over the carpet, his fingers scrabbling at the key swinging in the ignition. The engine sprang into life. He backed the car across the yard and then, spinning the wheel, shot forward and out through the entrance into the road.

Luckily no other vehicle was coming from either direction or he'd have slammed right into it. If by some miracle he'd avoided a collision the driver would still have seen him. It was important no one did. Lucas drove away furiously, not stopping until he reached the bottom of the hill, beyond the copse, where the entrance to a field allowed him to pull off the road. He fumbled for his mobile phone.

Thank heavens the call was answered.

'Listen!' he croaked. 'Don't go! I mean, don't go to that place, Cricket Farm, confound it! Where are you now? Then turn round and go back home. Don't argue! I'll explain later. Just do it, all right?'

He was sweating and fought for control of the bile that bubbled up into his throat. In his haste to get away from that place before anyone saw him, he must have left any number of traces behind: the tyre marks of the Mercedes; his footprints; his fingerprints on the pitchfork handle. Well, it didn't matter, did it? The chances were it would tip down with rain again before the day was out. They'd had enough lately to float Noah's Ark and the forecast had promised more. It would wash away the tyre marks and footprints. The fingerprints? Oh, come on, they would be smudged, incomplete. They might not even check the handle. Who? The police, of course.

Why should the police go to Cricket Farm? No one went there. Except himself, worse luck. No one would find the— no one would find *it* for weeks, months. The most important thing was that no one should ever know that *he* had been there. Only the two of them had known of their arrangement. He wouldn't talk and the other daren't.

A rattle and engine growl, becoming swiftly louder, announced that another vehicle was approaching at a fair lick. Lucas cursed aloud. It was coming down the hill past Cricket Farm and straight towards him. He had no time to pull out and drive off. He did the only thing he could. He flung himself down and hoped whoever drove by would assume the car was empty.

The vehicle rattled past. Lucas, emerging cautiously to peer over the dashboard, just glimpsed the rear of a horsebox. It was the sort designed for a single horse, with a ramp at the back of the trailer that pulled up to make a half-door, and usually towed by a Land Rover or similar; just what you'd expect around here. The trailer disappearing round the bend appeared to be tenantless, which explained why the driver had put his foot down. Some country type about his business and not interested in Lucas.

He'd got himself under control and began to plan his actions. First, get out of here. But was there anything he ought to do first? And what about afterwards?

A good citizen, of course, would phone the police and report the grisly find. But good citizens didn't have bad consciences; and Lucas? Well, Lucas's conscience had always been an obliging entity. It rarely objected to anything. What he had instead was a strong sense of self preservation which kicked in now with a vengeance. He'd made a mistake in coming here; he'd made a mistake in getting involved in the whole stupid affair. To contact the authorities would be another mistake, compounding all the others. He couldn't afford to make explanations. The police always promised to be discreet when they wanted to encourage faint-hearted witnesses. But there was never anything discreet about a couple of coppers, in uniform or not, trudging up to your front door – or office – or wherever they chose to appear. Being a pillar of society, inspiring confidence in others, was a big part of Lucas's stock in trade. Having some idiot telling everyone within earshot in the bar at the golf club or down the local pub that the police had been to see Lucas Burton ('honest truth, saw them myself as they were leaving'), wouldn't be forgotten in a long time. That was the thing about coppers: even if they were in plain clothes, it was always obvious to anyone with half an eye who they were. Even if he managed to spin them some convincing yarn, fob them off, his reputation would remain that little bit tarnished.

Well, then, how about an anonymous call? Not on his mobile. Far too risky, the call would eventually be logged and traced to the area, perhaps even to this phone. There were no public call boxes around here; the nearest would be in the next pub and someone would notice him, a stranger, and might even overhear. Scrub anonymous call. So, let someone else find it, or preferably not find it.

He got out of the car and walked slowly round it. It was plentifully splashed with mud and if someone saw him arriving home like that, they'd notice. There was a puddle of water nearby. He squeezed out his handkerchief in it and attempted to wipe off the mire but only succeeded in making it worse. He would have to hope no one saw him arrive back. He made a similar ineffectual attempt to clean up his shoes.

Eventually he gave this up and glanced at his wristwatch. He'd wasted almost twenty minutes! Was it possible? Someone else could have driven past and seen him making a fool of himself trying to wash a car with a pocket handkerchief. Spots of rain began to land on the windscreen and struck him in the face. Now it was going to tip down again. He was getting out of here, going home. He'd wash down the Merc, remove all traces of that wretched place, later.

He sped away reflecting that the unwelcome adventure had confirmed his feelings about the countryside. It always had a nasty surprise in store for you. If not cows it was dead bodies.

Chapter 2

The Land Rover and its attached empty trailer rattled past the sign that read *Berryhill Stables, Livery and Equestrian Centre. Prop. P. Gower.* It turned left immediately and carried on down the track until it drew up in the middle of the yard.

The loose boxes stood in facing parallel lines. The water trough was an old enamelled bathtub. Penny (aka P. Gower) herself and any available helpers laboured to keep the place tidy but it would be nice, she thought wistfully, if it looked just a little bit smarter. People would pay more to keep their animals in a 'proper' stable yard with brick buildings and a cinder all-weather exercise circuit and . . . oh, well. Penny sighed. Dreams were nice but cost money. You had to invest to make a profit, people kept telling her. But you can't invest what you haven't got. And she was pleased with what she had got. The yard might not be swanky but, when she'd bought it, it had been derelict. She'd worked wonders here. Sadly, few visitors realised it.

One or two inquisitive heads appeared over the half-doors at the sound of Penny's arrival, ears pricked. But Solo, who once would have been the first to identify the familiar engine noise and pop out his head to whinny a greeting, didn't appear.

She had visitors now. There were two cars, one parked near the 'office' and the other down by the gate into the paddock. The nearer one, a dark blue Passat, she recognised as belonging to Andrew Ferris. She hoped he hadn't been waiting for too long. The mud-splattered elderly Jaguar down by the paddock was also familiar and belonged to Selina Foscott. All she needed, Ma Foscott and child.

She climbed down. She could see Andrew, down there leaning on the paddock fence. On the further side she (with his help) had set up some low jumps. Andrew was watching, as if mesmerised, a small child atop a chestnut pony with white socks and laid-back ears. The pair approached a set of red and white parallel poles with the élan of a cavalry charge. Then, at the last moment, the chestnut swerved to one side and the rider carried straight on, to land with a thud Penny fancied she could hear, at the foot of the jump. The rider rolled over and sat up. The pony cantered off a short way and stopped, snorting like a dragon. A wiry figure in a Barbour descended on it and grasped the bridle in a way that meant no nonsense. The pony jerked up its head and stamped its front feet but didn't offer serious resistance.

'Charlie!' yelled the wiry figure. 'Don't just sit there! Get aboard!'

'Sorry, Andrew,' said Penny, joining him at the fence. 'I had to pick up the trailer from Eli Smith. He promised to fix the damage made when Solo tried to kick his way out.'

'And has he fixed it?'

'Oh, yes, Eli can fix almost anything if he wants to. Luckily he offered to do it or it would have cost me a fortune. He wouldn't accept a penny. I hope Charlie's all right.'

'I should think so,' said Andrew, glancing at the child with a dispassionate eye. 'They seem to bounce, don't they, kids?'

'With luck. That one has had plenty of practice falling off.' *'Come on, Charlie, look lively!'*

The small figure at the foot of the pole fence rose to its feet and plodded in a dispirited way towards the pony.

'It's a girl!' said Andrew, surprised. 'Isn't it?'

'Yes. Hadn't you realised?'

'They all look sort of the same in that gear, don't they? Now I can see it's got long hair. She must have had it tucked up under her hat and it's got loose. Why is she called Charlie?'

'Charlotte. But I think her mother wanted a boy. That's her mum, Selina Foscott, issuing the orders.'

'I thought that looked like old Selina. She's what you'd call a virago, isn't she? She doesn't strike me as very maternal, more like a drill sergeant. Charlotte, eh? Char*lotte* Fosc*ott*, not an altogether ideal combination of names.'

'First-class pain in the bum, that's Selina. Come into the office.'

As they walked back towards the loose boxes, Andrew said, 'Lindsey rode out about twenty minutes ago with a learner. Thin bloke with sticking-out knees.'

'Mr Pritchard. He's taken up riding to expand his personal horizons. Those are his words. He'd be better off taking up watercolour painting if you ask me. But he's keen and he pays.'

They'd reached her 'office' which was in reality the end loose box converted. A glance showed it also doubled as tack room. A row of saddles perched on pegs. Beneath hung the bridles. To show it was also the office, it contained a small table (referred to grandly as a 'desk') and a couple of old-fashioned wooden chairs. Shelves had been fixed up on the wall facing the saddles and held, along with various boxes of papers and some dented tins, a couple of hard riding hats. Because there were no windows, both halves of the door, come rain or shine, had to be hooked back to admit light when the office was in use. The glimpse of the yard also gave an illusion of space but in reality it was horribly cramped. Next door, on the other side of the wooden partition, Solo could be heard snuffling and stamping, occasionally bumping against the wall.

Andrew looked at it all and sighed.

'It's OK, Andy. I don't keep anything important or sensitive here, no accounts or tax records! That's all back at my place. There's just the appointments book for the riding lessons and odds and ends.' As she spoke, she took out her mobile phone and laid it neatly on the table alongside the dog-eared appointments book and a piece of paper on which was scribbled, 'Mick Mackenzie stopped by and left this'.

'This' was a white envelope.

'His bill,' said Penny. 'I don't have to open it to know what it is, but I do have to pay it. Mick's very good but he can't afford clients who don't pay their vet's bills.'

'Is it likely to be a big bill?' He looked concerned.

'Any bill is a big bill for me! The livery clients pay the vet's bills for their own animals, of course. But my trusty mounts have both had problems recently.' She glanced at Andrew. 'That's what you've come to talk to me about, isn't it, my dodgy financial situation? I couldn't trouble you to put the kettle on, could I? You're nearer.'

'Putting on the kettle' involved lighting a bottled-gas burner. Andrew obliged.

'This isn't safe in here, you know, all this wood – and animals in attached accommodation.' He indicated the gas bottle. 'It's meant for a patio.'

'Lindsey or I only light it when we take a tea break or have a visitor like you. It isn't going to blow up on its own,' Penny told him defensively.

'It would blow up if there were a fire and it engulfed this office of yours. Take the thing home with you at the end of the day, at least.'

'I wish you wouldn't talk about disasters, Andy. I've got enough of one with bankruptcy looming. And I can't lug a gas bottle about with me everywhere I go.'

'It's not as bad as that,' he said, 'well, not yet. But you've got to increase your income, Penny. Quite seriously, it's a matter of urgency.'

'I haven't got any free loose boxes. I can't take on any more livery clients. I could give up this office, turn it back into stabling, but I'd have nowhere to talk to clients when they come and want to discuss things, and Lindsey and I wouldn't have anywhere to keep all the gubbins. As it is I may have to buy a new riding pony soon, for the learners, if I hear of a suitable one that isn't out of my pocket. Solo's getting crotchety with age. He's never taken against the trailer before but the other day he went berserk. The vet says he might have impaired sight in one eye and if he's right, it's the end of Solo's usefulness for the riding lessons. He'd be a positive danger to a learner, in fact to anyone. The possibility is terrifying. I couldn't let him off the premises. Even here, if it is his eyesight, he'd be likely to kick out or shy unexpectedly. Handling him would become dangerous and my insurance wouldn't cover me if there were an accident as a result. It probably doesn't already, now Mick Mackenzie's drawn my attention to the matter.'

Penny made a gesture of resignation. 'Let's face it. The poor beast is useless, a liability.' She reached out and touched the unopened white envelope. 'Perhaps that's what this contains, not the bill. Just a final reckoning for Solo.'

'So he'd be for the bullet in the head?'

'I hate the thought. He could go into retirement in the paddock for a bit but in the end . . . a blind horse is a blind horse. Meantime, well, he's costing me money and not earning me any.' Penny twisted a length of brown hair round her forefinger and looked miserable.

'The riding lessons do pay, don't they? Can't you extend that side of things? Even without Solo?'

'Without poor Solo, no. Anyway, there's only Lindsey and me here to do everything. If one of us takes a pupil out, that leaves just one to deal with all the rest. Neither of us takes a holiday, not a proper one. Lindsey did take a fortnight at

Easter because her husband insisted, and I was pretty pushed to cope, I can tell you.'

'I came over and helped,' he said, hurt.

'Oh, sorry, I didn't mean that. I know you did and very grateful I was. I am grateful, Andrew, for everything, for your doing the accounts cut-price and volunteering to come over and shovel horseshit and build fences and all the rest of it. You're the best friend I've got.'

He gave her a meaningful look.

'Don't, Andy. You're married, remember?'

'Not so you'd notice. Karen's been in Portugal for the past week, floating down the Douro. Doesn't come back until the week after next and then it's only a few days before she's off again, Middle Europe, I fancy.'

'She works hard, Andrew. It can't be any fun shepherding tour groups around.'

'I know she works damn hard. I know she enjoys it. I wouldn't ask her to give it up. That would be selfish and pointless. But both she and I know that, as a marriage, we're pretty well washed up. It's only a matter of time before one of us calls it quits. I'm waiting for her to say it. She's waiting for me.'

'I'm not an agony aunt, Andrew,' Penny said firmly. 'Nor, even if you were free, would we make a success of it as a twosome: I might not be playing nanny to elderly well-heeled cruise-goers sailing up and down European rivers, but I spend all my time here.'

'My dear old mum,' said Andrew wistfully, 'used to read paperback romances in which couples got married for love.'

'I don't live in a paperback romance and neither do you.'
He pulled a face, rolling his eyes. 'Cruel, cruel world . . .'

'Yep, that's it.'

A shadow fell across the door and they both looked up.

'Raining again,' Selina Foscott informed them briefly.
'We've got Sultan under cover and Charlie's unsaddling. Oh,
here she is.' Charlie appeared weighed down with the saddle,
the bridle reins trailing in the dirt behind her. 'Right, chuck
it down in there,' ordered her mother. 'OK?'

This last query was addressed to Penny and before she could
reply firmly that no, it wasn't all right, Selina was already in
retreat.

'Sorry, we've got to dash. Look lively, Charlie, hop in the
car. Might see you tomorrow, unless it tips it down. If so, see
you some time next weekend.'

She vanished. 'See what I mean?' hissed Penny. 'Shove
Sultan under cover, unsaddle and dump everything in the tack
room . . . but no mention of rubbing down the animal or
washing the mud off his legs, cleaning out his hooves, anything
like that. No cleaning up that tack.' She pointed to the jumble
of leather on the floor. 'That's been left for me or for Lindsey
to do.'

'That's what she pays her livery fees for, or so she'd reckon.'

'She reckons wrongly. That is *not* what she pays her livery
fees for! She pays for the animal to be stabled here, fed, mucked
out and groomed, fair enough. We exercise Sultan if Charlie
can't get over here during school term to do it. All that is regular
maintenance and labour-intensive, not to say time-consuming.

It does not cover the pair of them coming over here on a dirty day like today, riding the animal round and round the field until it's thoroughly muddied up and sweating and then pushing off home! What's the difference between that –' she jabbed a finger towards the saddle at their feet – 'and dropping your dirty washing on the bedroom floor and waiting for someone else to pick it up and launder it? Anyway, taking care of an animal is part of having one. I'm not her ruddy employee!'

'Tell her.'

'You can't tell Selina anything.'

'You can tell her to take her pony and wretched child elsewhere.'

Penny sighed. 'She's determined to make a showjumper of Charlie – not that either Charlie or Sultan have any aptitude – and that means a succession of mounts for Charlie, all stabled here for years to come.'

'Increase the fees.'

'Daren't. I ask the most I can. You may not have noticed, but this isn't a de luxe establishment.'

'I love you.'

'See what I mean? I don't need more complications, Andy! No, you don't *love* me. You admire me for slogging away here against all the odds, when what that really means is that I need my head seeing to. The only other reason I keep going – apart from your support and Lindsey's devotion – is that Eli Smith rents me the paddock cheap and doesn't mind if I spill over and graze my horses in the next-door field that technically I don't rent. Not that he uses it for anything else.'

Andrew frowned again. 'Funny old stick, Eli, touchy, too.'

'Yes, he is, but reliable. Even he may get an offer for the land one day, so good he can't turn it down. Then, well, that will be that. I couldn't afford to buy it.'

The kettle had boiled and was filling the little room with steam. Andrew made the tea and handed a chipped mug to Penny.

'Ta,' she said as she accepted it. 'Funny thing, now that we're talking of Eli . . .' Penny stopped.

'What's that, then, the funny thing? Other than Eli himself.'

Penny sipped the tea, muttered, 'Ow!' and put down the mug on top of Mackenzie's veterinary bill. 'I drove past that yard of his as I was coming home here. You know, the place just up the hill – used to be the farmhouse and buildings. Eli stores all his merchandise there.'

'Is that what it is, all that junk?'

'He calls it that.'

'I call it accumulated rubbish. Why doesn't Eli live up there? At the farm?'

'Because the house is haunted, ask anyone round here, the old-timers, I mean. It was the scene of a horrible crime.' She paused.

'Oh, right, yes, I've been told about that. Eli's exploiting it, shrewd old bugger that he is. A rumour of a ghost is a pretty good way of keeping Nosy Parkers from sniffing round the place.'

'I don't know if the story originates with Eli, or why he should invent it if it does, but he won't live there or farm there, so other people think there must be *something* about the place. I'm certainly not saying Eli *believes* in spectral apparitions floating around in the middle of the night. All the same, his memory must hark back to a period of his life he'd want to forget. In that sense perhaps *he's* haunted, even if the house isn't, if you see what I mean?'

'Perhaps that's why some people see ghosts and others don't,' Andrew offered. 'The ghosts come from within, not from outside ourselves.'

There was an awkward pause. 'Look,' said Penny briskly, 'do you want to know what the funny thing is or not? I'd got past the yard and just a short way on there's an entrance to a field. A car had pulled off the road and parked in it, a pretty super-duper sort of car, a silver-grey Merc. Doesn't belong to anyone round here, I'm sure.'

'Driver nipped behind the wall for a call of nature.'

'Oh, no, that's the really funny thing. He was in the car, trying to hide, crouched down along the front seat by the dashboard. But I could see him quite clearly.'

'Aha! A mystery. I'll drive back that way and see if he's still there.'

'Doubt it.'

'If he drove this way, we'd have seen him.'

'No, we wouldn't. We were both hanging over the fence watching Sultan and Charlie. Talking of which, I'd better go and see to poor Sultan.'

Andrew said thoughtfully, 'Have you got a phone number for Eli?'

'Got his mobile number, why?'

'I'll give him a call and suggest he checks out his yard. I mean, as far as we know everything he keeps there is rubbish. But he's a canny old bird. He might have something valuable there, something the haunted-house yarn is supposed to protect from snoopers. Well, if there's been a stranger hanging around, a stranger who didn't want you to see him, Eli would want to know about it.'

Penny reached up on to the shelf and took down a grubby exercise book. 'Here you are, my useful phone number list. Eli's mobile is in there. Thanks again for coming over, Andy, and making the tea. But I really have to go and fix up Sultan.'

He was leafing through her address book as she left.

Chapter 3

'Why worry about tyre tracks?' demanded Sergeant Phil Morton rhetorically. 'Why not just drive all over the shop and destroy the lot?'

He drew in at the tail of a queue of vehicles that had parked on the roadside. Both of them could see that, ahead of the queue, other vehicles had pulled off the hard surface on to the grass verge before the entrance to the farmyard. Phil Morton was right to spot the offence and be annoyed. Other tracks would potentially have been obliterated. The two of them got out and Morton turned up his collar. Rain had been forecast – again – and had begun to fall in the form of a thin persistent drizzle. A lousy summer was creeping into a dismal autumn.

'Dave Nugent had the right idea in taking off for the Algarve with his golf clubs and a bottle of sunscreen,' muttered Morton, finding a new source of grievance.

'Dr Palmer is here,' said Jess as they passed a familiar Toyota. Phil snorted. 'Bet he's pleased, and all!'

'We're none of us pleased, Phil. Give it a rest.'

Morton was an inveterate grumbler. In the short time they'd worked together Jess Campbell had got used to it and normally she didn't mind too much. But it was Friday afternoon and she was tired. She'd been looking forward to the weekend.

They drew level with the two vehicles that had pulled on to the soft earth. One, Jess was dismayed to observe, was a police patrol car. The other was a battered lorry laden with junked household appliances, dented cookers, scratched washing machines and what looked like a commercial coffee maker. As they appeared alongside, the door of the cab opened and a squat figure in a disreputable sweater and grimy jeans climbed down and confronted them.

'Who are you?' he growled.

'Inspector Campbell,' said Jess. She indicated Phil. 'Sergeant Morton.'

Phil obligingly took out his ID and held it up.

Small dark eyes studied it carefully before swivelling back to Jess and subjecting her to the same comprehensive inspection before the answer came in a hoarse rumble from somewhere inside the tatty sweater. 'I'm Eli Smith and this here . . .' Mr Smith waved a sunburned hand, 'this here is my yard, my land, as it happens.'

'You're the gentleman who reported finding the body?'

'Yes,' said Smith. He pursed his mouth. 'A woman, then?'

'I understand the body is female,' retorted Jess, deliberately misunderstanding him.

There was a brief gleam of appreciation in the dark eyes. Eli Smith wasn't a fool. But, thought Jess, probably liked to act one.

'It is, as far as I could tell. I didn't hang about in there.

I called you lot. It is,' added Eli loftily, '*your* business. Mine is scrap.'

'So I see.' She looked up at the collection on the lorry. 'Where do you get it all?'

'It's legal!' said Smith immediately. 'I got receipts.'

'So you don't farm here, Mr Smith?' confirmed Morton wearily.

A flicker of contempt in the dark eyes. 'No, I don't. There's no money in farming no more. I'm holding on to my land until such time as.'

'As what?'

'Ah . . .' said Mr Smith, laying a callused finger alongside his nose. 'That's it, ain't it?'

Jess sighed. 'Tell us how you came to find the body, Mr Smith.'

Eli's manner changed. Beneath the teak hue of his skin, a dull red flooded across his features. 'On my property! That's trespass.'

'If you don't farm, what do you use the place for?'

'I store my merchandise here,' returned Mr Smith with dignity. 'Don't I?' he added.

'If you say you do. And do you live here, even though you don't farm the land?'

This earned her another look of disgust. 'No, I don't, and you wouldn't ask a tomfool question like that if you went and took a look at the house. It's all boarded up and empty and the roof is in a real bad state. Of course,' continued Eli twisting his blunt features into a pathetic expression, 'a poor old chap like me can't be expected to pay for all the repairs.'

'So why not sell the farm, then?' Phil asked. He didn't like standing around in the rain and had been shifting from foot to foot.

'I told you,' said Eli sulkily to him, 'I'm waiting on things, until such time, like I said.'

'*Barmy*,' murmured Phil Morton.

Jess had moved off a few paces to get a better look at the yard from the road and judge what a passer-by might or might not be able to see. She zipped her rainproof jacket up to her neck, stuck her hands in the pockets and wished she could pull up the hood against the persistent rain. Water was beginning to plaster her short-cropped auburn hair to her skull. But there was something undignified about a hood fitting closely over her head, which would make her look like a rambler who'd strayed into the scene out of curiosity. Moreover, people here needed to see who she was. It was like the king raising his helmet on the battlefield so that the troops could be reassured someone senior was in charge.

Give over! she thought. You're no Henry the Fifth; you're just an overworked police officer and this is Friday, for pity's sake. Why did these things always happen on a public holiday or at a weekend?

It's your job, by your choice, replied another little voice in her head. You gave up a normal life when you joined the force. She had a suspicion the voice belonged to her mother. Neither of her parents had understood her wish to join the police. They'd accepted it reluctantly, but her mother still resented what she bluntly called 'the waste'. Waste of what?

Jess had once unwisely asked her. 'Of the life you could have had!' had been the unkind reply. Jess hadn't asked again.

Her father, having worn a military uniform for most of his working life, had more respect for what she did, even though he also would have wished her to have chosen something else. 'I can't say I approve,' he'd told her when informed of her decision. 'It's not what I'd have liked for you. But if it's what you want, then fair enough. It's a worthwhile career. But you'll find it tough going.'

She wondered now briefly if he had thought she'd find it too tough, and would cry off after a while. She hadn't and he'd never commented.

Further back by the lorry Phil had again taken up the questioning of the witness. She could see them both from the corner of her eye and the body language spoke volumes. Phil was getting tetchy. As for the witness . . . he was sounding belligerent and stood there with his solid round head sunk between his hefty shoulders, glowering at Phil. It was a picture of defiance but it was a smokescreen. It was designed to hide something. Just for a moment she wondered if it was fear.

'So, Mr Smith, you came out here today to leave that load on your truck here in your yard. I understand that's what you told us when you phoned in!' boomed Morton much too heartily.

'Then you know the answer. How many more times have I gotta say it?'

'A chance visit, then? I mean, you don't make a regular call here?'

'As and when . . .' Eli looked shifty.

'But the only reason you came here today was to unload your truck? Did anyone expect you?'

'Who would that be, then? There's no one here.'

'But you didn't drive into your yard. You parked here, outside. That meant you would have to carry everything on that truck through the gate.' Phil indicated the loaded truck with its collection of domestic appliances. 'A weight like that and all on your own? You'd have a job on! Why not drive right in? Then you could climb up and just shove the things off the back. Wouldn't that make more sense?'

There was something terrier-like about Phil Morton. He wouldn't let go of any question until he thought he'd got a satisfactory answer. He was compact in build and only just the required height for a police officer. He was conscious of it. Jess liked Phil and respected his ability, but he wasn't always the easiest person to work with. Bull-baiting, she thought suddenly, that was what the two of them brought to mind, some picture in a history book of a long-vanished cruel sport. The larger powerful animal and the smaller but determined dogs snapping at it. It often worked as a technique with awkward and unsophisticated witnesses. But Jess wasn't sure it would succeed with Mr Smith.

'Thought I'd take a look round first,' said Eli defensively.

'That's what you usually do? Take a look round first?'

'Not necessarily but lately, well, there are all sorts of people around these days, you never know.'

'Anyone in particular?'

'Just general,' said Eli, now looking decidedly furtive. He rallied. 'Just as well I did, isn't it? Because there's a dead woman in my cowshed.' He scowled. 'This is nothing to do with me! I didn't ask to find her. She's got no right to be there and I hope, when you go, you take her with you. You ain't going to leave her lying there?'

'It's been a shock for you, Mr Smith,' called Jess, turning towards them and treating him to a sympathetic smile, designed to calm nervous witnesses. And the old boy was nervous. But what about? There was something, perhaps a lot, he wasn't telling them. 'What you need is a nice hot cup of tea as soon as you get home,' she suggested.

Phil gave her a look of startled disapproval.

'Shock?' Eli's bright dark gaze leapt from Morton to her. 'Oh, shock . . . it's that, all right. I've been through enough trouble. I don't need any more and not *here*. She's got no business here, no business at all! Someone's done it deliberate, dumped her, that's what I reckon. Some bugger done it on purpose for me to find, and *it's not right!*'

He was definitely getting agitated. Jess decided to let him off the hook for the time being. She signalled as much to Morton. 'Thank you for now, Mr Smith. I'll go and take a look. Perhaps you'd like to make a statement to the sergeant and give him your details?'

Eli eyed Phil cautiously. 'Will I have to sign it?'

'Eventually, sir, when it's printed out. You can come in and do that, or we could call round to see you,' said Morton.

'Oh,' said Eli, and looked shifty again.

'Some problem, sir?'

Eli sniffed. 'I'm not one for writing. OK if I just make my mark?'

White-suited figures picked their way around the sea of mud that had been a farmyard and could be seen moving inside the open-fronted cattle shed on the far side. A uniformed man was guarding the blue and white plastic tape tied between the gateless gateposts. As Jess approached, having donned protective clothing, the constable lifted the flimsy barrier so that she could duck underneath.

'What's your name?' she asked him.

'Wickham, ma'am.'

'Do you know who took the original report?'

'Someone phoned in to the station, ma'am. The station radioed Jeff Murray and me, out in the patrol car. So we came over here and found that old chap . . .'

Wickham indicated Eli Smith who was now indulging in some tirade and waving his arms about. Phil, holding his notebook in one hand, was making placatory gestures with the other, valiantly following her lead in trying to calm down the witness, but not having much luck. He looked as if he was swatting flies.

Smith was probably on again about it being on his property, thought Jess. This was the one thing that really seemed to shock the old boy: not the finding of a corpse, the sight of death, but finding it *here* in his cowshed. That's what had frightened him.

'And you both, you and Murray, went into the barn, cowshed, whatever it is?'

'Well, yes, ma'am. I mean, we didn't really believe him. We thought perhaps he'd been at the home-made cider.'

'Did he come with you?'

Wickham shook his head. 'Wouldn't. He wouldn't budge from the road here. He said he'd seen it once and didn't want to see it again. We thought that if a body was there, you wouldn't want too many people tramping round the place, so just Murray and I went.'

The constable shifted from foot to foot and looked for the moment as if he was going to throw up. 'It's horrible,' he said.

'Never seen a murder victim before?' The constable was very young. Jess guessed this must be his first time. There was always a first murder victim for them all. Violence and man's cruelty to man, nothing could prepare you for the shock of seeing it.

'No, ma'am.' He looked shame-faced. He didn't like having to admit it, especially to a woman. She did him the favour of not looking sympathetic. In any case, she had a bone to pick with him and his partner.

'Next time you're called to a suspicious death, don't park your car up on the soft verge. Leave it on the road. Now we've got your tyre tracks in with all the others.'

The youngster looked stricken. 'Yes, ma'am, sorry.' Hurriedly he added, 'But I did spot the paint, ma'am, and pointed it out to one of them fellers.' He indicated the Scene-of-Crime team.

'Paint?' she asked sharply.

In reply, the constable pointed at the nearer gatepost. A smear of metallic silver-grey paint glittered amid the rust. Jess stooped to look at it. This was done very recently and by a car driven by someone either in a hurry or very careless. She'd put money on his being in a hurry. Hurry to get in here or hurry to leave? It didn't come from Smith's truck. They'd get it over to forensics and find out what sort of vehicle had left it. Different manufacturers used different paints. The paint smear was a real piece of luck.

'Well done,' she said.

The young constable looked relieved.

Tom Palmer was coming out of the shed.

'Hello, Inspector Campbell.' He grinned.

Before Jess had taken up her present post, every pathologist she'd come across had been nudging middle age and their long, close acquaintance with death and violence had bred in them a certain detachment. Palmer, on the other hand, was young, still enthusiastic enough to bring a personal curiosity to his work. He was a Cornishman. It sounded in his voice and showed in his dark hair and eyes. Perhaps, three or more centuries ago, some shipwrecked Spanish sailor had swum ashore on the rocky Cornish coast and settled down with a local girl.

'I've finished here. Young female, late teens to early twenties. I'd say she's been strangled: bruises on the neck, burst blood vessels in the eyes, tongue protruding. She bit her lip in the struggle but she wouldn't have had time to put up much of a defence. She'd have passed out. I'll know more when I get her on the slab.'

'How long has she been dead?' Jess asked.

'At the moment I'd say your guess is as good as mine, but not very long. Rigor is passing off, so let's say thirty hours? I'll be in a position to tell you more later.' Palmer stripped off his thin rubber gloves. 'Rum old place, this, isn't it? Look at that house over there. Can't you see Dracula flapping out of its attic window one dark and stormy night?'

'I don't need Dracula,' said Jess. 'I've got enough to do with present-day horrors.'

She went into the shed. The girl still lay on the ground awaiting Jess's arrival, now that the Scene-of-Crime crew had done their stuff. After Jess had left, the body could be removed and become Tom Palmer's area of expertise.

Jess paused instinctively in respect. The presence of death inspired a decent demeanour. Not that it was unknown for police officers and SOCOs alike to indulge in black humour, seeking to defuse a stressful situation. But this was a dead human being, even though at first glance it might be mistaken for a discarded life-sized dummy with arms and legs crooked in awkward, uncomfortable positions. We don't all end up murdered, thought Jess sympathetically, but we all 'pass on', as adults in her childhood had always said, if they thought a child might be listening. Don't ask for whom the bell tolls and all the rest of it.

She moved closer and bent over the body. This girl wasn't

out of her late teens, she decided. Her features, even distorted as they now were, still showed signs of a youthful puppy fat. She must have been pretty before this happened to her. Her skin was unblemished; her long, thick hair was a natural-looking blond, though the staring eyes were brown. Dark smudges around them were less likely to be bruising than smeared mascara. Jess had a brief mental image of a young girl leaning towards a mirror, carefully applying her eye make-up.

She was also nicely dressed, to Jess's eye, in newish jeans, white T-shirt now smeared with mud, fairly new trainers. A raspberry pink showerproof jacket lay alongside her. It showed little sign of wear. She'd had money in her pocket when she'd gone out to buy all this new gear. If the shopping trip had been a recent one, they might be able to trace the jacket to a particular shop. An assistant might even remember the customer.

No jewellery, thought Jess. No earrings, no wristwatch. Absence of these things always raised the possibility of robbery as a motive. But muggers didn't generally strangle. They were more likely to carry a knife.

Jess became aware of the crime-scene manager standing beside her. Perhaps he was waiting to see if she'd look as queasy as the young constable. But Jess had practice in schooling her features so that they revealed nothing. She turned her head to look at him, raising her eyebrows.

'Did you take a scraping of that paint on the gatepost?'

'We took it and we took plaster casts of some tyre tracks.

Someone did a rapid three-point turn . . .' He pointed over her shoulder into the yard and an area of churned mud protected by a line of plastic mini-tents, like a row of garden cloches. Then he gestured in the direction of the boarded-up farmhouse. 'Do we break into the house? It's sealed up like it had the plague in there.'

'We'll have to check it out.' Jess frowned. Eli Smith was probably still engaged in battle with Phil Morton. 'I'll see if the owner has a key and tell him we're going to search his property.'

She went outside where Palmer waited. When she was sure no one else was looking, she drew a deep breath of air, hoping to dispel all the miasma of death. She didn't mind if Palmer saw her do it. He'd understand.

He smiled at her now. 'It could be worse,' he said.

'Yes, I know. But she's very young. You can take her away as far as I'm concerned,' Jess told him.

They generally were young, murdered women. Older women in steady relationships didn't go out with strange men, didn't frequent clubs and bars alone, didn't accept lifts from casual acquaintances. If the victim had been out and about 'in the line of business', she was also likely to be young. Streetwalking was a young profession, in many cases distressingly so. But there had been something depressingly 'normal' about the appearance of the girl in the cowshed. Not a tart, just a nice teenage girl. She ought not to be lying there dead this Friday. She ought to be planning her weekend, phoning her friends, making dates, getting ready for another shopping spree, all activities that Jess's mother would have deemed part of 'a normal life'.

And look where a normal life got the dead girl, thought Jess wryly. Another entry for the murder statistics, lying in mud and filth, her body soon to be dissected and studied, her life equally dissected and discussed; *if* they identified her. But they should be able to do that. Thirty hours was already long enough for someone to have reported her missing.

Beside her, Tom Palmer was nodding. 'Got the new man arriving on Monday? This has turned up just in time to greet him!'

'Don't I know it?' Jess grimaced as she spoke and Palmer chuckled.

He could afford to find it amusing, she thought. He didn't have a new boss about to arrive. A new broom, as the saying went, anxious to bring order, or rather, impose his version of order.

Morton was squelching towards them across the yard, glum satisfaction on his face. 'I jotted down his statement, for what it's worth. He just repeats he came here to unload his truck, decided to check out the yard first for reasons he won't be specific about and found the body. I'll get it printed up. It makes sense as far as it goes . . .' Phil's voice trailed away and he gazed morosely at his notes.

'But?' she asked. 'There has to be something else. Is that what you mean?'

'Dead sure of it,' said Morton, oblivious of the unfortunate turn of phrase. 'But he won't say. He's the sort of old chap who keeps what he considers his business to himself. He's told us what we need to know, in his opinion, and that's that.'

'Look him up on the computer,' said Jess. 'And while you're about it, enter the name of this place, Cricket Farm, as well, and see if police records throw anything at us.'

Phil raised his eyebrows and looked round the yard. 'Receiving stolen goods?' he hazarded.

'Not necessarily. More likely driving without a current tax disc or any insurance. I'm not suggesting he's public enemy number one. But he and the police have crossed paths before, I'm sure of that. We make him very jumpy.'

'If you ask me,' said Phil, who, all in all, was not having a good day, 'he isn't going to be much use to us. They're very close in the country. Don't like you to know their business. Do you reckon he's on the level about not being able to write his name?'

Jess said patiently, 'There may be any number of reasons why he can't write. He must be going on sixty or more. In his day, dyslexia was seldom diagnosed. That could be one reason. Or he may have missed a lot of schooling for some cause or other. Needed here to work on the farm? We don't know. He's illiterate, but that certainly doesn't mean stupid. Eccentric maybe and, I agree, not talkative about his business. Once he's accepted we don't care where he gets his old cookers and washers from, he might be more chatty.'

'Hey!' exclaimed Morton. 'If he can't write, he probably can't read. How is he going to read his statement before he makes his mark?'

'You should know the drill, Phil. You read it through aloud

to him and put a declaration at the bottom that you've done so – and also that you were the person who took the statement. You add a note that he's illiterate and then you sign it, with date and place.'

'He wants to know if he can go. I got his home address off him. He lives in that direction.' Morton pointed away up the hill. 'It's just before the crossroads, he says, off down a dirt track on the right, a cottage on its own.'

'I want a word with him first,' Jess said.

Eli watched her approach, an expression of deep mistrust on his face.

'Mr Smith,' she said firmly, anticipating some opposition, 'We'll need to go into the farmhouse.'

'Whaffor?' demanded Eli, thrusting out his jaw and blinking rapidly. 'The girl isn't in there. She's in my cowshed. What's the house got to do with anything?'

'We have to search all areas of a crime scene.'

These words had an unexpected effect on Smith. Beneath the weatherbeaten tan of his skin, she was sure he blanched. He looked panic-stricken.

'You seen it,' he croaked. 'You seen all you need to see. You seen my yard and my cowshed and you can see all you need of the house from here.'

'We haven't seen *inside* it. We have to do that, Mr Smith. We'll be very careful. We won't damage anything.'

'No, no,' Eli burst out, waving his arms wildly. 'It's boarded up. No one's been in there since— no one's been in there for nigh on thirty years.'

'It certainly appears to be boarded up,' Jess agreed patiently. 'But perhaps someone has found a way in and managed to conceal it.' Eli looked terrified. 'So I hope you understand we have to enter.'

'Locked,' said Eli unhappily. 'Even if you lever the boards off, you can't get in. No one could. If they did, I'd see it. No one has. It's locked, it's all locked.'

'Have you the keys?'

'I got 'em,' Eli admitted sullenly after a pause during which he chewed at his lower lip and studied Jess. He was probably wondering if a denial would thwart the police. He'd decided rightly it wouldn't. They'd break down the door. 'They're back at my place.'

'Then Sergeant Morton will go with you now and collect them.'

Eli didn't move.

'All right, Mr Smith?' Jess frowned. The old fellow was looking more than worried. He looked ill. Pearls of sweat had gathered on his forehead. She wasn't sure if he feared what they might find in the house or if some other reason inspired his distress. She hoped he wasn't working up to a heart attack. Gently she asked, 'What's the trouble, Mr Smith?'

He leaned forward as one about to impart a confidence.

'What are *they* going to say about it all?' he asked in a hoarse whisper. 'They won't like it.'

'Who are they?' Jess asked.

Eli blinked and rallied. He adopted something of his former

41

determined stance. 'The neighbours,' he said. 'Terrible ones for gossip, the neighbours.'

With that he turned, stomped off to his lorry and climbed into the cab.

'Follow him down to his cottage and get the keys, Phil,' Jess said. 'Don't ask him any more questions just now. He's in a bit of a state and he's elderly. But don't let him pretend he can't find those keys or anything like that. He does seem worried about his neighbours.'

'Neighbours?' Morton stared at her incredulously and indicated the dripping trees and empty fields around them. 'What's the silly old fool on about? He hasn't got any ruddy neighbours.'

Chapter 4

Lucas was at home. Normally, walking into the gracious late-Georgian terraced house he owned in Cheltenham filled him with the pride inspired by a trophy possession. It stood in a terrace of white or pastel-washed others. Its tall sash windows that had once gazed out on carriages, when Cheltenham had been a fashionable spa town, now rattled to the passing motor traffic. But it kept its air of superiority, of quality.

Lucas appreciated that. He'd started from nothing, with no advantages, and worked his way up, as he liked to tell new acquaintances. Everything he had, he'd got for himself. Besides this house, he also owned a small flat in London's Docklands. But he only used that as a pied-à-terre, somewhere to base his activities when business called him to the capital. The flat was 'new money' and that, for all its glitter and power, couldn't shake off the whispered reproach of being 'flash'.

Not so this house. True, it had been a little run-down when he'd bought it, five years earlier, but it had still kept an aura of being a dowager 'in reduced circumstances'. Because of its shabby state and antiquated fittings he'd acquired it at a very reasonable price. Since then he'd spent a small fortune renovating it and furnishing it. The cost had included the services of a very expensive interior designer. At first, Lucas hadn't been happy with the designer's choice of pale blues and yellows as a décor. It had seemed a bit too feminine. But now he saw that the designer had been right. The colour scheme set off the lofty ceilings, the sculpted cornices and ceiling roses and Lucas's own collection of period furniture.

Not that too many people saw the interior of Lucas's house. He lived here alone. He'd been married once, early on, as a very young man. It hadn't lasted long and he'd made up his mind that marriage wasn't for him. Apart from anything else, any divorce now would cost him millions.

Of course there were women in his life. He kept a legendary 'little black book' in which he recorded the telephone numbers of several available lovelies whom he could squire around London, as necessary. All of them knew they were just a number in his book, but when Lucas took them out, he spent money freely and if they were 'very good girls', they generally got an expensive present as well. It was a business arrangement, like any other in Lucas's life. The girls were happy enough. When one of them dropped out, he replaced her number with another. High-class tarts really, but exclusive enough to escape the derogatory description. They were all 'models' or 'actresses'. It was to his credit that he maintained a genuine sort of friendship with the girls. All of them thought him 'a great guy'. He actually liked them. He just wasn't going to enter into any permanent relationship with any of them.

There were also, now and again, affairs with married women, bored rich women with time on their hands, who liked a bit of an adventure. They knew Lucas wouldn't be indiscreet or boast. He knew they were just having fun. He – and they – liked the challenge, the frisson of risk. He had always trusted them not to be foolish and until now that trust had been repaid. But there was always a first time . . .

As for men, most thought Lucas 'a good chap'. Except for those who had crossed him and they growled about 'that sod Lucas Burton'. Lucas didn't take kindly to being crossed and usually got his own back. Otherwise, he was a man of his word, kept his wits about him and didn't give others the chance to put one over on him. Thus he had a trick of staying on civil terms even with those he'd outmanoeuvred in deals, so there weren't too many malcontents. Lucas, they all agreed, could turn on the charm 'in bucketfuls'. Even the few who cursed his name conceded that, though they said it sourly.

Lucas wasn't feeling very charming at the moment and walking into the house had failed to lift his spirits as it usually did. He felt bloody awful. He'd washed the mud off the Mercedes in the lock-up garage he rented. (The drawback of these period properties was that they had no garages of their own.) He'd also cleaned his shoes in the garage and would get rid of them as soon as possible. He pulled them off now and glowered at them; no longer expensive acquisitions but potential stool pigeons. That sort of farm dirt was traceable and the minutest speck would tell the police, if they ever got to him, that the car had been at Cricket Farm. He couldn't dispose of the Merc so easily, nor risk taking it, in its spattered state, to the car wash where it would attract notice and comment. So he'd done the most thorough job he could but knew forensic examination could still find something.

On his way home, he'd disposed of the muddy rags and his soiled handkerchief in a convenient skip. But he had a third problem. To his dismay, when cleaning up the car, he'd found a scratch on the left wing mirror. It wasn't a big scratch but it was in a highly visible spot. He wasn't altogether sure where he'd done the damage. It might have been in that damn farmyard or it might have been just after he'd driven off in a panic and pulled into the entry to that field to make his phone call. He hoped he'd scraped the wing mirror there on the crumbling drystone wall. He'd been in such a state he hadn't noticed. If he'd scraped against something at the farmyard, that would be a much more serious matter. It was a trace left at the scene of the crime.

'Scene of the crime!' muttered Lucas aloud, as he splashed whisky into a tumbler. Well, that's what the plods would call it when they got around to finding it. Sooner or later they would do that. The later, the better. But it was too much to hope the body would never be discovered. For a few mad minutes, when parked by that field, he'd allowed himself to be optimistic. But he was a realist. Sooner or later someone would go to the farm.

He'd have to deal with the scratch himself. He couldn't take the car into the usual place for maintenance. They knew him and would remember. Nor could he phone one of those fellows who came to your house and fixed up minor scratches. He'd have to do it himself. But heck, as a teenager he'd patched up a succession of old bangers. He'd do it first thing tomorrow. They wouldn't get to him, not if he did a proper job on cleaning and repair. Why the hell should they? Only if the other talked . . . that was another thing he had to see to tonight. Unlike the scratch, Lucas couldn't leave that job until the morning.

He drifted out into the kitchen, glass in hand. Lucas didn't cook, apart from making toast in the morning. He either phoned out for a home-delivery takeaway service to bring him something or he went out to eat. He didn't want to make any human contact tonight because he was agitated and someone might spot it. Nor did he feel hungry but he did feel sick. He should eat something.

He looked fruitlessly in the as-good-as-empty cupboards, containing only the scant necessities for his breakfast: the marmalade, coffee and tea, an ancient opened packet of sugar that had already lasted six months, a half-eaten packet of cornflakes and, for some reason, a tin of sardines. He couldn't remember buying the sardines. His fridge was equally devoid of anything except butter and milk, and half a dozen cans of lager. Why the hell wasn't there any cheese? Everyone else had cheese in their fridges.

For the first time, and with a real shock, it struck him how pitiful these oddments of grocery must look. He had always thought of himself as a man who didn't bother with domesticity. Now he had a sudden unwelcome vision of himself as an ageing singleton, no family, no wife or partner, no one who gave a damn, really. Not even the complaisant girlfriends. They didn't *care*. Once that absence of commitments had appeared freedom. Now it made him look – could it be – like a loser? He pushed the thought away. He wasn't himself. Who the hell would be after stumbling over a corpse?

Eventually he ran to earth a packet of chocolate digestive biscuits his cleaner must have put there to have with her endless cups of tea. She came three times a week and hardly had anything to do. Fortunately she wasn't due to come again until Monday. Perhaps it was she who'd bought the sardines. If so, he couldn't imagine why.

Lucas knocked back the whisky, made a large pot of coffee and retired with it and the chocolate digestives to his study, to plan what he should do. He needed a clear head in order to think.

Now he felt more normal, he could contact the person he'd arranged to meet – and had so urgently had to put off. That relationship was now definitely over. The other person might not be agreeable at first but would see sense; Lucas would make sure of it. Besides, the more he thought about it, the more he disliked the apparent 'coincidence'. Of all the places for there to be a dead body (*a dead body, a human one, just lying there . . .*) it had been waiting for him where they'd agreed to meet.

No, no, coincidences happened in films and in books. They happened in real life too, but he had to make certain. Could it be that he was the victim of some malicious practical joke? Had one of the people he'd outmanoeuvred in a business deal failed to be won over by his proverbial charm? Was this someone's idea of revenge?

Well, if he had been set up, he wanted to know who'd done it. And that person would find he was dealing with 'the other Lucas', the one who lacked all charm, the street-fighter he'd once been.

He didn't believe the person he'd been going to meet had done the dirty on him, because there'd be no reason for it. But someone else, who'd known of the proposed meeting; that was the most likely. Damn it, he'd sworn the other to secrecy and had thought they were of a mind on it. It was in both their interests. Surely no third party . . .

He took out his mobile phone, scrolled down the list of names in the address book, and pressed a number.

'It's me,' he said briskly when the call was answered. 'Are you alone? Then listen. Our association is over. Yes, over! There was a dead body at that farm. No, I'm not bloody drunk! Why the hell did you pick that place? I walked into some sort of a barn and there was a stiff. Yes, I'm sure! How should I know who it was? Sooner or later it will be found and the cops will be all over the place. I never went there, all right? You and I never agreed to meet there. That's the story and the way it stays. We're merely acquaintances with no personal history. Yes, that's what I said, just acquaintances; and we're going to stay that way . . .'

The person at the other end of the call broke in with vigorous protest.

'Shut up!' snapped Lucas. 'Now then, I wouldn't like to think I'd been set up . . .'

More vigorous protest.

Lucas overrode it. 'All right, I'm not accusing you! But if not you then who was it? Have you blabbed? Well, have you said *anything*? Let slip some hint, left some piece of paper lying around with my name or phone number on it, or the name of that blasted farm? Has anyone had a chance to over-hear when we've been talking on the phone?'

A pithy response to this.

'Well,' said Lucas. 'I don't like coincidences and I don't like being dropped in it. I do think I was set up – perhaps we both were – and I want to know why and by whom! You can take it from me, I'll find out.'

When Jess got home late on Friday evening, a crumpled envelope with an unfamiliar stamp greeted her on the mat just inside her door. She stooped to pick it up with surprise and pleasure. Simon had found time to write. Letters from her twin were few and far between. He was a doctor working for a medical charity in various world hotspots. The areas he found himself in were remote and dangerous, communica-tions uncertain and vulnerable. He had no free time. So this letter, scribbled at night probably by the light of an oil lamp, was a rarity.

She tucked it in her pocket to be read at leisure and savoured later, and back-heeled the door closed behind her.

Her flat was small but it suited her because, for one thing, it was low maintenance. Something she didn't have time (or the inclination) for was vacuum cleaning and dusting. On the other hand, she was by nature tidy and disliked living in a tip. So the flat was carefully furnished with essential pieces only and no ornaments except a framed family photo taken when she and Simon had been about twelve, in the garden of a rented holiday cottage in Cornwall.

The pair of them, their red hair glinting in the sunshine, grinned at the camera. Jess had both arms wrapped round the neck of the family Labrador. They had always taken him with them because no one could accept putting him into kennels. Not until he had gone to dog heaven, accompanied by a funeral elegy over his grave in their back garden, spoken by their father, had the family ventured abroad on holiday. It didn't mean they were untravelled. Her father had been in the Army and when she was a small child they'd all lived for a time on a NATO base in Germany. It was another reason, she supposed, that her parents had felt no need to brave the airports or ferries at holiday time. Perhaps it was also the reason both she and Simon had chosen unsettled adult lives. Simon did more travelling than she did but a CID officer hardly worked nine to five. Like today, the unexpected was always ready to pounce.

Jess smiled at the snapshot and tried to recall who, since they were all four in the picture, had taken it. She couldn't remember.

She walked into the bedroom and stripped off her damp, muddy clothing. When she'd showered, washed her hair and dressed in clean jeans and a T-shirt she felt a lot better. Her earlier tiredness had sloughed off with the Cricket Farm mud. Revived, she went back to the living room and switched on the local radio programme. There had been no sign of the press at the farm and possibly word hadn't yet reached the media. There was nothing on the local programme. She'd watch the TV news later; the regional bulletin might have got wind of the 'corpse in the cowshed' by then. There was a quirkiness about the location that might appeal to the compilers of the evening news slots. Tabloid headline writers would hail it as a dream.

In fact, she'd prefer it if the media didn't get hold of the news until the weekend was over. Later, if they couldn't identify the victim, they'd need media help, but at the moment she didn't want a camera crew scrambling around Cricket Farm. A judiciously released photo of the farm might jog the public's memory later.

More particularly, she didn't want reporters besieging Eli Smith this weekend. Jess was sure Smith was a deeply worried man. Anyone who found a corpse on his property wouldn't be happy about it. But Smith was jumpy. He was also a loner and he wouldn't deal well with intrusive questioning by eager reporters.

It had been arranged that Smith would come in and make his statement at ten tomorrow, Saturday. Phil Morton could take care of that. Theoretically Jess herself wasn't due at work until Monday morning, but she couldn't just let it all go over the weekend.

For one thing, early days in any murder investigation were the most important. Second, and no less important, Superintendent Ian Carter was due to take up his duties on

Monday and they'd have to have something to show for a weekend's investigations.

They knew little about the new man. He came to them from the other end of the country and they had no idea why he had chosen to relocate or been relocated. An acquaintance, a retired senior officer, had informed her Carter was a very experienced man. 'I think I played rugby against him, years ago,' said the same informant. She hadn't even seen a photo and her imagination had served up a large tweedy ex-rugger player, fighting a losing battle with his weight.

Her plans for the next morning, therefore, ran something like this: get up early and go for a jog. Come back and snatch some breakfast and then go over to HQ to see what was going on. Later, drive out to Cricket Farm and make a careful exploration of the area. There had been some kind of stables lower down the hill, past that little wood. They needed to interview anyone who had been there at all during the past week.

She had time to make supper before the evening news. She went into her kitchenette, put pasta on to boil and when it was ready stirred in a small tin of tuna and a jar of pesto. Then she settled down in front of her TV with her dinner on a tray, and Simon's letter spread out on the coffee table in front of her. She didn't own a dining table. Who would sit at it?

Eli Smith had a table. Phil Morton had been right and his home was an isolated one. Smith's cottage was one of four former labourers' cottages belonging to the farm and dotted about the landscape. Two were semi-detached and had fallen into too much disrepair to be habitable. The other two, single cottages three quarters of a mile apart, were still in reasonable shape. He lived in one and the other was rented out to Penny Gower. Technically she was his nearest neighbour but at a distance that meant he saw little of her, unless he went over to the farm. Then he'd sometimes drive down the hill and check she was all right at the stables.

He also liked to see the horses. They'd had plough horses at the farm when he'd been a boy. They'd later been replaced by a tractor. Modernisation, they'd called it. He'd been sorry to see the plough team go and he fancied his father had regretted saying goodbye to them. It was a rare occasion when he and his father had been in harmony. But the plough horses, Dolly and Florence by name, had grown old. There was no room for sentimentality in farming. Certainly there had been no trace of any such emotion at Cricket Farm.

Eli had his 'workshop' at the back of his cottage. It consisted of a corrugated-iron shed to which an electric cable was strung from the house. He could make as much noise as he liked in it. No one could hear. No one likely to raise any protest, anyway. Nor was anyone likely to come round and ask what he was doing out of curiosity. He couldn't abide Nosy Parkers. That was something else he'd learned in his childhood. Now the coppers, they were real ones for sticking their noses into everything. So, reasoned Eli, there was no cause to tell them more than they needed to know. Like, they'd *needed* to know there was a corpse in the cowshed. But that was it: no more, no less.

That evening Eli sat at the rectangular pine table in the kitchen with his family. He'd realised they'd know what had happened and would turn up, so he wasn't surprised. His father sat down at the other end facing him; his mother to the left and his brother to the right of him.

They didn't always join him but they'd come once or twice a week. When they did, he accepted their presence as one does accept visiting relatives. Thus, he wasn't particularly pleased to see them; but on the other hand they didn't make tiresome conversation. Fair enough, you wouldn't expect the dead to be chatty.

He much preferred their present taciturnity to the constant bickering and recriminations that had characterised these gatherings when they'd all been alive. Although even now, even silent, they still managed to needle him.

His brother, for example, insisted on attending wearing a rope round his neck. That annoyed Eli because it wasn't just tactless, it was inaccurate. Nathan had used his pillowcase, torn into strips and knotted together, to hang himself in his prison cell. Where would he have got a proper rope like that one? Typical of Nathan: always making out he was smarter than he was.

His mother sat sullenly, alternately glowering at the uncleaned cooker (Eli was blowed if he was going to clean it just to please her) and mopping at the bloodstain on the bosom of her frock with a tea towel.

His father stared down the table over Eli's shoulder and out of the window behind. There was blood all over his shirt, too, but he didn't bother with it. Eli fancied his mother kept patting at her frock with a cloth because she sat opposite Nathan and wanted to remind him of what he'd done. But Nathan, he just sat there grinning with the rope halter round his neck.

'I don't know what you've got to look so blasted smug about, Nat!' said Eli to him. 'Anyhow, there's been another killing, so you aren't the only murderer up at the farm. See? You're not so special!'

Nathan fingered his rope collar and smirked. You never could tell Nat anything. He always knew better.

His mother turned her sullen gaze from the cooker to him. She always did blame him for anything that went wrong at the farm. But he hadn't been the problem, had he? It had been Nathan. As for his father, he just carried on staring over Eli's shoulder, out of the window. But he'd heard the news. He'd screwed up his face in that way he'd always had.

'It's not my fault them coppers are going into the house!' Eli defended himself. 'I told 'em no one had been in there since Nat done what he done. But they had to have the keys. It's no use you blaming me.'

But they always did ruddy blame him.

'Clear off, the lot of you!' snapped Eli, tired of their wordless company and moved to rebellion by the unspoken but unremitting criticism.

They obligingly did so, fading into the grubby wallpaper

with its design of Chianti bottles. Damn silly design for a wallpaper, thought Eli, even in a kitchen. One of these days he'd get round to scraping it off and painting the walls.

'Better not, though,' he said to his elderly tabby cat, which had walked in. She didn't care for company, always shot straight out the door into the backyard as soon as they turned up. 'Better not change anything. They wouldn't like it and it'd only give them something else to glare at me about.'

The cat was prowling cautiously round the kitchen, making sure they'd all gone. She'd jump up on his lap in a minute, squeeze her head up between him and the table, and try to steal scraps off his plate.

Eli wondered whether, in time, the dead girl in the cowshed would join them at the table. After all, she'd been found on their farm. It made her sort of family.

Still, he reflected as he tucked into yesterday's leftover boiled potatoes fried up with bacon, now the family had buzzed off. He and old Tibs (she'd smelled the bacon and was getting ready to spring) had the place to themselves again . . . for the time being, anyway.

They'd be back.

Chapter 5

Saturday morning, Jess realised immediately, wasn't a good time to arrive at a busy stables, especially one that offered riding lessons as well as livery. She got out of her car and surveyed the two rows of dilapidated wooden loose boxes, their corrugated-iron roofs in need of some attention. When it rains here, she thought, it must make a hell of a noise. I suppose the nags are used to it. The space between the loose boxes formed a sort of yard, containing an old bath that had been converted into a horse trough, a stack of hay bales and a midden, the last steaming gently. At the far end several vehicles were parked and beyond them, Jess could see a paddock dotted with some low jumps.

She was early but work here had begun even earlier, since the aptly named 'mucking out' was already done and added its own particular warm odour to the acrid smell of horses. These appeared to be mostly out in the yard. A group at the far end was being tended by people Jess took to be the owners. They would be the livery animals. A very small girl whose arms only just reached up to the animal's withers was energetically brushing one of them, a stout pony. The two nearer animals were saddled up ready to be ridden out and a tall spindly young man was hoisting himself awkwardly aloft. The horse, sensing inexperience, put back its ears and stamped a hind hoof. The sturdy woman holding the bridle stroked its neck and uttered reassuring words, first to the horse, then to the rider.

'Steady, steady . . . All right there, Mr Pritchard?'

'Yes, fine, Lindsey!' he replied too cheerfully.

Lindsey released the bridle and Mr Pritchard's look of apprehension increased.

Jess moved over to her.

'Good morning, are you the owner?'

Lindsey turned a freckled face towards her. 'No, that's Penny, Penny Gower. She's in the office.' She pointed to the end of the row of loose boxes behind her. 'Is it about riding lessons or hiring a hack? Because if you haven't booked . . .'

'No,' said Jess, taking out her ID and holding it up.

'Oh, right . . .' said Lindsey. 'It's about that rotten business up the road at Cricket Farm, then?'

The unease that had entered her voice was picked up by the horse carrying the novice rider, Pritchard. It stamped its feet again and moved backwards.

'Whoa! Steady!' gasped Pritchard.

'It's all right, Mr Pritchard, smooth the neck!'

Pritchard leaned forward slightly so that he could just reach the horse's neck and patted it nervously.

Somehow, thought Jess, I don't think Mr Pritchard is going to progress to Horse of the Year Show.

'And you are?' Jess asked the young woman.

'Lindsey, Lindsey Harper. But I can't help you,' she added quickly. 'I was here Friday but only because Mr Pritchard was coming for a lesson. We didn't ride anywhere near the farm-yard, just across the fields over there.' She pointed into the distance. 'I don't go past it on my way home, either, sorry.'

'I'll go and find Ms Gower, then,' Jess said. She gestured at the other horses. 'Are those the owners tending them?'

'Yes, those are the livery animals. Most of the owners get out here at the weekend. Penny and I manage during the week. We also keep a couple of riding animals belonging to Penny. This is one of them.' She indicated the horse Pritchard rode.

Lindsey turned to the other saddled horse and put a propri-etorial hand on its mane. 'And this is my old fellow. I keep him here and he makes himself useful, don't you, eh?'

The horse swung its head towards her and stretched it out to nudge its owner's shoulder.

'He's getting impatient,' said Lindsey tactfully.

'Sure, don't let me hold you up.' Jess smiled up at Mr Pritchard as she walked past on her way to the 'office'.

Mr Pritchard, responding to the smile and outside interest, held the reins nonchalantly in his right hand, put his left hand, left elbow turned out, on his thigh and struck a pose usually shown by cavalry officers in old illustrations. His attempt to look dashing was less than natural but he was trying, give the man credit. Anyway, he wasn't really trying to convince Jess: he was trying to convince himself.

When Jess reached the office she heard voices. She wasn't

the first visitor and whoever was there ahead of her was female and sounded strident. That the office had previously served as a loose box was shown by the stable doors, both halves hooked back against the wall. Jess avoided the dented bucket lying on its side by the entrance and tentatively knocked, before stepping inside.

After the bright light outside it was dark in here. There was no window; the only light came from the yard behind her, so that she was temporarily blinded and stood there blinking like a mole. Her nostrils filled with a mixed odour of leather and sweat.

When the shadows cleared she saw that three people were already in the small room and her arrival made it crowded. As the 'office' obviously doubled as tack room, there was little enough room to begin with. One of those present was a young woman of much her own age, attractive in a very English and slightly 'horsy' way. Her untidy long light brown hair was tied back with a scarf. Another was a man Jess judged to be in his late thirties or very early forties. He leaned against the far wall with his arms folded. He wore riding breeches and boots and a pullover over a check shirt. He didn't look like a customer of any kind. His manner was too 'at home'. The remaining person, the nearest to Jess, was a woman of indeterminate age and of what Jess unkindly termed to herself a 'shrivelled' appearance. She was weatherbeaten and carried not an ounce of superfluous fat. Her hair was wiry and unkempt, her clothing well worn. She stared at the newcomer in an imperious way, challenging the interruption.

The younger woman, seated behind a battered old table, looked partly relieved to see a new arrival and partly wary. The conflicting emotions flickered across her face.

'Yes?' she asked. This, then, must be Penny Gower. Thank goodness the stable owner wasn't the wiry woman.

Before Jess could answer, the man detached himself from the wall, grinned and said, 'It's the fuzz. You've been raided, Pen!'

'Police?' demanded the wiry woman immediately. 'Have you come about that nonsense at Cricket?'

Jess ignored her and produced her ID again to show them. She was slightly discomfited at being identified so promptly and before she'd opened her mouth. It wasn't the first time it had happened and she ought to be used to it. They must be expecting the police to call, after the incident at the farm. But she'd found, as so many of her plain-clothes colleagues had, that the general public was remarkably well attuned to the presence of law officers.

'I'm sorry to disturb you when you're obviously busy, but perhaps we could have a word?'

The wiry woman didn't take kindly to being ignored. From the corner of her eye Jess saw her bristle and take up a combative attitude.

'Yes, of course,' Penny said. 'Sorry, Selina, I'll be out directly the police have finished with me.'

'Hah!' said the wiry woman darkly and marched out with a last laser glare at Jess. Probably, thought Jess, she was off to phone the chief constable.

'I'll push off, too,' said the man, not sounding as though he meant to do it. He didn't move.

'No,' Penny put out a hand to prevent him. 'Stay, please, Andy. Inspector, this is Andrew Ferris, a friend. He was here on Friday, too. You want to talk about Friday, I suppose? I'm Penny Gower, by the way.' She looked round her. 'Do sit down, there's a chair . . .'

Ferris now moved with alacrity, detaching himself from the wall to grab a rickety wooden chair, which he flourished towards the visitor. Jess took a seat as gingerly as Mr Pritchard had the saddle.

'I hope I haven't upset a valued client,' she said, indicating the yard behind her with a jerk of her head.

'Ma Foscott?' said Ferris, grinning. He had good teeth. He was a good-looking bloke, thought Jess. 'Don't worry about her, the old battleaxe.'

'Sh!' hissed Penny. 'She's probably lurking outside, Andy. That's Selina Foscott, Inspector. We have her daughter's pony here.'

Jess recalled the very small girl toiling away grooming the stout pony.

'She was also here on Friday, by the way.' Penny looked a little glum. 'Selina and Charlie were here every day last week.'

Damn! thought Jess. I've offended Mrs Foscott and now I've got to interview the old bat. She'll take pleasure in being awkward.

'I am here about the business at Cricket Farm,' she said

aloud, briskly professional. Ferris twitched an eyebrow and looked as if he might grin again, but decided in time it would be inappropriate.

Jess gave him a look to let him know she'd spotted the near-grin and Ferris responded by looking suitably meek, like a chastened schoolboy.

'I'm particularly interested to know if either of you noticed anything unusual on Friday, at any time of the day, or earlier in the week. I know you can't see the farmyard, but you are its nearest neighbour.'

Penny waved a hand around her. 'All this is Eli's land. Eli Smith, that is. Only the stables belong to me. I rent the paddock from Eli. The whole outfit was derelict when I bought it. The previous owner had been obliged to cease business, the horses had all left long since and no one had been interested to take the place on.'

'How did you know about it?' Jess asked, curious.

'Oh, well.' Penny looked slightly embarrassed. 'I was living in London and teaching. Being a teacher in an inner city school these days is no fun. Also I – I was in a relationship that was going nowhere.' She reddened.

Behind her, Ferris muttered, 'Who isn't?'

Penny went on, 'When I was a kid, we used to visit an aunt who lived down here. I always loved the area. She, my auntie, died and I came down here for the funeral. It happened that was also a half-term, so I took the week. I'd come on my own, because I – well – I felt the need to be alone for a bit. I was driving around and I passed by this place with a *For Sale* notice that had been there so long it had fallen into a hedge and was barely visible. No one had bothered to re-erect it. I stopped the car and came to explore. It – it sort of spoke to me. All in a terrible state, of course. But I felt I needed a change of direction. I didn't like my life in London and that *For Sale* sign offered me a chance of something quite different. My aunt had left me a little money, I'd always been keen on horses . . . well, I made a sudden decision and bought it.'

'It must have been an expensive business, getting it up and running again,' commented Jess. 'A lot of very hard work, too.'

'It took every last cent of Auntie's money,' Penny Gower said frankly. 'Together with what I got from my ex-partner for my share of the flat we were buying. I was rather lucky there in that he wanted to keep it on. Now I struggle along and survive, mostly because I've got very good friends. One of them is Lindsey Harper. You might have seen her outside?' She paused and looked at Jess.

'Yes, I met her.' Jess nodded.

'Lindsey keeps her own horse here and in addition comes in nearly every day and works her socks off, helping out.'

'She has no other job?' Jess asked curiously.

'Oh, well, her husband is pretty well off . . .' Penny said awkwardly.

'Rolling!' contributed Ferris, less inhibited.

'Then there's Andy here.' Penny turned to smile up at him.

Ferris returned the smile. The look in his eyes told Jess enough. Smitten, she thought sympathetically, he thinks she's the bee's knees. I wonder how she feels about him? Fond of him, I'd guess, but not in love.

'Andy not only comes over and helps with the heavy jobs, like building the jumps in the paddock. He also does my accounts on the cheap.'

'I'm an accountant,' explained Ferris. 'I'm self-employed. It lets me arrange my day pretty well as I want it.'

'In addition there's Eli,' Penny said suddenly. 'I mustn't forget him. Eli can mend things, anything. He's also the landlord of my cottage and, frankly, the rent I pay him is laughable. You've met Eli? Oh, that's a silly question. You must have done.'

'If you mean Eli Smith, then he found the – the victim.' Jess could have said 'body' but some witnesses went a bit funny at that word. Although both Penny Gower and Andrew Ferris, she guessed, were made of sterner stuff.

Penny leaned forward over the table. 'Eli is very kind,' she said with emphasis. 'He's a bit eccentric, but that's because . . .' She paused.

'Because?'

She looked embarrassed but then shrugged. 'You'll hear about it, I suppose. The Smith family used to farm Cricket together. I'm talking of years ago. There were the parents and two brothers, Eli and Nathan. I can't remember which brother was the older. One day, for a reason no one knows, Nathan shot dead both his elderly parents with a shotgun kept in the house. He was arrested but while awaiting trial managed to hang himself in his cell. Eli boarded up the house, left the farm to its own devices and has never lived there since. He uses the yard, though, for storage.'

'He told us about his scrap business,' Jess said thoughtfully. She'd asked Phil Morton to look up Smith on the police national computer. If he had, this is what he would have found. No wonder the presence of the police again at Cricket Farm made Eli Smith nervous.

'Andy and I feel a bit guilty!' said Penny unexpectedly, glancing up at Ferris for confirmation.

Ferris looked startled but then nodded loyally.

'Oh?' asked Jess and waited.

'Because it's our fault, or rather, it's *my* fault, poor Eli had the awful experience of finding another body at the farm. It was Eli, you see, who found his dead parents, and his brother watching over them, at the farm. Nathan, they say, was sitting at the kitchen table, just waiting for him to come home. I think Eli had been to market. He wasn't there when it happened, anyway. He just walked in. The shotgun was lying on the table in front of Nathan and there was blood everywhere. Can you imagine what it was like for Eli? Just walking in and finding a horrible scene like that?' Penny shuddered. 'And now he's had to go through it all again, walking in on a dead body.'

'Nathan must have flipped his lid!' said Ferris. 'I don't know why they didn't just plead insanity. The poor bloke hanged himself, anyway, in his cell.'

And there will have been hell to pay about that, thought Jess, and an official inquiry. Nathan Smith should have been the subject of suicide watch. His taking of his own life ought not to have been possible.

'Wonder why Nathan didn't blast off the shotgun at Eli, too?' Ferris asked thoughtfully. 'He must have had plenty of time to reload.'

'Why is it your fault Eli Smith found the body?' Jess asked Penny. Easy as it would be to be diverted by this gruesome account of a long-ago crime, she was here to investigate a modern one. They'd have to check out the earlier murders, of course. Three dead bodies, all on one farm, well . . .

Ferris and Penny Gower had begun talking together, eager to tell her their story. She wondered if they'd rehearsed it.

'Not your fault at all!' Ferris said indignantly. 'Honestly, Pen, you have to get over this way you have of worrying about other people. It was on Eli's property and who else should find it?'

'Of course I feel it's my fault, I saw the car!' Penny was arguing.

They squabbled until Jess brought them to order, again feeling she was being faced by an overenthusiastic class of eager but undisciplined kids.

'Right . . .' said Ferris apologetically. 'It's just that Pen . . .'

'No, *I don't*! But I'm fond of Eli and I have to worry. He's not a young man . . .'

Jess held up her hand. 'One of you! Ms Gower?'

In the end the story came out fairly coherently.

Penny had seen a strange car, a silver-grey Mercedes, she thought, an expensive car, anyway. It had been pulled off the road between the stables and the farm where there was an entry to a field.

'I was driving my horsebox back from Eli's place. Eli fixed some damage. I told you, Eli is very kind.'

'The Mercedes . . .' Jess reminded her patiently.

The driver had been in the car but behaving oddly as Penny drove past. Penny's impression had been that he was trying to hide. She'd told Andrew on her return to the stables.

Vigorous nodding from Ferris at this point and he took up the tale.

'I thought we, one of us, ought to inform Eli because, well, neither of us is sure quite what Eli keeps at the farm. Look here,' Ferris added hastily. 'I don't mean he keeps anything there he shouldn't. Frankly it looks like rubbish but it must have some value or old Eli wouldn't deal in it. Anyhow, I offered to ring Eli . . .'

'And I gave Andrew Eli's mobile number . . .'

'And I rang him. He said, "I'll take a look, then." Eli is usually a man of few words. But I thought, fair enough, I've passed on the news.'

Ferris frowned. 'I was going to cut the call, but then he suddenly added that he had to go out to the farm some time soon with some scrap, so he'd make it sooner rather than later and go today – that is, he meant he'd go that day, Friday. It's not like Eli to be so loquacious so I reckoned the news had worried him. The old boy did go and found the stiff. Penny's right. It was rotten for the poor old chap. Enough to send him off his chump, like brother Nathan. I'm sorry now I didn't wait up there and look round the place with him. But Eli's funny about anyone knowing his business. He wouldn't have liked it, if I'd offered to accompany him. He'd have thought I was being nosy.'

'What time was all this?' asked Jess, pulling out her notebook.

Penny and Ferris watched her actions with interest. Then they looked at each other.

'I must have seen him about a quarter to four,' said Penny uncertainly, 'or near enough. I left Eli's place about twenty to four. I know that because I looked at my watch. Andrew had told me he meant to drive over and I wondered if he'd be there when I got back, and he was. I drove quite fast home.' She flushed. 'I don't mean I broke the speed limit. I meant, I had no horse in the trailer so I hadn't to worry about that.'

'You didn't drive past Cricket Farm, Mr Ferris, on your way here?'

He shook his head. 'Nope, came the other way. But Penny got here about a quarter to four, like she said. It's only a minute or two from Cricket Farm to here by car. Old lady Foscott took her unappealing brat and went home about four, five past perhaps, and I decided to ring old Eli's mobile at about quarter past four or let's say twenty past.'

'Eli Smith didn't mention any of this to us,' said Jess. 'I don't mean the family history. I can understand why he didn't mention that. I mean, he didn't tell us you'd seen a car or that Mr Ferris had called him about it.'

Penny and Andrew exchanged glances. Ferris chuckled and even Penny smiled.

'Eli wouldn't,' said Penny.

'It's just his way,' they chorused together, looked at one another, and laughed.

'Sorry,' said Penny immediately. 'It's not a funny matter. It's just, well, Eli, you see. He isn't one to chat, not even to me, just like Andrew was telling you. He just says what he's got to say, the bare facts, and that's it. He fixed up my little horsebox. One of the horses freaked out and kicked a hole in it. I asked him if he'd do it. He came and had a look, just said, "Yes." I hitched it up and drove it to his place and he mended the hole in the side. Hardly a word spoken, except when he refused payment.'

She smiled. 'Besides, in not bringing me into it, Eli probably thought he was protecting me. In his way, he likes to keep an eye on me. He comes down here from time to time, he says to see the horses, wanders round and offers to fix anything obviously broken.' An expression of dismay crossed her face. 'Oh, I've just had a thought. I suppose Eli wouldn't be worrying anything could *really* happen to me, out here? I mean, there is generally someone here with me. Lindsey, or an owner or a pupil or Andy . . .'

The implications in the fact that a murdered woman had been found just a quarter of a mile away had suddenly struck her. Her mouth dropped open and she gazed at Jess in alarm.

Ferris put a hand on her shoulder. 'OK, Pen, take it easy. The cops will sort it out.'

Such confidence on the part of the public was welcome. Jess hoped they'd live up to it.

During the conversation in the office, Jess had been aware of various bumps and snorting noises from the loose box adjacent. Now, as she left and stepped out in the yard again, a horse put its head over the half-door.

'Hello, old chap,' said Jess and put up a hand to pat him.

'Careful,' said a male voice behind her, 'we think he may be blind on that side. Best to come up on him on the other one.'

Ferris had come out into the yard behind her.

'Oh,' said Jess, embarrassed.

'See here,' he went on in a low urgent voice, 'you don't think Penny is in any danger here? It is lonely. I know generally someone is around for most of the day but she gets here early in the morning and leaves late at night. She's alone at those times. Horses have to be cared for. I can't prevent her coming here and I can't be with her all the time. I've got a business of my own to run.'

'There's no reason to believe Ms Gower is in any danger from what you and she have told me,' Jess said slowly. 'But she did see the silver Mercedes and glimpse the driver. That makes her a valuable witness. If the driver of the Mercedes is involved, he probably realises that, too. The horsebox she was driving was a giveaway to where she was going.'

'So, he may look here?' Ferris nodded towards the stable yard.

'Ms Gower should just be prudent. We never release all information to the press at the start of an inquiry and the fact that she had sight of the parked car may just be one of the things we keep quiet about for the time being. In fact, it probably will be.'

'That would suit us fine,' Ferris replied.

Jess looked around her.

'If you want Selina Foscott,' he continued, pointing towards the paddock, 'she's down there with Charlie.'

'Charlie is the pony?'

'Charlie is her daughter. Good luck.'

He went back into the office.

Guard dog, thought Jess. Guarding Penny Gower. Both Eli Smith and Andrew Ferris felt they had to look after her. There were women like that, she reflected ruefully. Men felt they had to protect them. They had never felt that way, as far as she knew, about herself.

Charlie Foscott and her pony were circling the paddock and squaring up to the jumps. And 'square' was the word to describe the pony. It resembled a barrel on four stubby legs with what looked to Jess's untutored eye more than usual width between its front pair. The pony also gave the impression it might refuse at any moment and the rider, a fragile figure, looked as if she knew it.

Mrs Foscott saw Jess approaching and bellowed, 'Stop!'

For a moment Jess thought the order was directed at her but Charlie pulled up the pony immediately and Jess realised it had been barked at them. The pony put down its head and began to tear at what short grass was left amongst the mud. The rider sat aloft and stared across at Jess. She had her mother's arrogant look. Jess, who had been feeling rather sorry for her, stopped doing so.

'Right,' said Mrs Foscott clumping across the mud towards the gate. 'You want to interview me, I suppose?'

'If you've got a few minutes to spare, Mrs Foscott.' The woman wasn't going to be awkward. If anything, she was eager to talk. Whether she had anything of interest to say was another matter. Generally it was the garrulous witnesses who proved the biggest time-wasters.

'Do you know who she is?' asked Mrs Foscott.

Jess deduced the dead girl was meant. 'Not yet. Penny Gower tells me you were here every day last week, is that right?'

'Can't waste time,' said Mrs Foscott. 'There's a show coming up. Sultan's got to be ready. He got the blue rosette last time, you know, in his class.'

'Oh? Well done.' She couldn't care less if the animal had sprouted wings and flown over the jumps. Frankly, looking at Sultan, she couldn't imagine any other way he'd clear them. However, she supposed blue meant a very respectable second. But then, how many riders had competed in that particular class? Jess drew a breath and firmly brought the conversation back on track.

'On your way here, do you drive past Cricket Farm?'

Mrs Foscott nodded. 'Can't say I take much notice of the

place. Try not to; it's a real eyesore. It usually looks deserted. Sometimes Eli Smith is there or I see his lorry.'

'Did you see it on Friday?'

'No. If he went up there and found a stiff, he did it after I'd got home. Bloody nearly had an accident and didn't make it.' She scowled. 'I was pulling out of the entrance to the stables here and swoosh! A big silver Merc going like a bat out of hell roared down the hill and straight across my nose. I had to slam on the brakes. These road hogs think it's a country highway and they can drive like madmen because there won't be any other traffic. But there's precious little passing space and no wide verges.'

'What time was this, Mrs Foscott?'

'Oh, around four, slightly after. It had come on to rain. I put my head in the office back there,' Mrs Foscott waved a hand vaguely towards the stable block, 'to tell them I'd put Sultan in his box. Charlie dropped off the tack and then we were off home.' She scowled. 'I was easing my way out on to the road, looked both ways, couldn't see anything, thought it was OK to pull out and, like I told you, this maniac came roaring downhill. The idiot nearly took my front bumper off. Charlie shrieked like a banshee. She thought our number was up and for a moment so did I!' Mrs Foscott squinted thoughtfully at Jess. 'If I'd got his number I'd have reported him to you.'

Jess wondered whether Mrs Foscott thought CID officers also doubled as traffic cops. She realised the woman's detailed account was designed to make it clear the near-accident was not Selina's fault. Penny had driven past a suspect car, similar in appearance, not long before this second incident, Jess reflected. She'd told Andrew Ferris about it and he had phoned Eli Smith. But the Mercedes involved in the near miss with Mrs Foscott's car had driven past the stables about twenty minutes after Penny had seen it. That meant the driver hadn't immediately left the spot where she'd seen him parked. Why? Because he wanted to be sure he wouldn't overtake Penny again on the road? Or he had been doing something else? Phoning someone? Trying to clean up? Eli Smith's yard was very dirty.

'Now, look here,' said Mrs Foscott unexpectedly, reassuming the hectoring manner that seemed natural to her. 'How did that girl die?'

'We're not releasing details yet, Mrs Foscott, I'm afraid. Nor, frankly, do we yet know. We have to wait until after the post-mortem. We need to be sure about these things.'

'I know that!' the other woman snapped. 'I'm not an idiot. What I mean is, was she shot?'

'Oh,' Jess was startled. 'Not as far as we know. But as I told you, the post-mortem—'

She wasn't allowed to finish. 'Oh well, then,' said Selina Foscott in a satisfied way. 'Old Eli Smith had nothing to do with it.' She fixed Jess with a minatory glare. 'If old Eli wanted to kill someone for any reason – say he'd found the girl snooping round his farm – he'd blast her or anyone else with a shotgun.'

'Why?' asked Jess faintly.

Mrs Foscott looked grimly pleased at having at last taken the wind out of the inspector's sails. 'Because that's the Smith way,' she said simply. 'You've heard about it? The double murder at the farm?'

'Nathan Smith shot dead his parents, I understand,' said Jess.

Selina nodded. 'That's right. It's what Nathan did and it's what Eli would do.' She shook her head. 'I do remember the whole bloody business. No one was much surprised at the time, I recollect. The Smiths were a funny family. Never mixed with any outsiders. People like that, they don't have much imagination. If they'd found a way that worked, they'd stick to it. Believe me, if Eli wanted to kill someone, he'd do it the same way brother Nathan did. He wouldn't have the brains to come up with anything different.'

She stared at the silent Jess. 'That's it, then? You don't want me any more?'

Jess rallied. 'No, er, not just now, at any rate. Could I have an address and phone number for you, Mrs Foscott? Just in case I have to come back to you, about the Mercedes car you saw.'

'Certainly,' said Selina almost cheerfully. 'Glad to help.'

Out of earshot, Jess took out her mobile and rang Phil Morton.

'Phil? Get on to traffic. I've been told of an incident involving a silver Mercedes car on Friday some time between four and half past. If we've got anything in Gloucestershire, it's a healthy supply of speed cameras. If he was going like the clappers, and a witness says he was, then he may have gone through one. If his mind was on something else, like a body in a cowshed, he might not even have noticed.'

Lindsey Harper stood in front of the cheval glass in her bedroom and studied her reflection. The sun was setting and bathed everything in a mellow golden glow. It even lent some colour to her hair. Its natural shade was a sort of tallow yellow. Not a nice sexy blond, just tallow. She had it coloured regularly at a hairdresser's but spending so much time out of doors meant that it faded quickly to its original hue.

She was a big girl. Not fat; just tall and big boned, built more like a man than a girl. She'd always been like that. When she'd been a kid, strangers regularly mistook her for a boy. A big, strong, sensible, outdoor type; that about summed her up.

She sighed. She'd returned from the stables an hour earlier and showered, changing into a dress for the benefit of her husband, Mark, who was due in at any minute. He'd been away on a business trip and was driving back this afternoon. Her mother had drummed it into her head, years before, that a woman should make herself look nice for her husband. But dresses didn't suit Lindsey. Trousers, jodhpurs, riding boots, chunky pullovers and sleeveless body-warmers became her far better.

'I look,' said Lindsey to the reflection in the mirror, 'like an upright piano someone's draped a sheet over prior to doing a spot of decorating. You can see the shape of me, all square angles, and the dress looks like a rag.'

And that was annoying because it had been a jolly expensive rag.

There was a slam of the front door downstairs and footsteps in the hall. Mark was home. She hadn't heard the car, so he must have parked out front. Her bedroom was at the back. She knew, without seeing him, what he was doing. He was going into the drawing room and pouring himself a whisky.

She gave the dress a last shake and went downstairs to join him.

'Oh, there you are,' he said carelessly as she came in. 'Thought you might still be out at the stables.'

'I came back early. I wanted to be here when you got home.'

This declaration of wifely affection was disregarded. 'Care for a drink?' he asked.

'Gin and tonic, please,' said Lindsey, giving up on the 'little woman' approach. Who was she fooling? Not herself and probably not Mark. 'Much traffic?'

'Usual.'

'Trip a success?'

'Yes, I think so.'

He brought her the drink and she sat down on the sofa and sipped it. He threw himself into a nearby armchair. 'What's for dinner?'

'Lamb curry!' Lindsey said promptly.

He showed some interest at last or, to be more accurate, he looked surprised. 'Cook it yourself?'

'Well, I cooked the rice. The lamb curry is from M and S.'

'Ah, frozen?'

'No, tinned. It's very good. You said you liked it, last time.'

'Oh, yes, fine by me.'

He'd already lost interest. He didn't care what it was. He didn't really care that she hadn't cooked it. When they'd first come to live here he'd suggested they hire a cook. They'd hired just one and she'd been a disaster. Since then Lindsey had muddled along with the help of a daily woman to dust Lower Lanbury House's cavernous Victorian rooms.

'There's been a murder at Cricket Farm,' she said.

He had leaned back and closed his eyes. Now he opened them again. 'That's old news. It happened donkey's years ago.'

'No, not Nathan Smith murdering his parents. A new one. They've found a body.'

There was a silence. Mark stared at her. Then he said, 'Don't talk so bloody daft.'

Lindsey felt a hot flush crawl up her throat and face. She gripped the gin and tonic. Another woman would have chucked it at him. But she was still trying to hang on to this marriage.

What the hell for? asked a little voice in her head.

Mentally she answered it. *For as long as it takes to get out of it with dignity and a decent settlement. I know my husband well enough to know he's a vindictive blighter.*

Aloud she said, 'Eli Smith found the body of a young woman in one of the outbuildings at the farm. The police came to the stables today. Actually, it was just one woman police inspector.'

'Lord help us!' said Mark drily. 'Is that all the local cops could manage?'

Lindsey drank most of the gin and tonic before she replied, so that she couldn't hurl it at him.

'She talked to Penny and to Andrew Ferris and to Selina Foscott.'

She had his attention now. 'And to you?' he asked sharply.

'No, not really. I told the inspector I couldn't help. The body was found on Friday. I was there on Friday but I went nowhere near Cricket Farm.'

'That's all right then,' he said. 'We don't have to bother about it.'

Lindsey had planned what she was going to say this evening. Planned it before the matter of the body at Cricket Farm had come up and provided an unexpected topic of conversation, or what passed for conversation between her and Mark. She'd intended to ask him, casually, to tell her more about the 'business trip'. Lead up to the real question. But it was a waste of time trying to do that. Perhaps surprise would work better now that she'd put him off-balance with the news about the murder.

So she just asked, keeping her tone casual, 'Have you got a mistress, Mark?'

He goggled at her. 'Have I *what*? What sort of bloody question is that?'

'Pretty straightforward, I should have thought.' She felt sick with nerves but she wouldn't let it show.

He was rattled. He got up and went to pour himself another whisky.

'What's put that damn fool idea in your head?'

'You're away a lot. You never talk about it. You—'

He spun round. 'I am away on business, working to earn the money to keep you in the style to which you are accustomed!' He indicated the room around them.

'I didn't choose this house!' she defended herself.

'You didn't refuse to come and live in it, either. You didn't refuse to marry me.'

'No,' Lindsey said regretfully. 'I was flattered. Why did you ask me? Actually, I know why. You wanted a wife to fit in with your county-set aspirations. You thought I'd do that. And I have done, haven't I?'

Mark was listening now, calculating. She could almost hear wheels going round in his head.

'What's brought all this on, anyway?' he asked. 'Haven't you got enough money? Do you want to buy another horse? Then buy one.'

'I might!' Lindsey snapped, her self-imposed control evaporating. 'Penny needs another riding horse at the stables.'

'I didn't mean one for the Gower female. Why not buy yourself a decent competition animal? Try a spot of eventing.'

'And keep myself out of your way even more?'

Mark walked over to the sofa and stood over her. Quietly he said, 'You need a goal, something to keep your mind from dreaming up crazy fancies. So carry on mucking out those smelly nags if it makes you happy but think about taking up some form of horsy competition. I'll concentrate on earning the money that pays for it all and leaves you free to spend your time as you wish.' He smiled but it didn't reach his eyes, 'I don't have a mistress, as it happens, but if I did, do you really think I'd tell you?'

He reached out and chucked her under the chin.

'Silly girl,' he said. 'Let's not have any more of this, all right?'

Chapter 6

'He's in the building!' whispered Joe Hegarty hoarsely, as she passed by his lair on Monday morning.

He was leaning over the ledge that parted him from those coming and going by way of the main doors; his round head turned up to her and his fingers gripping the edge of the counter. He looked, to Jess, like one of those grotesque corbel heads that lean out from nooks and crannies in churches, to fix intruders with their stone gaze.

'Thank you,' she said.

'He's a grey-haired fellow,' added Joe, who was hoary-headed himself.

'Fine, Joe, I'll no doubt be meeting Superintendent Carter very soon.'

The mild put-down passed completely over Hegarty's head. He only had a few months to go to retirement and, frankly, didn't care about seniority any longer. He'd be a civilian soon, an ex-copper. When that long-awaited time arrived, whether inspector or superintendent, it would be all the same to him. He wouldn't have to say 'sir' or 'ma'am' to any of them. He was, Jess thought with amusement, already practising.

She was however grateful for the warning and slightly annoyed by the information it contained. It was natural that the new boss would be prompt to arrive in his office on the first day, and she had made sure not to be even a minute late herself. She checked her wristwatch: a full ten minutes early. But Superintendent Carter had been earlier still. Was he hoping to catch them all out? She considered turning back to ask Joe what time the superintendent had arrived, but decided against it. It would give Hegarty great pleasure to know that she was jumpy.

And I am nervous, she admitted to herself as she climbed the stairs. It wasn't just because she had a new boss but because they had a new murder investigation underway. How they had handled it so far, and would handle it in the coming weeks, would set the tone of how Carter saw his team. If they were efficient, he would be easier on them in future. If they messed up, he wouldn't forget. They wouldn't be allowed to forget, either.

Usually at this early moment on a Monday a few people would be hanging about in the corridors exchanging greetings and trivial details of how they'd spent the weekend. There wasn't a soul to be seen now. Partly this was because two were on holiday and one on sick leave. Partly they were all lying low, toiling assiduously at their desks.

She looked into the room that Morton shared with Nugent (at present in the Algarve muffing his golf shots). Phil looked up sharply as she came in.

'It's only me,' she said with a wry grin.

'He's in,' said Morton. 'He walked in here, introduced himself, informed me he'd hold a meeting at ten o'clock and walked out. Man of few words, our new super, I fancy! Since there's only you, me, Stubbs and Bennison here at the moment, it'll be a cosy meeting.'

Jess sighed. 'Where are we at?' she asked.

'Well, Doc Palmer phoned in about three minutes ago and told me he's doing the post-mortem at nine thirty this morning.'

Jess hissed annoyance. 'Well, one of us had better be there and that means one of us will miss the superintendent's ten o'clock briefing. Have you told Carter?'

'I was going to, but then you came in. It'll be me, I suppose, who'll have to go and stand at Palmer's elbow,' added Phil gloomily. 'You'll have to be here.'

'Yes, and you'd better get going. Palmer always starts on time.'

'I always get morgue duty,' said Phil. 'I've got this for you, by the way.' He flourished a folder. 'You said to look up Eli Smith so I came back here on Friday night to check him out. I reckoned he'd be in on Saturday to give us his signed statement and if he was on the National Computer, I needed to know. I entered that farm, Cricket, as well for good measure and it turned up trumps.' He allowed himself a satisfied smile. 'I printed it out for you.'

'Thanks. And did he come in and give his statement?' Jess took the folder of papers. 'I think I know what this is, by the way. Double murder at the farm, right?'

'Oh, heard about it, have you?' Phil looked disappointed. 'Twenty-seven years ago, and yeah, the old chap came in and made his mark, like he said he would. I still can't get over him not even being able to write his own name. He didn't have anything to add to what he told us at the scene.' Phil indicated the folder. 'With that history no wonder he's so cagey. I've always said you've got to watch 'em in the country. They get up to all sorts.'

Jess opened the folder and glanced down at the first page.

'What's up?' asked Phil sharply.

Jess managed to wipe the shock from her face. 'Nothing,' she said.

But of course it was something; something that struck her whereas it might not strike Phil. Penny Gower had said she didn't know which of the brothers, Nathan or Eli, had been the elder. But Penny didn't know much of the detail of the Smith tragedy. The fact was the brothers had been twins. Like me and Simon, Jess thought, feeling discomfited. Except that they were twin boys.

There was a closeness between twins. She had always known, when they'd all lived together under the family roof, what her brother was thinking. He'd had the same almost telepathic link with her mind. They'd anticipated each other's replies, reactions, intentions. It had been a shock, when they grew up and went their separate ways, to find that neither of them knew any longer just what the other one was doing. But she knew that Simon, on his rare visits home, spoke to her of his medical work with a frankness he couldn't, or wouldn't, use when talking to his parents. Their father probably had some idea of the dangers Simon and his colleagues ran. Their mother imagined all manner of perils – and probably had little idea of the real ones.

And Nathan and Eli? Had Nathan's increasing slide into mental disorder and murderous intent communicated itself to Eli in the weeks beforehand? How much of a shock had it been for Eli to return and walk into that blood-spattered kitchen? Or had the massacre appeared to him as the culmination of a long brooding gestation in his brother's mind? Had his initial thought been, that Nathan had finally done it? Did Eli feel guilty? Did he think he ought to have known, have felt his brother's inner anguish and frustration? Had Nathan ever expressed a threat towards his parents? What about the subsequent suicide? Had Eli had any premonition of that?

She paused in the corridor on the way to her office as another thought struck her. Hastily she leafed through the remaining sheets. Had Nathan and Eli been identical twins? It didn't say. Eli's alibi for being absent from the farm at the time of the deaths was that he'd been attending a local cattle market. People had seen him there. But the Smiths were loners as a family. They hadn't 'mixed', so Selina Foscott had said. Selina had a childhood memory of the tragedy. She must be a local and for all her odd way of conducting a conversation and habit of taking charge of it, she might yet prove a mine of information. So if the Smith brothers hadn't been friendly with anyone they might not have exchanged more than a few words with fellow farmers at the cattle markets they visited. Could Nathan and not Eli have been absent from the farm when tragedy struck? Had Eli's finger triggered the fatal blasts from the shotgun?

Jess shook her head. That would mean Nathan had taken the blame for Eli's crime. Why should he do so? No, Nathan was the murderer and had been driven by remorse, depression or mental instability to take his own life afterwards. But it was hard to expel Selina's brusque comment from her head. *Believe me, if Eli wanted to kill someone, he'd do it the same way brother Nathan did.* Because, thought Jess, that was what a twin would do.

The possibilities opened up by the information in the folder running through her head, Superintendent Carter slipped her mind. Until, that is, she walked into her office, with the opened file in her hands and her eyes on the printed page, and the scrape of a foot caught her ear. She started.

A man was standing on the far side of the room, his head turned towards the window. She could only see that he was tall and stood very straight, putting her in mind of some of her father's military friends. He had thick, iron-grey hair and wore what looked to her inexperienced eye like a fairly expensive suit. She didn't need training in detection to work out who he was.

The surprise fanned the embers of her lingering annoyance. If he wanted to see her, why not leave a message that she should go to his office when she got in? Or wait until the ten o'clock meeting? Why come in here, snoop around her office, and catch her on the hop like this? She was beginning to think she didn't like the way Carter did things – and this before she'd seen his face or heard him utter a word.

So when he did turn round and said, 'Good morning,' politely enough, she returned his greeting fairly stiffly.

She thought he looked puzzled, just very briefly, and realised that she was glaring at him. She managed to assume a neutral expression.

'Superintendent Carter? I – we're very pleased to see you.'

'Thank you,' he said, 'and you're Inspector Jessica Campbell. It's nice to meet you.'

He held out his hand and Jess shook it. He knew how to shake hands with women, she noted. He neither mangled your fingers in a manly grip nor balanced your hand in his palm as if it were a Fabergé egg.

Pleasantries satisfactorily over, then. But he looked younger, when you saw his face, than the grey hair suggested, probably only in his mid-forties. Some people went grey early. Jess held up the folder in her hand. 'Sergeant Morton has just given me this. You'll have been told we have a new murder case?'

'Yes, and that's relevant, I take it?' He nodded at the folder. He was still speaking calmly enough but there was a definite awkwardness in the air. They were like strangers at some particularly chilly drinks party, standing around trying to find something to say.

Briefly Jess's mind went to Alan Markby, who'd been her senior officer in her previous job. She'd thought Markby an imposing figure when they'd met but he'd gone out of his way to put her at her ease. This man, she decided quickly, didn't have Markby's skills with people. The nicely judged handshake had been misleading. But then, it was Carter's first day. It wasn't a question, as it had been when Markby met her, of the senior man interviewing a new member of his team. Now the senior man was new and, in a curious reversal of roles, almost being interviewed, certainly judged, by those already here.

She pulled herself together and replied briskly. 'Yessir. The body is that of an unidentified young woman. It was found by a man named Eli Smith who owns Cricket Farm, where the deceased was discovered in a disused cowshed.'

'Disused?' He twitched an eyebrow.

'Smith doesn't farm there any more. He still owns the land and uses the yard for a scrap-dealing business. He's a sort of scavenger. When we got out there on Friday his lorry was laden up with all kinds of metal junk, old cookers and so on. He lives nearby but not at the farm. The old house there is boarded up.' She held up the folder. 'This is why. He used to live and farm there with his parents and brother. Then, twenty-seven years ago, the brother took a shotgun and shot dead both parents. Eli wasn't there at the time. He was attending a cattle market. Plenty of witnesses saw him there. Perhaps he was lucky or the brother, Nathan, might have shot him too.'

'So, murder has struck three times at the farm? A rather grisly coincidence. What sort of person is Smith?'

'He's a funny old chap,' Jess told him. 'He must be in his mid- to late sixties. He told us that he went to the farm to drop off his load of scrap, so his discovery of the body was purely chance. But I spoke to a woman called Penny Gower on Saturday morning. She runs a livery stables and riding school further down the hill from the farm. She saw a strange Mercedes car parked between the farm and her stables, pulled off the road, on Friday afternoon. The driver was crouched down inside it as she drove past, as if he didn't want to be seen. She mentioned this to a friend, a man called Andrew Ferris, who was at the stables. He decided to call up Eli on his mobile because he thought it might just be dodgy. That's what took Smith out there, about an hour later, to check over his premises. He did have a load of scrap too, so he was killing two birds with one stone. But he didn't mention a phone call from Ferris when we interviewed him. I put this to Gower and Ferris. They both said that would be "Eli's way" and seemed to find it amusing.'

She tapped the folder. 'This does go a long way to explaining that and some of the things Smith did say. The place holds a terrible memory. He was very upset about the body being on his property, and even more distressed that we'd be unbarring the abandoned house and going inside. But then, with a history of murder there, he'd know people might think yet another body an odd coincidence. He expressed worry about what the neighbours would say. Although, as Phil Morton pointed out, he doesn't have any neighbours. He lives about three quarters of a mile away in an isolated cottage. Oh, and he's illiterate.'

'A likely suspect?' Carter asked in that same calm way.

'Doubt it,' said Jess firmly, dismissing her own recent conjectures. 'He'd put her somewhere else, wouldn't he? Not so near his own property, especially not in his cowshed. There's plenty of land. He could have dumped her body anywhere. He could have buried her in one of the fields. No one would have known.'

'So could anyone else,' Carter said.

She realised he was watching her closely as she spoke. His eyes, she thought, were hazel and the look in them cool. It spooked her almost as much as the first sight of him standing by the window had done.

'Yes, it's strange that the murderer should dump the victim in the cowshed,' she agreed. 'Unless, of course, he killed her there and just abandoned her body.'

'It would still have been more sensible to move her. If the yard is used for any kind of business, the likelihood of someone stopping by would mean an increased chance of discovery.'

There was a silence. 'You're saying,' Jess said slowly, 'that the body was left there to be found?' She frowned. 'Funny, Eli Smith said that it had been left "on purpose". But he meant, I thought, on purpose to get at *him*. Someone who knew about the earlier murders, and holds some grudge against Smith.'

'And have you checked that? Someone with a grudge against Smith?'

There was something unsettling about the level expression and the unwavering calm tone.

'We'll talk to him again. But no, as yet we haven't. I have spoken to a local woman, Selina Foscott, who was a child at the time of the farm murders and remembers the Smith family as loners. Isn't it unlikely someone would go to the length of killing a young woman just to embarrass Smith? Besides,' Jess went on, ignoring a faint twitch of the other's eyebrows, 'there is another possible suspect.'

'The driver of the parked Mercedes?'

'Yes, he was spotted again very shortly after the first sighting. That is to say, Selina Foscott was driving out of the stables on to the road when a silver-grey Mercedes shot across her bows. She just avoided a collision.'

'What are we doing about finding this Mercedes driver who was so shy?'

'We' not 'you'. Jess appreciated that.

'Phil Morton's got on to traffic division, sir, in case a speed camera picked him up – and we do have a scraping of metallic silver-grey paint from the gatepost at the farm, so it looks as though our man *was* there that afternoon. Forensics will confirm if the paint comes from a Mercedes. He's a definite suspect.'

'When's the pathologist doing the post-mortem?' Carter asked suddenly.

Blast! She'd forgotten. Jess felt herself flush. 'At half-past nine this morning, sir, so . . .' She consulted her wristwatch. 'He's starting about now. Sergeant Morton has gone down there to attend. I know you wanted to see everyone at ten, but now Morton's out and we have two on leave and one sick—'

'Oh, scrap the ten o'clock briefing,' Carter interrupted. 'I'll see everyone who is here when Morton gets back. I'm interested to see Cricket Farm and where the body was found. Could you drive me out there, do you think?'

'What, now?' Jess asked.

'Yes, now,' he said. 'Unless you have something more urgent to do?'

'Um, no,' said Jess, stuffing the report on the Smith killings into the mini rucksack she carried everywhere in lieu of a shoulder bag. 'That is, I'll be happy to show you the scene of the crime, sir. I'll see if I can find the keys to the house. Phil Morton had them. They might be in his desk.'

'Good, and on the way out there, you can tell me anything else I should know.'

Whatever that meant.

Cricket Farm appeared abandoned but plenty of signs of the activity that had taken place there over the weekend remained. Blue and white tape still fluttered across the entrance. There was no man on duty guarding the spot so presumably the technical boys had finished. Sightseers might come later, drawn to the scene by gruesome curiosity, but as yet they hadn't found their way to this fairly remote place.

Jess and Carter ducked under the tape and she showed him the cowshed where the body had been found. A roughly chalked outline on the dirty floor could still be made out, but it was already partly obliterated. No more rain had fallen but the next time it did, it would blow in here and the chalk markings, the last sign of the dead girl's presence here, would disappear for good.

'No idea who she is, then?' Carter asked, staring down at the spot.

'Not yet. No one of that description has been reported missing. I would have thought she was a local girl, out here. It's a bit far from town. On the other hand she was quite smartly dressed in a casual way. A woman's pink jacket, presumably hers, was beside the body and it looked new. I got the impression from the way she was dressed that she'd gone out planning to meet someone.'

'A man?' Carter turned his head and surveyed her. She realised with shock that his eyes, which she'd thought hazel in the artificial glare of her office, were actually green in this light.

'A man, possibly. Or she might have planned to go out with a girlfriend on a shopping spree or to take in a film.'

They moved out into the yard. Carter nodded towards the house. 'What about in there?'

'I don't know that they found anything, sir. Sergeant Morton didn't mention it but I only spoke to him briefly this morning before he dashed off to the morgue.'

'Hm,' said Carter. 'Well, we'll have a conference later.

Now we're here, we might as well take a look.' He set off towards the sombre bulk of the building and after a moment's hesitation Jess followed him.

The house seemed to loom even more unwelcomingly as they neared it. The front door, with its coat of faded peeling brown paint, had been unboarded as had two of the downstairs windows. Splintered holes in the frames showed where the boards had been wrenched off. Upstairs the boards remained in place but didn't cover the windows completely.

Jess took out the bunch of keys she'd found in Morton's desk, helpfully tagged with a small label in Phil's hand reading 'Cricket Farm'. A second attempt found the right key and the door creaked open. They went in.

The first thing to strike Jess was the overpowering odour of damp, dust and decay. It swept over her in what the Victorians would have called a miasma, filling her nostrils, clinging to her skin and infesting her hair and clothing. She would smell of this house for the rest of the morning, if not for the rest of the day. When she got out of here the first thing she'd want to do would be shower and change. But she'd have to wait until this evening for that.

Carter made no comment but he coughed and put his hand over his mouth and nose.

Only the light from the open front door illuminated the place and the gloom wasn't helped by the hallway's ancient wallpaper patterned with brown roses. Even new it wouldn't have been very attractive. Now great strips of it had peeled off in the damp atmosphere and hung in unsightly strands like skin after a bad attack of sunburn. On the plaster behind, black mould had formed. They looked into the two small rooms to either side of the hallway, those with the unboarded windows looking out on to the yard. One appeared to have been the family sitting room and contained a rotting three-piece suite and a faded carpet, freshly marked with mud from the recent intrusion. There was a hole in the seat of one of the armchairs. It looked as if something had gnawed its way into the horsehair stuffing, which had been pulled out and lay scattered around like tangled twine, black and shiny.

A rodent's nest, thought Jess with a shudder. *Let's hope it's abandoned.*

Above the fireplace hung a discoloured mirror. Two china vases, probably of Edwardian date, stood on the mantelshelf, veiled in cobwebs. Between them a silent clock waited in vain for a hand to rewind it. It had stopped, she noticed, at ten minutes past four; in a creepy coincidence about the time Selina had had her near miss with the silver Mercedes.

The other room had been a dining room with a square oak table, a thick layer of ancient dust forming a dull grey tablecloth, and four high-backed chairs. Two more matching chairs stood against the wall, suggesting that the table was extendable. Again all appeared to date from the period just before the First World War. There were two lithographs on the wall, faded and yellowed. The nearer one showed two female figures in vaguely antique draperies, one veiled. They were standing by a fork in the road. The veiled one was gesturing to the right-hand track. The other, apparently younger one, pressed one hand to her breast and with the other was pointing down the same right-hand path. Jess peered at the wording underneath.

'"Ruth and Naomi",' she read out. '"Whither thou goest I too will go."'

She glanced across at the companion picture on the other side of the room. It appeared to have a similar Biblical subject.

'They never bought anything new,' said Carter unexpectedly. 'The grandparents must have farmed here. Perhaps the great-grandparents did, and last of all the parents. Eli, is he called, the present owner? Eli and his brother would have farmed here after them, had everything gone according to plan.'

And if Nathan Smith hadn't put an end to it all with a double blast of a shotgun.

By common consent they moved out of the room and proceeded to a long wide kitchen that ran across the back of the house. Off it a small stone washhouse contained a mangle, the operation of which would have needed the strength of a navvy, and a large grey-enamelled cylinder perched on claw feet.

'A copper,' said Carter, taking off the lid and peering inside. 'I don't mean one of us! I mean, for boiling the white linen. This must be sixty years old at least. They never got round to buying a washing machine.'

They moved back into the kitchen. Plates on a wall rack were covered in dust. Saucepans hung, similarly begrimed, from hooks. A yellowed calendar pinned to the wall was twenty-seven years out of date. Thick cobwebs hung across the window like net curtains but the spiders had long departed. In the corner stood two pairs of gumboots caked in long-dried mud and a tatty old mackintosh hung behind the door.

'Eli just locked the place up, after the original investigations had finished, and left,' said Jess wonderingly. 'He simply walked out leaving it all exactly as it was. It's like Miss Havisham's house in *Great Expectations*.'

Carter looked at her curiously. 'Have you read the book? Or just seen the film?'

'Both,' said Jess, nettled. 'I've got an English degree.'

'I've only ever seen the film,' said Carter, unperturbed. 'But I was a botantist.'

A botanist! For a moment Jess almost fell into the trap of asking what on earth had drawn a man with an interest in field studies into police work. But, as she knew herself, men and women joined the police force for all kinds of reasons. She'd had hers. Carter had had his. What would have been the alternative for him? Schoolmastering? Still, she wondered that he hadn't gone into forensics.

Carter was searching about on the floor and peering at the surface of the pine table. 'Is this where it happened? Here? Did one of the brothers blast his parents into oblivion in this room?'

'Nathan was sitting in the kitchen,' Jess told him, 'when Eli came back from the market. The shotgun was on the table here. The parents were dead but I'm not sure if he shot them in here. Perhaps it was out in the yard. Let me take a look at the report Phil Morton printed out for me.' She pulled it out of the bag and took it to the cobwebby window for the little light admitted to fall on the printed page. 'Mr Smith senior was killed in the – oh, in here!' She looked up and met Carter's eyes. Then she looked down at the pine table he'd been studying.

Beneath the dust, were those spots of dried blood?

Jess took a deep breath. 'The mother was killed through there in the washhouse. The bodies hadn't been moved, just lay where they fell.'

'Do you believe in ghosts?' Carter asked unexpectedly and accompanied his question with a slight smile, as if to indicate he wasn't serious.

But if Superintendent Carter asked you a question, Jess had already decided, it was because he wanted to know your thoughts.

'If I were to start believing,' she replied, 'it might be in this kitchen. It's not hard to imagine Nathan sitting here.' She tapped the back of a chair. 'And Eli over there by the door. Only Eli's not dead, of course.'

But he is, she thought suddenly. In his own way Eli died the day he came home and found Nathan sitting here covered in their parents' blood. This empty house was Eli's tomb. Oh, his physical body walked around out there. His spirit had been left here, trapped, mummified with all the other mouldering dusty remains.

Carter smiled again but only nodded.

They climbed the creaking staircase to the first floor. Up here there was only the light seeping through the gaps between the boards across the windows; and an occasional brighter patch where a board had loosened and dropped off altogether. An unpleasant acrid odour pervaded the air. Carter took a small torch from his pocket and the beam danced around them. It illuminated a double bed decked with mouldering sheets and rotting satin eiderdown; a dressing table thick with dust but still bearing a glass tray and matching cut-glass pots; a dressing gown hanging on the back of a door, its tasselled belt trailing on the floor. Nearby lay a long-dead and desiccated mouse.

Jess uttered a small exclamation and pointed at the wall. Carter swung the beam of the torch over to the spot and it showed up the paler oblong on the darkened wallpaper.

'Have you noticed, sir?' she asked. 'There are no family photos anywhere. Eli left those two lithographs downstairs and the calendar in the kitchen. Everything else was left just as it was. I bet we'd find clothes in that wardrobe. But it looks as though he took away the family portraits before he locked the place up for the last time. I wonder if he still has them. Or whether he destroyed them.'

They made the final ascent up a narrow rickety stair to a door into the attic space. As Carter opened it, the acrid odour they'd already noticed increased and swept unpleasantly over them. From the darkness came an angry rustling and the beat of wings. Something swooped by and touched Jess's hair. Her heart leaped up into her mouth even as she identified it.

'Bats,' she gasped.

'Protected species,' observed Carter. 'That will give Smith a headache if he wants to move back in here some day.'

They descended the stairs to the entrance hall.

'There's no evidence,' said Carter now, 'of anyone having broken in and camped out in here, not recently or ever. You'd think an empty house would attract tramps or hippies. There are no empty cans or syringes. No signs of a disturbance.'

'You mean, Eli might have disturbed an intruder and lost his temper?' Jess asked.

'He might have done. But there would be some sign of a more recent presence than twenty-seven years ago. Until the police came in on Friday, this place stood untouched, exactly as when Eli locked the door and boarded it up. Just as you said, like Miss Havisham's.'

They moved back into the yard and Jess turned to lock the front door, feeling a distinct lightening of her mood. It was a horrible house and she hoped she'd never have to go into it again.

Carter, ever one for the unexpected question she decided, now asked, 'You were on Alan Markby's team over at Cheriton?'

'Yes, sir.'

'What made you move here?'

'Finding somewhere to live mostly,' Jess confessed. 'I couldn't find anywhere in Bamford or in the surrounding villages. I'd hoped to buy Meredith's house. That's Meredith

Mitchell who was then engaged to Mr Markby and is married to him now. But she took her house off the market because, as I understood it, he sold his and the house they were buying together wasn't ready. They needed Meredith's place to live in. That left me in a grotty rented flat. Then I heard that someone of the rank of inspector was needed here so I put in for a transfer.'

'And have you managed to find somewhere to live here?'

'Yes, sir. I've got a flat in Cheltenham. It's the first floor of an old house that's been converted into flats.'

'Good,' said Carter.

Jess gave way to curiosity. 'You know Mr Markby, then, sir?'

'What? Oh, yes. I've met him on and off over the years.'

With that Carter walked off towards the gate on to the road.

Doesn't mind asking personal questions, thought Jess, but doesn't like answering them. Fair enough. It's a privilege of rank.

But she was still curious.

Chapter 7

The evening sun bathed her office and, along with lending life to dead wood, showed up where the cleaner had missed the corners. Jess sat with the file on the double murder at Cricket Farm open on her desk before her. It was the end of a long day and, truth to tell, she could go home. She could take that longed-for shower and put on fresh clothes. Around her, others were on their way to do just that; the building was emptying. Footsteps sounded in the corridors and the occasional voice called 'Goodnight!', echoing off the walls and ceiling. She could hear cars leaving the car park and one or two arriving. The night shift was coming on.

'Go home, too, Jessica!' she whispered to herself. But the file drew her to it. Its sad, dreadful story now rolled out in her mind's eye against the backdrop of that abandoned house. Its mouldering curtains and dusty furniture and, above all, its rank smell filling her nostrils, took her back there. She tried to imagine the scene as it had been that fateful day as she opened the file. She was telling herself it was necessary to the present inquiry, as indeed it was. Eli Smith had found this new body. But she knew morbid fascination was what drove her.

Here were the witness statements; this one from Mrs Doreen Warble:

'I'd cycled over to Cricket Farm on Thursday afternoon, to get the eggs. I always buy my eggs from Millie Smith. If you buy them from the farm you know they're fresh. I never buy eggs in a shop. Anyway, I've known Millie for years, since we were children. She doesn't – didn't – get many visitors. Cricket was never a welcoming place, couldn't be, with Albert, her husband, there. But it was another reason for going there for the eggs. Millie liked to see me and she always made a bit of cake when I was coming. I'd sit with her for an hour and tell her what little bit of news I had. Albert didn't like it. He thought our cup of tea and women's gossip was time-wasting!

'I have to remember to use the past tense, now she's gone. It's hard to believe she's not there, nor Albert. It's like the Prayer Book says: in the midst of life we are in death. You never know, do you, when you'll be taken? I just hope I die in my own bed and not like poor Millie did.

'I'll miss our weekly chat. I don't know where I'll go for my eggs now. Whoever takes on the farm, if it's Eli or someone else, I'll never be able to go there again. I'll always see it like it was Thursday.

'It was quiet in the yard but that wasn't unusual when I got there. It was getting on towards five o'clock. The chickens were pecking about like they always do. The cows weren't in yet for milking. They'd bring them in shortly so I wanted to be away before that. They make such a mess on the road and I have to ride through it on my bike. In fact, I was a bit later than I'd intended. I shall always wonder, now, if I'd arrived half an hour earlier whether things might be different. Millie might be alive – or I might be dead, too, if I'd walked in when Nathan was blasting off that shotgun.

'I didn't look round particularly. I'd no reason to and I was in a hurry, being a bit on the late side. I propped my bike against the side of the house and walked round to the back door. That's what I usually did.

'Just as I reached the door, it opened and Eli walked out. He stood in front of me so that I couldn't go nearer. He looked really strange, his face very white and his eyes staring. He said nothing. So I asked him, was he all right? I had to ask him twice, the second time almost shouting at him to get his attention because he seemed to be looking right through me.

'His gaze sort of cleared then and fixed on me then. He said, "Mum and Dad are dead." My blood ran cold, it really did. But at the same time I didn't believe him. How could I? Both of them? Like, if one of them had been taken suddenly, with a heart attack or had a bad accident, that would make sense but not both! Accidents on farms happen. So I told him straight off, "Don't talk nonsense, Eli!"

'"You can go in and see for yourself, if you want to," says he. "But it's no pretty sight."

'I began to think then that something terrible really had happened and I was frightened. I asked him where Nathan was. He told me "in the house" and sort of jerked his head backwards towards the door. I asked if Nathan was all right. He said that Nathan was "as right as could be", given that he'd gone out of his head.

'I can tell you, I was terrified by then. I couldn't run away because my legs wouldn't work. I was rooted to the spot. I don't know how I stayed upright. I was just frozen with fear, that's the truth.

'But then I thought to myself, I had to find out what had happened for Millie's sake. "Come on, Doreen!" I told myself. "You can give way later but not now!" The fact is, I think I'm – I was – the only friend poor Millie had. I never did care for her husband. He's – he was – a real old misery. I know they say, don't speak ill of the dead. But there's nothing much good you can say about Albert Smith. He hardly ever spoke, wouldn't give you the time of day. He'd just sort of grunt if you said hello. Never did see him smile. When Millie was a young girl she was really pretty and lively. But after she married him, she just went down. He killed off her spirit, long before this happened.

'So I told Eli that I must go into the kitchen and asked, was his brother in there? Because I didn't fancy meeting Nathan if he was roaming round out of his head. You see, I didn't understand then that Nathan had killed his parents. I thought perhaps Eli meant that finding them both dead had sent Nathan barmy. I still didn't quite believe they were both dead, to tell you the truth. I didn't know then about the gun.

'Eli said he thought Nathan had gone up to the bathroom to wash. That did sound a bit odd, but so did everything else. All I wanted to know was that Nathan wasn't in the kitchen. So in I went into the house, and Eli didn't try and stop me.

'I hope, as God is my witness, I never see another sight like that. It looked as if there'd been a battle in there, blood all over the place. One of the chairs was lying on its side and beyond, sprawled out on the floor, on his back, was Albert, although most of his head was blown off, so it could have been someone else. I knew it was Albert from his watch chain. He always wore his own father's gold watch and chain across his waistcoat. Summer or winter I never saw him without his waistcoat and the gold chain across it.

'I couldn't see Millie and I called out her name a couple of times. Eli came in behind me then; and said his mother was in the washhouse.

'I edged round Albert, making sure I didn't touch him, and into the washhouse. I was sort of prepared this time, if anyone can be prepared for a sight as horrible as that. Poor Millie was sitting on the floor with her back against the copper. He – Nathan – must have pointed the shotgun at her and just blasted her away.

'I realised then what had happened. I knew that

Nathan was in that house somewhere and he probably had the gun still with him. So I turned and ran through the kitchen and outside where it was safer.

'Eli had gone out again and was standing there. He said to me, "I told you so." I asked him, where was the gun? Did Nathan have it? He said, no, it was on the kitchen table. I suppose it must have been there, but to be honest, I didn't notice it. It was dark in that kitchen even in the middle of the day and my eyes had gone straight to Albert. Then I'd gone into the washhouse, so I just didn't look to see what was on the table.

'I told Eli we must fetch the police. But he didn't seem capable of it. So there was nothing for it, I had to get on my old bike, and ride down to the Hart, the nearest pub, and tell the landlord what had happened and get him to phone you.' [Witness means the police.] 'I didn't phone from the house because I didn't know where Nathan was, only that he was wandering around in there somewhere out of his wits. I didn't know where the gun was, if Nat had it or not. Eli said it was on the table but I didn't notice it. Perhaps Nathan had come back downstairs after Eli went outside and picked it up again. Anyway, even if Nathan hadn't been there, I couldn't have brought myself to go back in again and step over Albert in the kitchen, knowing poor Millie was sitting out there in the washhouse with a hole in her chest. Besides, I had it in my head we mustn't touch anything. Perhaps that's only in detective stories.

'The police told the landlord to make me stay with him at the Hart until they got there. Well, I didn't need persuading, did I? I wasn't going back up to that farm! The landlord gave me a brandy. My hands were shaking so much I could hardly hold the glass. I shall never know how I rode my bike there without falling off it. I couldn't have ridden it all the way home. My son came later with his car, put my bike in the boot, and drove me home. I don't think I'll ever get over it.'

Poor Doreen Warble. How brave she'd been. Jess sighed and turned to the next statement, that of Eli Smith.

'I'd been to market. We were selling a couple of cows. I got a fair price for them. Dad would say it wasn't enough but he always said that. He was grumbling about prices that morning, before I left. It was all just as usual: Dad moaning, Mum getting ready to do a load of laundry, Nathan slicking his hair down in front of the mirror with some stuff he'd bought in town. Dad said it made him smell like a tart's boudoir and grumbled about that, too.

'When I got back, usual time, around half past four, I walked into the house through the back door. We always go that way. We hardly ever go in and out the front door. I could smell the blood. I knew something had been slaughtered and I wondered if someone had killed a chicken or two. Then I saw Nathan sitting at the table with a silly sort of smile on his face and the gun lying in front of him. His shirtfront was speckled all over with spots and splashes of blood. I asked him, "What have you done, Nat?"

'He said he'd shot both Mum and Dad. He pointed at Dad who was lying on the floor. I asked where Mum was and he said she was in the washhouse. I went to look and sure enough, there she was. I walked back into the kitchen and asked him why he'd done it. He said, "It was time," just like that. It was time. He wouldn't say any more. He got up and looked down at himself, all spattered with blood, and said, "Best go up and wash, then." He went out and I heard him going upstairs to the bathroom, running the taps.

'I went outside and lit a cigarette. I must have smoked two or three, just standing there, not knowing what to do. I was shaking all over, my insides too. Then Doreen Warble came for her eggs. I told her what had happened and she sort of took charge. She's a good woman, Doreen. Mum thought a lot of her.'

Jess closed the file. Had it been a quarrel over something as trivial as the scented hair oil Nathan was using? Had his father uttered one insult too many? *It was time . . .* The straw that broke the camel's back had been added to the burden of years. Nathan had put an end to the grumbling forever.

She went home to bed.

* * *

Mud, Muck and Dead Things

In other circumstances, Lucas would have been feeling happy on Monday morning. He had made a good job of the scratch on the wing mirror, if he said so himself. The activity took him back to his youth, when he'd worked minor miracles on all kinds of old bangers, patching them up.

'Ah, happy days . . .' murmured Lucas. Then he thought, *No, they weren't! They were bloody miserable.* All the same, he'd always loved working on the old cars.

At least, back then, he hadn't needed to worry about corpses littering the place. He gave the wing mirror a final polish and stood back to admire his handiwork. But his self-congratulatory glow faded as he heard a tap on the closed up-and-over door of his garage.

He felt a stab of panic. Surely, not the cops?

'Who is it?' he called, trying to sound casual.

The voice identified itself, muffled through the door.

'Damn!' muttered Lucas, but he went to push up the door and gesture his visitor inside before he hauled it down again.

'I told you we were through!' he said sharply. 'What the hell are you doing here? I don't want any contact with you.'

'I'm here,' was the mild reply, 'because you told me never to go to your house. I thought I'd take a chance and try your garage. Been fiddling with the Merc?'

'I'm not fiddling,' Lucas began sourly, 'I've been polishing out a scratch probably made at that blasted farm. At least, it's possible I made it there. I hope to hell I didn't but anyway . . .'

It occurred to him that the less his visitor knew, the better.

'Just making sure she's in good order,' he added, far too

late he knew, and draped the polishing cloth carelessly over the wing mirror.

The other leaned against the car and that annoyed Lucas even more.

'You know what they teach them at cop school?' he asked unpleasantly. 'Never touch the car. If a copper has to stop a motorist, he bends down at the window or he asks the chap to get out of the motor. But he doesn't touch the car. Why? Because people are proprietorial about cars and they get upset. It's a primitive thing, instinct to defend your territory.'

'I've never thought of you as primitive, Lucas,' said the visitor, but moved away from the car.

'I don't bloody care what you think,' said Lucas. 'Just tell me what you're doing here.'

'I thought we ought to talk this over.'

Lucas relapsed into the idiom of his youth. 'Then you thought wrong, sunshine!'

He was uneasily aware that this whole business was having a deleterious effect on the carefully burnished persona he'd built up over the years. It was sloughing off like an outgrown snakeskin, gradually revealing the original Lucas, underneath. It was a shock.

'I mean,' said his visitor, 'if you really found a body . . .'

'Of course I really found it!' snarled Lucas. 'Do you think I'd make up something like that?'

'No, no, of course not!' the other soothed. 'But there was nothing on the news last night.'

'Then no one else has found it yet.' Lucas tried to conceal

his relief. The longer it went on without the body being found, the harder it would be to tie him to that wretched farm.

'In that case, perhaps you've been thinking you ought to report it to the police?' Both the question and the voice bugged Lucas.

Lucas himself had worked hard to eradicate the echo of south London from his speech, even though nowadays the accent had become quite fashionable. It hadn't been the trendy way to speak when he was growing up; it had been an indicator of not being 'one of us', and it had shut him out of a lot of places he'd wanted to be. So he'd worked hard on sounding what had been called in his youth 'posh'. But he knew it didn't ring true and he envied and resented the easy middle-class confidence of a voice like this one, echoing in his ear.

'Are you out of your head! How do I explain what I was doing there?' he exploded.

'Tell them you'd stopped to explore the place out of curiosity. You're looking out for land for development.'

The fact that he had had just such a thought for a moment or two while at the farm made Lucas angrier. Was he that easy to read? A person who's easy to read is also easy to manipulate. His earlier suspicion resurfaced.

'I've been having a bit of a think, too.' He glowered at the other. 'I'm beginning to wonder just why you chose that farm for our meeting!'

'I knew of it!' His companion was defensive now. 'It's pretty well deserted. The owner doesn't live there. He stops by occasionally but only rarely and it would have been really bad luck if you'd run into him. But if you had, I'd trusted you to think up some story quickly. You could have told him you were looking out for building land, the same as you could tell the police, if you go to them now.'

'I am not going to the police!' roared Lucas. In a quieter, but more chilling voice he added, 'And *you* know why. We're neither of us going to the cops, are we? Just get out of my life, right? And I'll stay out of yours. But if I find out who set me up—'

The polishing cloth slid from the wing mirror to the ground with a rustle, interrupting him, and he concluded the sentence with, 'Anyone who set me up will be sorry.'

As he spoke, he automatically stooped to retrieve the cloth. That was a mistake he'd never have made when younger.

Chapter 8

'Hello, Inspector, come to hear the gory details? I've just finished my report. Got it here, somewhere . . .' Tom Palmer hunted among the papers on his desk. 'Cripes, I remember now, I gave it to my secretary. But I can remember it all, if you've got any questions?'

He stopped shuffling the papers and looked up at Jess, black eyebrows raised.

This was a morgue and her business here this Tuesday morning was death and destruction but Jess found herself returning his cheerful smile. Then she forced herself to assume professional seriousness.

'I have already spoken to Phil Morton. He tells me you're satisfied with manual strangulation.'

'Take a pew!' Palmer indicated she should take the chair opposite and seated himself again. 'Oh, yes, quite satisfied. There is the characteristic fracture of the hyoid bone. There are bruises on the throat consistent with the pressure of fingers, but not of nails. So our strangler had short fingernails.' He held up his own hands, the backs of them sprinkled with fine dark hairs, and made gripping movements with them.

'A man, then, you think?'

'Some women have quite large hands and keep their fingernails short,' Palmer said reproachfully. 'I knew a girl once, well, doesn't matter. But she had hands like a navvy.'

Jess found herself hiding her own hands. They weren't large but she did keep her fingernails short. 'Spare me the details of your love life,' she begged. 'However odd it may be.'

He chuckled. 'I mean, it wouldn't require that much strength or time to kill someone by throttling them. That's what you tell kids, isn't it? Never put your hands round a friend's throat in play. If you grip your victim round the neck –' (more demonstration with his own hands) – 'he or she will lose consciousness quite quickly. Pressure on the carotid artery, you see. Blood doesn't reach the brain. Also the victim can't breathe.' Palmer rolled his head and gasped realistically. 'He or she will pass out and the murderer can finish the job at leisure.' He put his hands down on the desk.

'Thanks for the demo,' said Jess.

'You're welcome. So, yes, a woman could do it, especially a fit woman. Of course, there would be an initial struggle. Our corpse has a badly bitten lower lip and I would say that occurred during the brief fight back. She bit her own lip. But if the murderer surprised his victim or if she had no reason to think she should fear him, her reaction would be slow. If it is a "him", then perhaps a certain amount of rough and tumble was usual in their, er, physical contact.'

The pathologist cleared his throat and showed a momentary unexpected confusion.

'Sexual activity?' asked Jess immediately.

'No sign of recent activity.' Palmer was brisk again. 'She wasn't a virgin but then a modern girl . . .' Palmer avoided her eye. 'She was young. I'd say eighteen or nineteen, twenty at the most.'

'And how long had she been dead? And was she moved?'

'I would say my original guess of thirty hours that I made at the scene is probably correct, or as correct as we can say. One can never be exact about these things, despite what telly detectives and paperback whodunits tell us. So many factors come into it. In this case, the body lay in that cold shed, open to the night air and raindrops swept in by the wind. But her clothing wasn't soaked, only damp,' added Palmer suddenly. 'When did it rain?'

'It started to rain on Friday, the day she was found,' Jess replied. 'Before that, although we've had a lot of rain recently, I don't think it had rained for forty-eight hours. I remember thinking it was a welcome break.'

'Hum, well, you're the detective! As to whether she was moved, well, I'd say she was, but quite soon, within the five hours after he killed her. She was then deposited in that cowshed and, after that, she wasn't moved again until we took her away. So, for my money, she was killed elsewhere and after taking a few hours to think what he could do with the body, he decided to put it in the cowshed.'

'So he knew about the farm and that it was more or less abandoned,' Jess said thoughtfully. 'It also means he had to have kept the body somewhere between killing her and moving her.'

'Boot of his car?' suggested Tom. 'He'd have needed a vehicle to move her. And he might not have known about the farm. He could have driven round for four or five, maybe six, hours with the body in the boot, wondering what the hell he's going to do with it. Then, suddenly, he passes the farm. It looks deserted. He gets out of the car, takes a closer look and decides it's excellent for his purpose.'

'But what *was* his purpose?' Jess pursued, after a pause to consider this plausible scenario. 'He left her very near the entrance to that barn. Anyone taking a casual look would have seen her. OK, he threw her jacket and some sacking over the body but it was still obvious something was there, probably something that was hidden because it wasn't meant to be there. Short of painting a line of arrows leading to it, he couldn't have made it more obvious.'

Tom scratched his mop of black curls and pulled a face. 'You work out his motive, Sherlock. I don't know what his purpose was. I'm the sawbones. Post-mortem hypostasis is consistent with her having lain in that position for most of the time after her death. Lividity is fairly well fixed; leading me to think she was moved early on. You know what I'm talking about, of course?' Up went the black eyebrows again.

'Yes, Doctor, on death the blood stops circulating and settles at the lowest point to form pink or red patches. After a short while they become fixed. They ought to be underneath the body. If they're on top she's been moved.'

'Yeah, OK, of course you know! As a general principle, yes. We don't attach so much importance to *livor mortis* now as they did years ago. But basically what you say is right and still holds true. The fact that she lay in such a cold place may account for the deep red colour of the patches. She'd had a meal not long before she died, by the way.'

'Do we know what she ate?'

'Probably fried food. The fat register of the stomach contents is high. Beef, potato and some other vegetable. If I had to guess, I'd say steak and chips. Perhaps garnished with salad. The sort of meal you get in pubs.' Palmer grinned again. 'And there are hundreds of pubs in Gloucestershire which serve it.'

He was right, unfortunately. 'She was found at five o'clock,' Jess mused aloud. 'Deduct thirty hours or so and you get a time around lunch the previous day. Perhaps she had a date and he took her out to lunch in a local pub. We'll have to ask around. It's a good start. Thanks, Tom.'

'It's a guess!' said Palmer quickly, alarmed. 'I could be wrong.'

'We have to start somewhere,' Jess told him. 'What about her personal possessions? Anything to identify her?'

Palmer gestured towards the neatly wrapped items laid out on a shelf nearby. 'Sorry, don't think you're going to get much joy there.' He went across. Jess followed him.

The girl's clothes were laid out in individual plastic bags. There were no loose items. Struck, as she had been when she'd viewed the body, Jess ran down a list in her mind: no jewellery, wristwatch, notebook or diary, mobile phone, purse. Nothing, not even a lipstick. She frowned.

'Odd,' she muttered. 'Are you sure this is all?'

Beside her, Tom stared down at the pathetic collection and

123

nodded. 'I thought it a bit strange, too. There's no money. Everyone carries money, don't they? Even if they have a credit card on them, and especially if they don't.'

'He – I'm still saying "he" for convenience,' Jess began. 'I have taken note of what you said about the murderer possibly being female. So, he checked over the body and removed any personal items. He's a cool character, isn't he? He wasn't panicking. Most people, if they'd realised they'd inadvertently strangled someone, would panic. But I don't buy your theory that he drove round for five hours in ever-decreasing circles looking for somewhere to dump his victim. It's too long. Two hours? Three? Yes, possibly. Five? No. He drove her somewhere else where he waited, with her body still in the boot, until he felt safe to go to the farm. Of course, I'm assuming for the time being that the motive wasn't simply robbery. A mugger would have left her where she fell and run.'

'That's not something for me to decide,' said Palmer, suddenly cautious. 'Manslaughter or murder? That's up to you and the Crown Prosecution Service.'

'All right, I know! I'm the detective!'

A scenario was unrolling rapidly in her brain.

He took her out to lunch. She was happy, trusting . . . Somehow he persuaded her to go with him to some lonely spot where he killed her. There must be a dozen such places within range of the farm. He waited until evening, removed all identifying items, put her in the cowshed, threw her own jacket over her and, because that wasn't big enough, a handy sack as well . . . and scarpered. This isn't manslaughter. We're looking for a murderer.

But is he the man in the silver Mercedes? Did the murderer start to worry after he left her? Did he decide to go back and check again? Was he surprised no one had found her? Could he just not keep away?

'Her clothes all look new to me,' said Palmer, poking his finger into the nearest plastic sack. 'But I'm no expert on ladies clothing.'

'They look new to me, too,' Jess agreed.

So, had she recently come into extra money? Had the man who bought lunch also bought the new clothes? Had she got a new job and better wages? Was she a student who had got herself a part-time job to pay for new things?

Jess picked up the package containing the pink jacket.

'This is the most distinctive item and, I'd say, the most expensive. We'll go public with that one. Get a picture of it in the press and, with luck, on the telly.' She stood for a moment with the plastic package in her hands, frowning.

'I'd still like to know why he left her so near the entrance to that barn. It's as if he wanted her found. There are a dozen better hiding places at Cricket Farm.'

'Have you ever tried to move a dead body?' asked Tom. 'Let me tell you it's bloody heavy. "Dead weight" isn't a term used in jest. He may have staggered as far as the entrance of the barn and decided, sod this, and just dropped her there. To strangle doesn't take strength so much as persistence and pressure. He may not have been physically very strong.'

'Or "he" may have been "she",' said Jess.

*   *   *

125

The news of the 'Body in the Cowshed' was out. Late that afternoon Carter and Jess held a hastily assembled press conference and appealed for help in identifying the victim. They passed out photographs of the pink jacket.

She was a small stocky girl with a mop of tawny blond hair and smoky grey eyes. Phil Morton fancied he could almost see the smoke rising from them. He wished they looked at him in a more friendly fashion. It was Wednesday morning.

'Miss Svo-bo-dova . . .' His voice tailed off.

She leaned towards him, her manner even more aggressive. 'Svobodová!' she corrected.

'I was never very good at foreign languages,' confessed Morton.

She looked as if she believed him.

He tried again. 'Svobod-ova . . .' He held up his hand. 'You'll just have to put up with the way I pronounce it, all right? Or can I just call you Milada? That's a bit easier for me.'

'You can call me whatever you like,' she said. 'But do not pull a face.'

'I wasn't!' denied Morton, feeling that he was getting the wrong end of this interview.

'You were. You cannot see yourself. I can see you. You have a name, Sergeant?'

'Morton,' he told her.

'Tsk!' She waved it away irritably. 'You have a first name? You were baptised?' She frowned and stared at him in manifest doubt.

126

'Yes, I was!' snapped Morton, 'I was christened Philip, after my dad.'

'Good, well then, I can say "Philip Morton" and not pull a face. So you can do the same for me.'

'What can we do for you, Milada?' Morton asked wearily. 'You said you wanted to talk to someone about the recent discovery of a body.'

She threw herself back in her chair. Her belligerent expression faded and looked mournfully at him. She had full, well-formed lips, noted Morton, but now they turned down and he wished, for some reason he couldn't quite articulate, they would turn up, smile at him. He wished the smile could be reflected in the grey eyes.

'It's my friend,' she said. 'I'm certain.'

'Why do you think that?'

'She's missing. I can't find her. I have to do her shift as well as my own.'

Morton picked up his pen and retrieved his notepad. 'Where do you both work and what is your friend's name?' A note of apprehension entered his voice.

'Eva Zelená,' she said. Morton breathed a sigh of relief. 'We both work at the Foot to the Ground. It is a pub and a restaurant. I know it's a strange name but . . .' She shrugged. 'It's in the countryside and a very lonely place but lots of people come.'

'I think I know the place,' said Morton. 'Or I know where it is, at least. I hear it has very good food but a bit pricey. How long have you both worked there?'

'She was working there before me. When I came she had been there, oh,' she frowned again briefly, 'I think about two months. I also have been there two, nearly three months, so she's been there five months.'

'And do you both live there? Or where do you live?'

'Oh, yes, we share a room in the attic.' She pointed upwards. 'But it is a big room. It runs almost the whole length of the building and there is a little shower room up there for us. It's really quite nice.'

'And when did you last see Miss Zelená?'

'On Thursday morning, last week, before breakfast. It's her day off, Thursday, so she got up very early and told me she would go to Cheltenham. I asked her how she would get there. The Foot to the Ground is what you call "miles from anywhere" and there is no bus!' She looked indignant.

Looking indignant, Morton thought, seemed to come naturally to her. Nevertheless he felt he had to apologise for the inadequacy of rural bus services. 'Like that everywhere now, I'm afraid.'

'She told me she had a lift. Someone she knew, who lived not far away, was going to Cheltenham. She would walk down to the corner at nine o'clock and this person would pick her up. The Foot to the Ground is in a very narrow road but it joins a bigger road, which goes to Cheltenham. There is a –' She held up the forefinger of her left hand and put the forefinger of her right hand across the tip of it.

'A T-junction,' supplied Morton. 'Yes, there is. I know the spot. Yes, I have been to the Foot to the Ground. Not recently.

I haven't seen you there.' And he hadn't recognised the dead girl in the barn. But he hadn't been to the Foot to the Ground for at least six months. Neither of these two girls would have been working there then. Pity he hadn't been more recently. He might have met Milada when she wasn't so stroppy.

'This person,' Milada was saying, 'would also bring her back in the evening to the bottom of the road. But she didn't come back and Mr Westcott is very angry. He says she has buggered off. But I know she has *not* buggered off!'

'Mr Westcott?'

'He owns the pub. I told him, she most definitely has not buggered off because she would tell me, if she wanted to leave. Anyway, she left all her clothes and –' Milada rummaged in her shoulder bag and produced a small book with a flourish. 'She has left her passport! She would not go without passport!'

'Ah, now!' said Morton, taking it. 'That is interesting. Czech Republic. That's where you come from, too?'

She nodded.

He opened the little passport and studied the photograph. It could be the dead girl, but it had been taken in happier times and the dead face he remembered had been distorted and discoloured.

'If you don't mind,' he said. 'We'll keep this. I'll give you a receipt for it and if your friend turns up, you can give her the receipt and she can come in and claim it back, all right?'

'Keep passport!' she said impatiently. 'She can't use it now! She's dead so she won't come back!'

'Going off for a few days without warning is one thing,' argued Morton. 'Being dead is another. Does she have a boyfriend?'

Milada pursed her lips and made a side-to-side motion of her head. 'Perhaps. I think so, yes. But I don't know his name or who he is. She didn't say. But several times, when she had time off, she went to the corner, to this T-junction, and this person picked her up.'

'You saw the car?' Morton asked eagerly.

'Only once. I was outside the Foot to the Ground and I looked down the road towards the corner, just to see if Eva was still standing there, because it was starting to rain. But then a silver car went past; I mean it crossed the end of the road where the Foot to the Ground is. There were two people in it but I couldn't see the driver. I think the passenger was Eva.'

'What kind of car?' Morton pressed. 'Have you any idea of the make?'

'No, I don't know cars. Only Skoda.'

'BMW? Renault? Mazda? Toyota? Mercedes . . . ?' Morton lingered on the last name, aware he was leading a potential witness but there wasn't a judge here to hear him.

She shook her head and his hope was dashed. 'They are foreign,' she said. 'I only know Skoda.'

'Big car? Little car?'

'Not very big.'

Damn. That didn't sound like the mystery Mercedes they were looking for. But seen from several hundred metres away, it might have appeared smaller to Milada who, by her own admission, didn't recognise makes of cars.

'Why,' he asked, 'do you think Eva didn't talk about her boyfriend?'

She shrugged. 'I don't know. She was a quiet person. It was her business.'

'Ten to one, he's married,' said Morton a little later to Jess. 'He's a furtive blighter, at any rate. He meets her at the end of the lane when he could easily drive up to the pub and pick her up outside. Even when it's coming on to rain, she has to go down to the corner and meet him. He didn't want anyone to see him and you can bet he told her not to tell anyone his name.'

Jess was studying the passport photograph of Eva Zelená. 'Nineteen years old,' she said. 'It's about the right age and it does look like her. But probably a lot of East European girls look a bit like this. We'll have to get someone who knows her down to the morgue to identify the body. Would Miss Svobodová be willing to do that, do you think?'

Morton looked worried. 'Couldn't we ask this bloke, Westcott, who owns the Foot to the Ground? He was her employer. It wouldn't be nice for Milada, Miss Svobodová, to have to go and look at a dead body, especially if it is her mate. They shared a bedroom. Just imagine, switching out the light tonight with that empty bed alongside yours and an image of a corpse's face in your mind.'

It was rare for Phil to be so thoughtful about the difficulties of others. Perhaps Milada Svobodová was like Penny Gower: one of those fragile-looking women (in reality as tough as old boots) that men want to protect. Stop being sour, Jess!

'Hm. I'll have to go out there and talk to Westcott and anyone else there who knew the missing girl. But she hasn't been missing long and despite her resemblance to this...' Jess waved the passport. 'And despite what our informant tells us, she could yet turn up. If she does have a boyfriend, he might have suggested they drive into Wales for a couple of days and off she goes.'

'Not if he's married,' pointed out Morton.

'So his wife is away visiting her sick mother or something like that. There could be a dozen reasons why he has an un-expected opportunity to take off with his girlfriend. Yes, the girl in this passport does look like our victim. But that could still be coincidence. The other possibility is the sex trade. She's young, she's pretty, and she's a visitor from abroad with no family here. Someone could have struck up an acquaintance-ship with her with bad intentions. She wouldn't be the first foreign girl forced into prostitution. Anyway, I'll drive out to the Foot to the Ground and see what's going on.'

'I could go,' offered Morton. 'Milada has to get home somehow. She's still downstairs, having a cup of tea. She got a lift here with a delivery van driver, who'd dropped off supplies to the pub's restaurant, but she's got to find her own way back.'

'I'll talk to her first,' said Jess, standing up. 'And then I'll run her home.'

Morton looked disappointed.

'I want to see where the missing girl lived and talk to her other co-workers and this chap Westcott. Cheer up, Phil. I'm sure you'll see Milada again.'

'This is the Foot to the Ground!' declared Milada in proprietorial fashion. She waved grandly at the low rambling building.

It was an old place, sitting atop a high point in the hilly landscape and gazing out over grassy slopes and clumps of trees. In the distance more trees clustered thickly on the skyline like an invading army strung out along the ridge. The road on which the pub stood was little more than a lane now but was probably once the main highway. It was a quiet area, certainly, but on the way they had passed a scattering of stone cottages and one or two older houses, mellowed into the landscape and sitting behind high walls and wrought-iron gates. Just before the pub stood another row of terraced cottages in grey stone. Beyond them an abandoned, shuttered building that looked like a Nonconformist chapel built some time in the mid-nineteenth century was now crumbling away in isolation. It was surprising no one had bought it up cheap and turned it into an expensive unique residence. It showed a community had flourished here once. There still was one, of sorts. But Jess wondered how many of the cottages were second homes, weekend boltholes. She noticed little sign of any life.

Like so many other old pubs the Foot to the Ground had been added to and altered over the centuries. The different sections didn't match yet made a chaotic but attractive whole. An architect, thought Jess, would have fun picking out the medieval parts or the Georgian ones; and what even she could see was the Victorian or Edwardian exterior plumbing.

'Our food is very good!' insisted Milada, doing her bit for her employers.

Jess had quickly decided that Phil's desire to spare Miss Svobodová's feelings was not based on the young woman's fragility. Her manner suggested not so much the clinging ivy as the women's rights campaigner. Watch your step, Phil!

'Phil, Sergeant Morton, tells me it's expensive.'

A desire to talk up the business struggled with natural Slavonic thrift on Milada's face.

'English people pay a lot for everything,' she said, unanswerably, 'so I think it is not a lot for them to pay for a really good meal. You pay a lot of money in England for a bad meal.'

Also true.

'Fair enough,' admitted Jess.

Milada ran a professional eye over her. 'The fish is particularly good and always fresh.'

'And you're a very good waitress,' said Jess. 'Do you think Mr Westcott is here at the moment?'

Milada glanced at her wristwatch. 'The bar is open. He is here. I should also be here, half an hour ago. You will explain to him it's not my fault I'm late?'

Inside the Foot to the Ground it was dark. Already a couple of wall lights had been switched on to brighten up the gloomier nooks. The floor was paved with uneven slabs, a century or two old, and most of the furniture looked as if it had been there a few years. But everything gleamed with wax and brass polish. It looked welcoming, and despite the official nature of her visit Jess found her gaze wandering to the blackboard on which was chalked 'Today's Specials'.

A tall thin man with a moustache appeared from behind the bar and looked at Jess apprehensively.

'He is Mr Westcott,' hissed Milada for Jess's benefit. More loudly, and for her employer, she declared, 'The police!' She accompanied the pronouncement with a sweep of her arm towards Jess, rather like a magician producing a rabbit from his top hat.

'Oh, no, what have you done now, Milada?' groaned Westcott. 'You'd better come into my office, er, Officer?'

'Inspector,' Jess told him.

'Bloody hell,' said Westcott.

He ushered Jess into a tiny cluttered room and pulled out a Windsor chair for her.

'I knew Milada was going to the police,' he said. 'I'm really sorry she bothered you. I tried to talk her out of it.'

'Did you? Why?' asked Jess.

'Of course I did. Load of nonsense. Milada's got it all wrong. Look here, this dead girl they found at one of the farms around here, that's not Eva, can't be.' Westcott squeezed himself into a corner, perching on a wobbly bar stool that had probably been relegated here in case some customer fell off it.

Jess could already guess why Westcott was so determined

135

the dead girl wasn't his missing waitress. Bad publicity. He didn't want the police all over the place, questioning his customers. That's what would happen if the girl did turn out to be Eva.

'I appreciate your difficulty,' she began carefully. She didn't want to antagonise the man. Not yet, at least. She'd give him every chance to be cooperative. 'I understand it's a worrying thought for you. But Eva *has* gone and she *has* left her passport behind, and all her clothes, Milada says.'

'Oh, she'll send for them, or turn up to collect them when she feels like it. She's got herself another job, most likely.'

'Didn't she like it here?'

'She was paid well and the work isn't that hard!' said Westcott hastily. 'But the place is a bit out of the way and she didn't have her own transport. She grumbled about that a lot. Ten to one, she's working in Cheltenham. She'll roll in here, calm as you please, in a week or two, and pick up her stuff. You know what these youngsters are like.'

'I believe,' Jess told him, 'that she was regularly collected at the end of the lane, down by the T-junction, by someone who possibly drove a silver or metallic grey car.'

'The girls scrounge lifts off anyone. I'm always running them into Cheltenham.'

'Some of your customers might have given either of the girls a lift on occasion?'

Caution crossed his face. 'Ah, well, I wouldn't know about that. Frankly, Inspector, I don't fancy you quizzing them. People drop in for a quiet pint or a nice relaxing meal. They don't want to be asked a lot of personal questions, some of them sounding a bit, well, as if something dodgy was being suggested. My wife and I have worked hard building up a good reputation for the restaurant. We're doing quite well now and the last thing we need, begging your pardon, is a load of police officers going round the tables asking diners where they were at such and such a time.'

'If it's murder, I have to ask everyone the same questions, Mr Westcott. And we do our best to be tactful.'

'I keep telling you, it's not murder!' he insisted. 'That's just a bee Milada's got in her bonnet. She's bloody obstinate, is Milada. You can't argue with her.'

'But you tried?' Jess imagined the scene.

'I told you I tried. She was going to rattle your cage – sorry – she was going to trouble the police to no purpose. Wasting police time, that's an offence, isn't it? Eva isn't dead. She's cleared off for her own good reasons.'

'What reasons?' Jess demanded immediately.

Westcott clutched his brow. 'I don't know, do I? You see? As soon as you – the police – start asking questions, even the simplest answer gets jumped on and twisted and made to sound as if, well, in my case, as if I'm hiding something. But I'm not. No one here is. How do I know what goes on in a nineteen-year-old waitress's mind?'

'Did she speak good English? Milada speaks good English.'

'Yes, she spoke good enough English. They all do, enough to do the job here, at any rate. She was bright. I seem to remember she told me once her father was a schoolmaster or a professor or something like that back home, something educational, at any rate. She'd come to the UK to improve her English. But they all say that. They come to earn good money.'

'You pay them well?'

'Yes, we do by current standards. But you've got to remember that what seems a modest wage here, seems a lot to them. They've come from a different economy.'

English people pay a lot for everything . . .

'Could I see her room?' Jess asked suddenly.

Westcott looked relieved that she seemed to have switched her interest from him. 'Course you can. Milada's stuff is up there too. They shared.'

'I'll ask Milada if she minds,' Jess said, getting up and making it into the bar ahead of him, before he could get there and speak to Milada first.

Milada had found time to change. She wore navy trousers and a navy T-shirt emblazoned with the name of the pub.

'I take you up there!' she said immediately, abandoning her post at the bar and running up a narrow staircase at the rear of the room.

'Oi!' yelled Westcott after her, 'What about your customers?'

'I come back! You can mind bar for only three minutes!' called back Milada, obviously not in any awe of her employer.

Had Eva been equally self-assured?

The room was, as she had described to Phil, a converted attic space, running the length of this wing of the building. The ceiling was low and raftered. But the laminated pine flooring had been installed not so long ago and still looked new. There was plenty of room. The two beds weren't very close together and two small built-in wardrobes fitted under the eaves.

'This is mine,' said Milada, pointing at one of them. 'This is Eva's. You see?' She threw open the door with a flourish. 'All her clothes, everything!' She darted across to one of the beds and scooped up a framed photograph from a small bedside cabinet. 'Look! Her parents, she left her parents' photo.' She jerked open the little drawer in the cabinet. 'See? She left earrings, bracelet . . .' As she spoke, Milada was picking up the items and displaying them for Jess's benefit. 'She left pills.'

'Pills?' Jess moved quickly to take the little pack.

Birth control pills. Eva *had* been in a relationship. Or given to casual sexual encounters. Jess preferred the first explanation. The pills had to be taken regularly. She hadn't just left on a whim, as Westcott wanted the police to believe. These pills would have gone with her, as would her jewellery and probably her family photo. Jess picked it up and was poignantly reminded of the picture of her own family she'd been looking at so recently in her own flat. Suddenly the missing girl was real, not just a name. And if she was the girl found at Cricket Farm, this worthy kindly-looking couple, smiling at her from a photograph, were about to have their lives devastated.

'I'll just look round, if you don't mind. You'd better get back down to the bar,' she said. 'I think Mr Westcott is already a little upset.'

'I handle it,' said Milada serenely. But she left and could be heard noisily running down the uncarpeted wooden stairs.

Jess looked round the room and went to a door at the far end. It opened on to a small shower cabinet, toilet and wash-basin. On a shelf stood a jumble of make-up items: several little bottles of nail varnish (all of them in shades of pink), shampoo, hairspray, and Velcro hair rollers. All the sort of stuff you'd expect to find; a snapshot of a teenage girl's life. She wondered how much of it was Eva's. There were a couple of glasses with a toothbrush in each. Using a tissue, Jess turned them in the light. The blue brush head gleamed with moisture. It had been used that day: Milada's. The other one, pink, was bone dry: Eva's.

She had a cold feeling in the pit of her stomach. Somehow, she knew that the girl found at Cricket Farm was Eva. She ought to feel pleased that they'd apparently identified her so soon. But she only felt deeply depressed.

Jess rummaged in her backpack. Pulling out a plastic evidence bag, she slipped the tumbler with the dry pink toothbrush into it. They ought to be able to get a decent fingerprint and she'd send the toothbrush to the lab with a view to obtaining the missing girl's DNA. The latter would take a little time to come through. If there were a usable fingerprint, they'd get that more quickly.

She turned aside and went to the dormer windows. They gave on to the yard at the back of the pub. Standing at one of them, she had a good view down on to a number of wooden tables and benches forming an outside drinking area. Before the recent ban on smoking in enclosed premises, it would have been used mostly in the warmer months. Now determined smokers would use it all the year round. Perhaps for that reason an outside heater had been installed, ready for when the chill evenings set in.

At the moment the only person out there was a young man, dressed in the same uniform as Milada, marking him out as a pub employee. As if he realised he was being watched from above, he looked up and met Jess's gaze. For a moment they stared at one another. Then the young man looked away and moved to busy himself at some task.

Jess went downstairs. The bar had filled up and she wondered if word had got round that something interesting was going on. For such a sparsely populated area, people had popped up from all over the place. Where had they all been on her drive here? Hiding? She felt eyes follow her as she crossed the room and went outside.

The young man was brushing the yard with a great deal of energy and concentration. Jess got his attention by standing in the path of the sweep of his broom and forcing him to stop. He looked up, opened his mouth as if he wanted to ask her to move, then closed it and stood silently staring at her.

Jess produced her warrant card and held it up. His eyes flickered towards it but he said nothing.

'Now you know my name,' she said in a friendly voice. 'May I know yours?'

'Dave – David Jones,' he said, barely audibly.

'How long have you worked here, Mr Jones?'

'Nearly a year.'

'You like it here, then?' She smiled at him.

He didn't return the smile. 'It's all right.'

'If you've been here that long, you must have known the waitress who suddenly left recently.'

He bit his lip and suddenly turned and leaned his broom against the nearest table. Turning back, he said more loudly, 'Eva? Of course I knew her.' He had a pleasant, educated voice but it was tense.

'Were you friends?'

He had control of himself now, his early edginess less obvious when he replied. 'We were friendly, if that's what you mean. We all work here. We all get on well.'

'Was she a nice person, Eva? Good natured? Helpful? Cheerful?'

'Yes! She was a nice person, as you put it!' he snapped unexpectedly.

Jess was startled. She'd struck a nerve. 'Did she chat about her private life? Did Eva mention anything to suggest she might be unhappy here?'

'No!' Jones said almost savagely. 'She's reliable, hard working and decent. She's here because she wants to improve her English and she's really pleased the job has accommodation included. Jake Westcott is talking through his hat when he says she's taken off without a word. Eva wouldn't do that! She *was* happy here. I would have noticed if she wasn't.'

He seemed to realise Jess was taking note of his energetic reactions and asked less vehemently, but still with emotion,

'Do *you* think something has happened to Eva? Milada thinks so.' Anxiety overtook him on the last words and made his voice wobble.

'I don't know,' Jess told him. 'Milada came to see a colleague of mine. That's why I'm here. Milada thinks she might have had a man friend. Did she talk about that?'

'Not to me,' Jones said stiffly. 'I told you she didn't talk about her private life and as far as I know she was perfectly happy. I don't know where she's gone, but there has to be some explanation. Perhaps she's had an accident and is lying unconscious in hospital, unidentified. That happens. I know it does. I've seen it. There was a case in the hospital where I was training.'

He'd been a medical student? What was he doing here? Whatever the reason, he wasn't happy, not happy at all. He fancied the missing girl, Jess speculated. But she had a boyfriend, Mr Secret with the Silver Car, and, for her money, Jones did know about that, even though he didn't want to admit it now.

She looked round the yard. 'This is a lonely spot. Scenic but cut off. Do you live here too, like the waitresses?'

He shook his head. 'I live over there.' He pointed over her shoulders towards a clump of trees behind which a chimney stack was just visible. 'Greystone House.'

She wasn't sure, with a name like that, whether the building was an institution or a private house. 'What is that?' she asked.

'What?' he stared at her bemused, then almost smiled. 'It's my parents' home.'

'Is your father a landowner?' It wouldn't surprise her. This boy was definitely no yokel. She guessed at a public school education. Why on earth he was working sweeping a pub yard she had no idea. It was something to find out.

'No,' Jones told her. 'He's a barrister.' Now he did smile mockingly, enjoying her momentary discomfiture.

Right, so young Jones had legal advice and representation on tap. But did he need it?

Jess decided bluntness would play best with this young man. 'Why are you working here? If you've been here a year, it's not just a temporary job.'

'I studied medicine,' he told her. 'I was all right until we started going into hospital wards.' He raised his head and stared at her. 'Have you ever been on an amputation ward? Have you seen someone quite yellow because of liver failure brought about by alcohol abuse and seen in their eyes that they know they are dying, leaving those they love, and they've done it to themselves . . . and yet, if you offered them a drink, they'd take it? I had a sort of breakdown. I dropped out. I work here now. I like it. Usually,' he stared very hard at Jess, 'usually no one gives me any hassle.'

'And you don't take hassle well?'

'What do you think? No, I don't – can't cope well with pressure and I couldn't cope with the reality of medicine as a profession. The theory of the thing is fine, even cutting up dead bodies I could manage, although I didn't like it. But hanging round hospitals watching real people suffer, the distress of the relatives . . .' His gaze slid by her and out into space, seeing something that was only in his mind.

'Medicine wasn't a good choice for you, then,' observed Jess. 'My brother is a doctor.' She named the charity for which Simon worked and saw a spark of interest in David Jones's eyes.

'I'd like to be able to do as your brother does,' he admitted. 'I had some idea, when I took up medicine, that I might do that, go out and work for one of the charities in the Third World. But I couldn't stick the course. So here I am.'

'Not for ever, you'll find something else,' she heard herself assure him.

'Yeah, sure. My father keeps hinting at the law. My mother hints at the church. Me? I just want to carry on sweeping up the yard, as you describe it. I do other jobs around the place, you know. Serve in the bar, act as cellar man, run errands.'

'You've got your own transport?' Jess asked quickly.

'My motorbike.'

'And you run errands for your employers on that?'

Jones hesitated. 'No, there's a van, belongs to the business.'

'I see. Tell me,' Jess asked. 'Are there any photos around, of the pub and its staff, of Eva especially?' She could hardly ask: *Do you carry her picture around with you?* I bet you do, she thought, some snapshot taken when she wasn't looking. But you won't admit that, either.

'There are the leaflets,' said Jones unexpectedly. 'They're in the bar, advertising us. Jake Westcott had them printed a couple of weeks ago. There's a picture of us all in them.'

Advertising material! A bit of luck, at last. 'I'll go and ask him, then,' Jess said. She nodded to Jones. 'See you again.'

'Yeah, I bet,' he said sourly and turned to pick up his broom.

A dark red 4x4 turned into the pub's car park as Jess walked back towards the building. It joined a couple of other vehicles that hadn't been there when Jess had arrived. The regulars were arriving for their lunchtime pints. A heavily built man, probably in his late forties, climbed down from the 4x4. He wore the uniform of the country gentleman: corduroy trousers, ancient but quality pullover over a shirt and a cravat. A venerable cap crowned his head. That looked as though it might have belonged to his father, too, thought Jess, amused.

Too late, she realised he'd become aware of her scrutiny. He raised his eyebrows and walked purposefully towards her.

'Problem?' he asked brusquely.

Jess was obliged to produce her warrant card. He studied it carefully before returning it to her.

'Police, eh? This anything to do with that missing girl of Jake's?'

'I'm talking to . . . ?' Jess returned politely.

'What? Oh, Mark Harper.' He nodded towards the pub. 'My watering hole,' he said briefly.

Harper? Now, where had she heard that name before? Of course, Lindsey Harper, who worked with Penny at the stables.

'We've been informed that one of the waitresses employed here appears to have gone missing,' Jess said casually. 'Is that the missing girl you mean?'

'That's the one. Old Jake's pretty fed up about it. It doesn't surprise me. I've told him a dozen times; if you take on these

146

foreign girls you can expect trouble. Oh, they're all pretty and they work hard, grant you that. Customers in the restaurant like having them hover around. But you don't know a thing about them, I told Jake, nothing of their past history. You're obliged to take anything they tell you in good faith and for all you know, they could be spinning you a real yarn. That's what I said to him and I stick by it,' he concluded. 'Been proved right, haven't I?'

'Were you referring to this particular girl? When you spoke to Westcott about it?' Jess asked.

'No, to the whole shooting match, all of 'em.'

'But you knew this girl?'

Harper was slower to answer this time. He eyed Jess and expelled a puff of air between his lips before replying. 'Don't know any of them. I buy my pint from one of them at the bar from time to time, that's all.'

'Do you know the name of the missing one?'

'No! Yes, wait a bit, Jake called her Eva.'

'You never got talking to Eva at the bar? Asked her how she was settling in, that sort of thing?'

'Why the dickens should I?' His manner was growing aggressive. 'They come and go, so what's the point of asking them if they like it here? Jake will be lucky to see her again. She might turn up for her things, I suppose, or if she's owed any wages.'

The last point was a good one. If Eva were owed money, she would come back for it. But sadly, her return seemed increasingly unlikely. Jess remembered the distorted face of the dead girl in the cowshed.

'Could you describe Eva?'

'Of course I bally can't!' His voice rose and rang round the area. 'They all look the same to me. Why are you asking me all this? I don't know where the silly little trollop has gone.'

'Trollop?' Jess asked sharply. 'Why do you call her that?'

Harper stared at her again and blinked. 'Decent girl doesn't take off and leave her employer none the wiser as to where she's gone or if she's coming back. Now, if you've finished quizzing me about her, perhaps I can go and get my pint?'

He strode off towards the door of the pub. If that's Lindsey Harper's husband, thought Jess, no wonder Lindsey prefers spending her time with Penny and the horses.

Behind her a quiet voice said, 'He really is a complete shit.'

She turned to see David Jones. He must have overheard everything. So must anyone else in the car park area. Harper hadn't troubled to keep his voice down. Jones had addressed his comment to Jess but his eyes were on the door into the bar through which Harper had vanished. They glowered with an intense dislike.

'What does he know about any of the girls? About Eva or Milada or any of the others? He's got no right to talk about them like that! He probably made one of his cack-handed passes at Eva and she snubbed him,' he went on.

'He makes passes at the girls?'

Jones glanced at her. 'He's not the only one. He's got less finesse than most, so I've never seen him have any luck. They suss him out the moment he comes into view.'

148

'But he's a regular?'

'Oh, yes, Jake is impressed by him, don't ask me why. Money, I suppose. Harper isn't short of dosh.' Jones gave a bitter little smile and turned back to his work.

Milada was busy behind the bar. Harper had his pint and retreated with it to a corner where he was giving another regular the benefit of his opinion. He ignored Jess. Westcott was nowhere to be seen.

Jess caught Milada's eye and raised her eyebrows. Milada responded by rolling her own eyes towards the closed door of the office.

Jess walked across, tapped briskly and marched in. Westcott had been on his mobile phone, but snapped it off the moment she appeared.

'Oh, Inspector! Everything all right?'

Jess ignored the question. 'I understand, Mr Westcott, that you had some promotional literature printed, showing a photograph of the pub and its staff?'

'What?' He looked surprised and then relieved. 'Oh, right, yes . . .' He opened a drawer and took out a stack of leaflets. 'There you go, help yourself.'

Jess opened one of the leaflets.

'The Foot to the Ground,' she read, 'is an ancient hostelry and although never on a coaching route, was a recognised spot for travellers on horseback to stop for refreshment. It's thought this may be the origin of the name. Certainly the inn had this name as early as 1741, the earliest recorded mention of it. The building itself is much older, on medieval foundations, and may once had been intended as a halt for pilgrims on their way to Glastonbury.'

The potted history continued, followed by a mouth-watering description of its culinary specialties, and at the end, at last, a photograph of its owners and their staff.

Westcott dominated the group from the middle. Next to him stood a fair-haired woman. Milada and an older man were to his left. David Jones and the girl whose photo appeared in the passport, Eva Zelená, stood to his right. All of them! thought Jess exultantly. If she showed this around, who knew what reaction it might spark, who might be identified by whom.

'Who is this?' She indicated the fair-haired woman.

'My wife, she does the cooking. She's in the kitchen now and very busy. The lunch trade has started arriving. This isn't a good time to interview her. If you want to see her, I suggest you come back around five.'

'My colleague may come.' Jess next tapped the image of the older man. 'And this?'

'Bert, he's my handyman, electrician, plumber, carpenter, the lot. But he's off sick at the moment with a bad back.'

'That's awkward for you,' she commented.

'Dave Jones is pretty helpful,' Westcott said, 'and reliable. He can do almost anything around the place. He's learned a lot from Bert. I don't know what I'd do without him, frankly.'

Ah, yes, David Jones, the former medical student, who had almost certainly been sweet on Eva (who had been involved with someone else), and who would know all about the carotid arteries. But you don't need medical knowledge to strangle someone, thought Jess. Still, Jones had to go on the list. He'd had a nervous breakdown of some sort, too. He couldn't cope with what he called 'hassle'. Like being crossed in love? Would he cope well with that? Hardly. He drove the pub's van. He could transport a body. They would have to take a close look at that van, if the dead girl turned out to be Eva.

On the other hand, he'd been quite open about his nervous state, almost keen to tell her his history. Because he calculated she'd find out, anyway? He had a barrister for a father and he would know how the law worked.

'What do you think?' Westcott urged. 'About Eva, I mean. She can't be, you know, the girl . . . the one who was found, can she?' He lacked his former confidence now and was almost pleading.

Jess stacked the leaflets carefully together. 'Well, Mr Westcott, we're rather hoping you can help us there. I'm sorry to have to ask you this, but as you'll understand, there is no relative in this country we know of who could be asked instead.'

Westcott was growing steadily paler.

'We're wondering if you would help us by taking a look and seeing if you can identify her.'

He opened and shut his mouth a couple of times wordlessly. Then he croaked, 'Look at this body you've got?'

'Yes, I'm sorry, but we'd appreciate it.'

'You think it's Eva, then?'

'We don't know, Mr Westcott. But it's a possibility. You were her employer and she also lived here for several months.'

'Oh sod it,' said Westcott, sitting down heavily in the Windsor chair. 'I knew this would bloody happen. I told Milada . . .' He looked up at Jess pathetically. 'I've never seen a dead body,' he said.

Lucky you! thought Jess unsympathetically.

She made her way out into the bar. Harper had snared another hapless listener to his views. His pointed refusal to glance towards Jess was insulting and ignorant, she decided. But more importantly, did it indicate her questions had made him uneasy? Was he now behaving like a schoolchild in class? Don't catch the teacher's eye, she'll ask you something. She'd suggest to Phil Morton he call on Mr Harper at home and have an informal chat.

David Jones had come indoors and taken up a position behind the bar counter with Milada. Either he'd been called in because they were getting busy or he didn't want to be caught alone outside again by Jessica. He, too, avoided the inspector's eye and entered into a lively conversation with a customer. Jess, however, managed to intercept Milada's interested glance. Milada didn't mind questions; she had quite a few of her own. She wanted to know what was going on. Jess rolled her eyes towards the exit and walked out into the yard. As expected, Milada came scurrying after her.

'What do you think?' She stared hard at Jess. 'You think I'm right? Mr Westcott won't believe it but I know better!'

'We'll see,' said Jess soothingly. She took the evidence bag containing the tumbler and toothbrush out of her backpack and held it up. 'Can you confirm for me that this is Eva's?'

Milada's eyebrows shot up in surprise but she said promptly, 'It's pink. It's Eva's. Everything she buys is pink. I told her, buy another colour sometimes, but she just said she liked pink.'

And when she bought a new jacket, thought Jess, Eva bought a pink one.

Chapter 9

'So, now we know the identity of the victim,' said Carter the following morning, leaning back in his chair. 'Eva Zelená. Jake Westcott, her employer, was in no doubt about it . . . before he passed out?'

'Bit embarrassing, that,' admitted Jess. 'He just said, "Yes, that's Eva," and then pitched forward flat at poor Tom Palmer's feet.'

'Didn't hurt himself, I trust?'

'Oh, no, we brought him round and he was all right, only a little annoyed at being made to look a fool, as he put it. He repeated that the dead girl was Eva. He's not in any doubt. When her parents get here, perhaps we can get her father to confirm it, but I think we can go ahead on the basis of Westcott's identification.'

'Fine,' said Carter laconically. 'Just so long as he hasn't any reason to sue us.'

'He was the obvious choice, in the absence of a family member,' Jess pointed out. 'Besides, his waitress *had* disappeared, leaving everything behind, so we needed to know if the dead girl was the same one. Otherwise we'd have to start looking for a live Eva Zelená, wasting time and effort.

155

We've also managed to get a couple of partial prints from the glass I took from the bathroom. Not good enough for evidence in a court on their own, I'm afraid, but as back-up evidence very useful. I do think we can be sure of her identity. In due course we ought to get a DNA reading from the lab. So I've gone ahead and informed the Czech Embassy in London. They, in turn, are informing her parents in Karlovy Vary and telling them the inquest is set for the week after next, to allow them time to get here.'

A slight frown creased Carter's brow. 'They do understand at the embassy that the preliminary inquest will consist simply of a statement of the facts surrounding the discovery of the body and the identification? When the parents get here they'll understand what it means when the coroner adjourns for us to make our enquiries? We can't yet explain what happened to their daughter. There won't be any answers.'

'I hope so,' replied Jess cautiously. 'I did ask that it was all set out for the Zelenýs, but that bit's out of my hands now. Naturally the parents want to come here at once. I would, if it was me, and someone told me one of my family had been murdered abroad.' She shut her mouth tightly after the last words and stared away from the superintendent out of the window.

It was what she – and her parents – feared for Simon. One day, they'd get a message, like the one the Zelený family had received. (Phil Morton, who seemed to be getting quite an authority on Czech grammar, had informed her that 'Zelená' was a feminine version of the surname.) When Simon wrote, he constantly assured them he was safe. But he wasn't, couldn't be, in the hellhole where he was working. Bullets had an indiscriminate way of hitting anyone in their path: refugees, medical volunteers, Red Cross officials, cameramen . . . Bullets, and the men who fired them, made no distinction between persons. Sometimes the aggressors even targeted foreign volunteers. They wanted no witnesses reporting their deeds to a wider world.

When she looked back at Carter he was watching her in a careful way which made her wonder just how much he knew about her and her family circumstances. There was no way he ought to know about Simon. On the other hand, her brother's work wasn't a secret. She didn't talk about it, from a superstitious fear of making something bad happen. But others might.

'Ah, well . . .' murmured Carter, stretching out a hand to pick up the enlarged copy of the staff photograph from the Foot to the Ground's promotional literature. 'I dare say you're right. So what do you intend to do with this?'

'Show it to people. I thought I'd start with Mrs Foscott. If anyone in that photo has been hanging around in the neighbourhood of the farm or the stables, Mrs Foscott might have noticed them. She's . . .' Jess hesitated then plunged on. 'She's a bit of a battleaxe but she's shrewd and observant. Also she's a local. She's knows all the gossip.'

Carter folded his hands and stared at her again in the careful way Jess found so off-putting. At last he said, 'Fair enough. But watch out. She might do a bit of gossiping herself.'

He handed over the photo. Jess wondered if she ought to tell him that David Jones, shown in the picture, was the son of Barney Jones, barrister-at-law. She didn't yet know where Carter stood when it came to bothering the sort of people a police officer might find himself facing in court. She decided to keep the information to herself for a little while longer.

Predictably enough, the Foscotts lived in a large rambling shabby house surrounded by an untidy garden. There were two cars parked on the weed-strewn gravel drive when Jess got there: Selina's elderly aristocrat of a Jaguar and a newer, smarter, Lexus. Jess wasn't surprised when the door was opened by Mr Foscott, presumably the owner of the Lexus.

He was a tall, spindly man with thinning fair hair and glasses. He peered through them at Jess's ID and then at Jess.

'Can't tell you anything about the murder. Wasn't there. Never go near that farm or the stables. You'll have to ask my wife.'

'Er, yes, I came hoping – is Mrs Foscott at home?'

'Oh yes, come in.' He turned away and ambled into the house, leaving Jess to follow him. '*Selly!* Policewoman here to see you!' He glanced back at Jess. 'An inspector!'

With that he disappeared, leaving Jess alone in the hall. She looked around her. The interior of the house matched the exterior. Nothing had been painted or papered or in any way 'done up' for years. Pictures of horses or of Charlie from toddler stage onward atop a pony – and horse memorabilia, like rosettes and a couple of horseshoes – had been tacked higgledy-piggeldy to the walls. A saddle cluttered the floor next to the umbrella stand. The house smelled faintly of horse. Mr Foscott didn't need to go to the stables. His wife and daughter had brought the stables home with them.

Selina could be heard approaching with a noisy clatter of feet and an off-scene yell of, 'Well, I can't afford new boots, you'll have to make do with the ones you've got!'

She burst out of a door and carried on seamlessly, but this time addressing Jess, 'Kids' feet grow! I think the old Chinese were on to something, binding feet! Come in!'

Jess found herself ushered into a large sitting room with a tiled Victorian fireplace and faded rugs. There was an eclectic collection of furniture: a large three-piece suite covered in equally faded cretonne covers, a huge chesterfield which looked as if it had escaped from some gentlemen's club, sundry small tables, all laden with books, horsy magazines or newspapers, and a rather beautiful early Victorian or late Georgian writing desk. All surfaces not covered with discarded paper were dusty.

'Sit down. Want a drink?' demanded Selina hospitably, indicating one of the armchairs in its cretonne robe. 'I'd offer you a gin and tonic or something, but I suppose you don't, not on duty. We can rustle up some tea or coffee? *Reggie!*'

'No, no, please!' Jess put out a hand in alarm to forestall the inevitable demand that Reggie Foscott put the kettle on. 'I won't have tea or coffee, but thanks all the same.'

She sat down in the armchair. It proved an alarming experience. The seat sank beneath her with a loud twang of springs and she found herself trapped in a deep depression. Her knees stuck up in front of her, the arms of the chair rose to either side like starting gates and something was digging uncomfortably into the small of her spine.

'Comfy?' demanded her hostess, flinging herself on to the chesterfield.

'Yes, thank you,' Jess replied, thinking it must be obvious she wasn't.

'I'm not surprised you've turned up,' remarked Selina with satisfaction.

'Oh?'

'It's no use talking to anyone at the stables about Cricket Farm. They're all newcomers. Penny's aunt lived here for years; but Penny only came occasionally until the old girl croaked and left her everything. Then she bought the stables. Lindsey – have you met Lindsey?' Selina paused to raise her eyebrows.

Jess confirmed she'd met Lindsey.

'She's local but her husband is a newcomer. He turned up about ten years ago.'

How long, for goodness' sake, did one have to live here before one ceased to be a newcomer? wondered Jess. Probably if you weren't born here you never became a local. It struck her that, although there was quite a social gulf between Eli Smith and Selina Foscott, they were united in being natives of this area. That counted for a lot.

'That would be Mark Harper?' Jess asked. 'I have met him.'

'He's made a lot of money in the City,' said Selina darkly. 'They bought Lower Lanbury House and he turned himself into a country gent. Must have spent a blasted fortune on it.

Even got a sauna and Jacuzzi. Oh well, each to his tastes. Lindsey is a sensible woman. But she's a local. I was at school with her mother, Wendy. She was older than me, of course. Very good horsewoman, Wendy, and so is Lindsey. What can I do for you?'

Jess took her cue. She leaned forward awkwardly and delved into the indispensable green backpack lying at her feet. 'I was wondering if you'd look at this photo?'

She ought to get up and take it over to Selina on the chesterfield, but had a horrible feeling that, without an undignified struggle, she couldn't.

Selina obligingly hopped off the chesterfield, seized the photo and retreated with it. 'Who are this lot, then? Oh, that's a pub not far from here. Don't go in pubs myself but I know where all the old ones are. That's the Foot to the Ground, isn't it?'

'Yes. The photo shows the staff and the owners.'

'Who's the owner? This chap with the moustache? Looks like a second-hand car salesman. Good Lord!' With this exclamation, Selina raised the photo closer to her face and scowled at it. 'This is Barney and Julia Jones's boy.' She jabbed a finger at the assembled staff.

'Can you show me which one you mean?' asked Jess, although David Jones was the only young male in the line-up. But in court, lawyers tripped you up over sloppy identifications.

Selina turned the photo so that Jess could see it and tapped David Jones's image. 'This one. Can't miss him. What's he doing in this?'

'He works at the Foot to the Ground.'

'Well I never,' said Selina, the wind momentarily taken out of her sails. She rallied. 'I remember now. Julia told me. Young David went off to study medicine but he cracked up. I didn't know he was still around. She's a bishop's daughter, you know.'

When talking to Selina, a certain mental agility was called for. 'Mrs Jones?' asked Jess.

Selina nodded vigorously. Then she put down the photo and stared hard at Jess. 'Why are you showing me this?'

Jess ignored the question. 'Apart from David Jones, do you recognise anyone else?'

'No,' said Selina briefly, glancing down at it. She redirected her basilisk stare at Jess.

'None of the women? Please look carefully.'

Selina obliged by studying the line up again. 'No, none of them. The girls are pretty.'

'Yes,' said Jess. She could have pointed out Eva, but didn't. That sort of thing often had the effect of making witnesses 'remember' seeing the victim, whereas before they had been sure they hadn't. When the photo of Eva Zelená was released to the public, Jess had no doubt that, if Selina remembered seeing her, she would be in touch at once.

'Young David's not involved in this, is he?' demanded Selina.

'We have no reason to believe so.'

Selina pursed her lips and flapped the photo back and forth. 'I'd like to know why you're showing this around. You're not going to tell me, are you?'

'No,' said Jess, unable to repress a slight smile.

Mud, Muck and Dead Things

A gleam entered Selina's eyes. 'No objection to me mentioning it to his mother?'

'She probably already knows I've been to the Foot to the Ground,' said Jess. 'I expect her son has told her.'

Selina looked positively cunning. She held up the photograph. 'One of these girls is the dead one, isn't she? The one at the farm? Don't deny it. I can see it in your face.'

Oh, well, the best-laid plans . . . thought Jess with a sigh.

'Yes, she is.'

'Which one?'

Jess surrendered. She managed to haul herself out of the armchair in a tussle during which the chair, as if possessed by some demon, seemed determined to retain her. It gave a series of angry twangs before finally ejecting her. She went over to the chesterfield to collect the photograph. 'This one,' she said.

'Well, well,' said Selina thoughtfully. 'I wonder what Julia and Barney will make of that!'

So do I! thought Jess. Especially when their son tells them we took the pub's van away today for examination and forensic tests.

'What's the matter with him, then?'

The voice, sounding unexpectedly close behind her, made Penny jump away from the paddock gate on which she'd been leaning and spin round.

'Oh, hello, Eli. I didn't hear you.'

In silent reply Eli pointed at his gumboot-clad feet. Then he nodded towards the horse in the paddock. 'Off his feed or what?'

'No,' Penny sighed. 'Eating like the proverbial horse, if you'll excuse the pun.' Eli looked puzzled and she went on hastily, 'The vet says he's losing the sight of one eye. Actually, now I can see for myself something's wrong. When the light shines on the eye, there's a misty look to it.'

Eli sucked his teeth and surveyed Solo for several minutes. 'Very likely he is, then,' he said at last. He continued staring at Solo for a little longer then said, 'That'll be it, then, for him?'

'That will be it, Eli, as you say. I can't afford to keep a useless horse and he is now useless.'

Eli turned his attention back to Penny. 'I come down to see if *you* were all right.'

'Fine, thanks, Eli, apart from all my troubles. How about you?'

'Me?' Eli gave a low growl like a restless volcano. 'I got a ruddy body in my cowshed.'

'She's not still there?' Penny was shocked.

He shook his head, crowned with a greasy flat cap. 'No, they took the poor lass away. But they've been all over my property, those coppers. Do you know?' The volcano was getting angrier. His voice rose and he jabbed a stubby fore-finger at Penny. 'They've bin in the house!'

'The – er – house at the farm, Eli, or your cottage where you live?' she asked cautiously.

Eli considered this. 'Both,' he announced at last. 'That sergeant came to my cottage to get my keys to the house up at Cricket. I told him, that's boarded up. Ain't no one been in there for years! But he reckoned the police had got to look all over it. They got no business! Anyhow, I give him the keys and off he went and he's not brought them back!' The volcano erupted with a furious shout.

Solo, grazing in the paddock, threw up his head and turned his head, ears pricked, towards the gate.

'Not that it matters,' Eli went on more calmly. 'I got another set. I'm going to lock the place up again, that's what I'm going to do.'

'I'm sure they will have locked up behind them, Eli.'

'That's not secure,' said Eli obstinately. 'I've brought down a load of planks and I'm going to nail 'em over the door and fix it proper!'

'Perhaps you ought to ask the police first, if they've finished . . .' Penny began.

'I don't have to ask no policeman what to do on my property! That house has been boarded up twenty-seven years come Thursday next week. So I've got to get it fixed up again before then.'

'Why before then, before Thursday of next week?' asked Penny unthinkingly.

Eli took off his cap, studied the grimy lining, and replaced it carefully on his greying curls. 'Third Thursday in the month,' he said, 'was always market day. Cattle market, I mean, back in the days when we had a cattle market.'

Oh, dear heaven . . . thought Penny, understanding now. It was on a Thursday that Eli returned from the market to find his brother had committed a double murder. The anniversary of that tragic event must be coming up. *He's afraid to leave the house unbarred next Thursday. What does he think will happen there if he does?*

An atavistic terror gripped her briefly before she shook it off. The events of so long ago had obviously affected Eli's mind. It was no reason to let it affect hers.

The slam of a car door caused them both to turn their heads to the sound.

'See what I mean,' grumbled Eli. 'Now that woman police inspector is here again to bother *you.*'

Jess had hoped to find Penny Gower alone but when she saw Eli Smith with her, she wasn't displeased. Now she could show them both the blown-up staff photograph taken from the Foot to the Ground's leaflet.

Eli was glowering at her as she approached but Penny smiled a wary welcome.

'Hello Inspector Campbell, can we help?'

Mrrr . . . from Eli.

'I don't know. I hope so. I was wondering if I could show you this photograph – you too, Mr Smith, if you've got a moment.' Jess turned her nicest smile on him but it bounced off.

The horse in the paddock behind them, seeing a growing number of people gathering by the gate, moved away. 'He's thinking I've arrived for a riding lesson and he's going to have to do some work!' said Jess, meaning it as a joking remark to encourage a relaxed atmosphere.

Her words fell into the silence like a lead balloon. Two pairs of eyes were fixed on her with stony expression.

'Hardly likely,' said Penny. 'He's out of service, as you might say.' She smiled again but it was forced. 'But Solo doesn't know that, does he?'

'He's sick?'

'He's going blind.'

'I'm sorry,' Jess said awkwardly. Put your foot in it, Jess! Of course, that was the horse she'd attempted to pet on her first visit. Ferris had warned her. Time to move on hurriedly to the business that had brought her. She produced her photo and passed it to Penny who studied it carefully.

'Do you recognise anyone there? Has anyone resembling a member of that group been seen in this area recently? I'm sorry the definition is so poor. It's taken from a much smaller version in a publicity leaflet.'

Penny shook her head. 'Sorry, can't help. I don't know any of them. Is it the staff of a pub round here? The two girls and the young guy are wearing some sort of shirt with a logo and that looks like a pub behind them.'

'Yes, but you don't recognise them? The pub is called the Foot to the Ground, do you know that?'

Again a shake of the head. 'Sorry, no, it must be about the one pub around here I haven't been to. Andy Ferris and I have about done the rounds of the lot! I've heard of it but I've also heard its food is pricey.' Penny handed the photo back.

Jess handed it to Eli. He took off his cap and held it aloft

167

while he scratched his curls with his index finger, and studied the photo. He held it some distance from him in his other hand.

Long-sighted, thought Jess.

'I recognise the dead one,' said Eli at last. He replaced his cap.

Penny gave a squeak.

'You recognise the dead girl in this line-up? Which one?' Jess asked.

He jabbed a finger at Eva. 'This 'un. She was in my cowshed.'

'Had you ever seen her alive, before you saw her dead in your barn?'

'No,' said Eli. 'You say this pub is the old "Foot"? I haven't been in there for years. They made it too fancy and put the prices up. The beer costs too much for a poor old chap like me and I hear the food is fancy too, nothing sensible like a pickled egg.'

'This girl's name,' Jess said, 'is, or was, Eva Zelená. Have you ever heard that name?' She glanced at Penny to include her in the question.

'No,' they chorused.

Jess turned her attention back to Eli. 'You seem very sure, Mr Smith. But you only saw her when her face was distorted. You refused to take a second look, when the first police officers arrived in the patrol car. You told them you didn't want to see her again.'

'Course I'm sure!' said Eli testily. 'I'm not blind nor daft! I know that girl in my cowshed is this one here –' He jabbed a finger at Eva in the pub line-up. 'Course, she wasn't smiling like she is in this photo. But you wouldn't expect that of her, not lying dead on the ground. Her eyes were popping and her mouth was open . . .'

Another, louder squeak from Penny Gower.

Eli glanced at her. 'Yes, well, you saw her yourself, Inspector, when she was lying in my cowshed. She might not have been looking on top of the world, but she looked near enough like that.' He indicated the leaflet. 'If it was me showing you that picture, would you say, that's her?'

'That's difficult for me to know,' admitted Jess.

'Well, it ain't difficult for me. I might be just a poor old country feller, but I can recognise a face. That's her.'

'But you never saw her *alive* around here? Or anyone else in this photograph?'

Eli gave her an exasperated look, as someone who has been pestered by a child. 'No. I already told you. I don't know none of 'em. Not living and breathing, any road. I only ever saw the one of them, that young girl. And that was just the once, dead *in my cowshed*!'

With that Eli stomped away.

'You'll have to excuse him,' Penny begged. 'He's really very upset. It's because all this reminds him of the murder of his parents, and of his brother who shot them. It's – it's a sort of anniversary of the horrid business.'

'Is it?' asked Jess, surprised.

'He told me just before you arrived. He said it would be twenty-seven years on Thursday of next week. He didn't say it like that, that it was an anniversary. But it was clear that was what he meant.'

Jess mulled over the information. The date must be in the file and she must have read it. She ought to have remembered and made the connection. Pull yourself together, Jess! It wouldn't be surprising that Smith wasn't quite rational on the subject of the double murder. He would be very conscious of the approaching date, just one week away. Could he have found Eva wandering round Cricket farmyard – for a reason not yet known – lost his presence of mind and attacked her?

But what would Eva be doing at Cricket Farm and, moreover, how would she have got there? She had no transport of her own.

The silver Mercedes, thought Jess. *We have to find the silver Mercedes.*

Penny was looking embarrassed and scuffing the toe of her riding boot against the fence post at the entrance to the paddock. Solo had now removed himself to the far side and was a miniature horse in the distance.

'Inspector? There's something I'd like to say, now I've got the chance and there's no one here but us. It's nothing to do with this case you're investigating. It's personal to me . . . and to Andrew Ferris.' Penny spoke rapidly and her face had reddened.

'Look,' Jess said soothingly. This wasn't the first time she'd heard this kind of preamble to some personal confession. It mightn't be anything illegal or even questionable. But people, usually the most innocent ones, felt they had to justify themselves. 'I'm not interested in people's private lives if it's nothing to do with my investigations,' she went on. 'I do understand how it seems to witnesses. We ask all kinds of questions, a lot of them intrusive. I get embarrassed, too, believe me, asking them! But I really am only after information of use to me in finding out who killed that poor girl.'

Penny caught at a stray lock of hair that had escaped from a grip and was blowing across her face. She pushed it back behind her ear.

'Yes, I know. But there's still something I want to explain.'

'Go ahead, then,' Jess invited, curious.

'I just don't want you to get the wrong idea about Andrew and me. We're good mates. He's been marvellous helping me out. He's a countryman at heart, even though he works in an office. He likes being here with the horses and mucking out, building jumps, riding round the fields. We are lucky with having the use of Eli's land, most of it lying fallow. There are some sheep grazing way over there . . .'

Penny pointed beyond the paddock and Solo tearing energetically at the grass. 'Not Eli's sheep, another farmer's. Eli rents him a couple of fields. But that's all there is. Otherwise you can ride out there all day and not meet anyone. It's peaceful here. Present events apart, of course. But that's all we are, friends. Andrew is married. It's no secret it's not much of a marriage. His wife is away a lot of the time. She's a tour guide escorting parties around Europe. They don't have any kids. I think they're sliding towards divorce but it isn't because of me. Andrew's had a lot of unhappiness. But when he's with me, he's happy. I've had my share of unhappiness, too. That's why I'm here, hiding away in the countryside. We've both been hurt by relationships. I don't mean to sound like an agony aunt.' Penny pulled a face. 'I just want to put the record straight.'

'Consider it done,' Jess said.

'Thanks,' Penny said briefly. She pushed herself away from the gate. 'I'm sorry neither Eli nor I could help you with that photograph.'

'Oh, someone will eventually,' Jess told her, hoping it was true.

Phil Morton, given the task of checking out the pub regulars, had decided to tackle Mark Harper first. To that end, he'd driven out to Lower Lanbury House that Thursday morning, on the off chance the gentleman might be at home; or just to take a look round, if he wasn't. But the dark red 4x4 was parked outside the portico front entrance and as Morton got out of his car, the front door opened. A tall, solidly built man appeared and stopped short when he saw the visitor. Then he walked towards him, jangling car keys in his hand.

Just caught him on his way out, thought Morton. *Wonder where he's off to?*

'Something tells me,' the man said, when he reached Morton, 'that you're another copper.' His tone was insulting.

'Mr Harper?' Morton asked icily, producing his ID and holding it up. 'Sergeant Morton. Have you got a couple of minutes?'

Harper reassessed the likely amount of difficulty he'd have with this one and decided to be amenable. 'Certainly,' he said at last. 'You'd better come into the house. There's no one there. No need to stand around out here.'

Where someone else might arrive and see us . . . thought Morton drily as he followed Harper to the house. He cast an eye up at the portico before passing under it. *And that would never do, would it?*

'Your wife is out?' he asked when they stood in a room obviously serving as a study.

'Yes,' Harper said brusquely. 'Sit down, Sergeant, if you want.' He gestured at a chair and seated himself.

'You know we're enquiring into the disappearance and murder of a waitress employed at a local pub, the Foot to the Ground,' Morton began conversationally.

He was interrupted.

'I already spoke to an Inspector Campbell. She came to the pub.' Harper's tone indicated he thought the matter done and dusted. He didn't know Phil Morton.

'Yes, sir. But when Inspector Campbell spoke to you, we only knew for sure that one of the waitresses was missing. We now know the body of the young woman discovered at Cricket Farm to be that of the waitress. We have an enlarged photograph showing the girl when she was alive. You told Inspector Campbell you couldn't recall which one she was, so I wondered, if you looked at this . . .' Morton produced his copy of the group photograph and held it out. 'It might jog your memory.'

Harper took it reluctantly. 'Oh, I know where you got

this! It's from that leaflet Jake produced to advertise the restaurant.'

'This is the dead girl,' Morton said, leaning forward and pointing at Eva Zelená. 'Do you recognise her now?'

Harper glanced back at the photograph. 'No, well, I might, vaguely. But they all look much the same, those girls of Jake's. I've told the inspector all of this. I don't know why you're here.'

'We have to track down anyone who had any contact, however slight, with the victim,' Morton explained, retrieving his photograph.

Harper seemed glad to give it back to him. 'Well, contact doesn't come any slighter than mine with her! I probably bought a couple of pints from her at the bar.'

'Were you surprised to hear she'd left unexpectedly?'

'No, and I explained that to your Inspector Campbell, too. They're foreign, all those girls. I've warned Jake he knows nothing about them. There's no telling what they might do. She probably—' Harper broke off.

'Yes, sir?' Morton asked with interest.

'Doesn't matter. I told you, I didn't know her.'

'We're interested in any theory, sir.'

'Are you? That desperate, eh?' Harper grinned at him mockingly. 'Well, if you want my guess, she was probably on the game.'

'Why should she be working as a prostitute, sir? She had a job and accommodation.'

'She could have been moonlighting. All those girls, well . . .' He shrugged.

'But you have no evidence of that?' Morton asked silkily.

Something in his voice warned Harper he'd stepped on dangerous ground.

'No, no evidence at all. I shouldn't have said it. I wouldn't have said it if you hadn't pressed me.'

'Never paid her for sex yourself?'

'*What?* Hell, no! You have no right to suggest that! As if I'd be so stupid as to play around so close to home!' He leaned forward. 'Look, this is a waste of time. I wasn't even in the area last week. I didn't get back until Saturday.'

'Where were you, sir,' asked Morton politely, 'last week?'

'In London, on business!' Harper snapped.

'Someone there verify that for you?' Morton opened his notebook.

Harper reddened in rage. 'Bloody hell! Do I need an *alibi*?'

'Routine, sir, I assure you.' Morton held his Biro poised.

'Well, I – I had a meeting with my bank manager on Thursday morning. He'll confirm that.'

'How about the rest of Thursday, sir? And Friday? You say you didn't return until Saturday.'

Harper sat back in his chair, his hands resting on his thighs. 'Look here,' he said, 'this is confidential, right?'

'It's a police inquiry,' Morton reminded him.

'I know that!' Harper exploded again. He made an effort to be calm. 'I mean, if it's not relevant to your enquiries, it won't go any further than your notebook and Inspector Campbell?'

'If it's not relevant, sir. So if you can just give us a name and address and we can clear all this up . . .'

'I have a friend,' Harper told him reluctantly. 'I stayed with her for a couple of nights. I don't want – there's no reason for my wife to know about this. The lady is someone I've known for a very long time, since before I married. She – well, you needn't know the background to it all. She is technically married too, but separated. Her husband lives abroad. I don't want her alarmed or embarrassed. Her husband is a diplomat. The wrong kind of newspaper reporting could cause a lot of trouble.'

'We'll be very tactful, sir,' Morton promised him. 'Now then, her name and address?'

Harper watched him write it down, a very unhappy man.

'Tell me,' Morton invited, when he'd finished writing, 'when exactly did you hear about the murder, sir?'

'When?' Harper glared at him in exasperation. 'When do you think? When I got back home from London, on Saturday afternoon, as I told you. My wife told me the news. She keeps a horse down at Berryhill stables and spends a lot of time down there, lending a hand. My wife is a very keen horse-woman. Your Inspector Campbell had been there, too.'

'It didn't occur to you, when you heard from your wife that a body had been found at the farm, that it might be that of this missing girl?'

'No, why should it be? Jake Westcott was convinced the missing waitress had gone to Cheltenham, probably to take up another job. Why should I think differently?' Harper leaned back in his chair. 'I think I've answered all the questions I'm going to, Sergeant. As I wasn't in the area when all this happened, and as I've given you a satisfactory explanation for my absence, I really see no way in which any more can be gained by your continuing with this interrogation. If you wish to do so it will have to be at some other time and with my solicitor present.'

From the front step, Harper watched his visitor drive off then turned back into the hall, slamming the solid oak door behind him.

'Blast!' he said forcefully, the word echoing round the high ceiling.

'Something wrong?'

Harper looked up and paled. His wife was standing in the doorway of the dining room, next to the study. She was wearing her usual daytime uniform of jodhpurs and sleeveless body-warmer.

'Who was that?' she asked.

'I thought you were at the stables?' He stared at her, nonplussed.

'I was delayed . . . I had to deal with some post. I was using the dining-room table as a desk.'

'Oh? Well, it was a copper. Nothing to worry about. They've identified that body you were on about, the one found at Cricket Farm. It's one of Jake Westcott's waitresses. They're interviewing the regular customers.'

'Did you kill her?' his wife asked in that blasted casual way she'd developed lately; springing unexpected and awkward questions.

'Of course not! Are you out of your mind? The cops don't

suspect *me*. It was just a routine call. Anyway, I wasn't even here last week.'

'That's right,' she said agreeably. 'You've got an alibi.'

There was a silence. Harper scowled at his wife and glanced from the open dining-room door behind her to the open study door near him.

'How much of that did you overhear?' he asked cautiously.

Chapter 10

The fluorescent light tube above her head hummed gently. From time to time it flickered. Jess hoped it wasn't preparing to implode. Outside someone going off duty shouted a greeting to someone coming on shift. The call echoed down the corridor with the tap of footsteps. She was alone in her office again, and grateful to be in a small cell of privacy. She spread out the papers from the Cricket Farm Murder file and took up her reading.

Transcript of an interview between Inspector Harris and Nathan Smith. Also present Sgt Welland and Mr P. Samson, Mr Smith's solicitor.

Insp. H.:	You are Nathan Smith and you reside at Cricket Farm?
Smith:	Yes.
Insp. H.:	Can you tell us what happened there yesterday afternoon, Thursday?
Smith:	I shot Dad and Mum.
Insp. H.:	Was it an accident?
Smith:	No, I meant to do it.

Pause for consultation between accused's solicitor and accused.

Mr Samson: Mr Smith is not confessing to premeditated murder.

Insp. H.:   It was on the spur of the moment?

Mr Samson (to his client): You don't have to answer that at this time.

Insp. H.:   Why did you do it? Did you have a reason to kill your parents?

Smith: It was time.

Insp. H.:   What do you mean, it was time?

Smith: Things had been building up to it and the time had come.

Insp. H.:   Whom did you shoot first?

Smith: My father. I heard him coming. I was in the kitchen. I took down the shotgun and loaded it. He came in and I loosed it off at him.

Insp. H.:   Did your father have time to say anything?

Smith: He said, 'What the bloody hell are you doing with that?'

Insp. H.:   What about your mother?

Smith: She was in the washhouse, next door. She came running when she heard the shot. I swung round and pointed the shotgun at her. She backed away through the doorway, back into the washhouse. I followed her and I shot her, too.

Insp. H.:   Why? Why kill your mother?

Smith: I had to. She would never have let it rest.

Insp. H.:   What did you do next, Nathan?

Smith:	I went into the kitchen and waited for Eli to come home from market.
Insp. H.:	Did you intend to kill your brother, too?
Smith:	No. What would I want to do that for? Cows would need to be brought in for milking soon. Anyhow, I picked that Thursday because Eli wouldn't be there until later. I got no quarrel with Eli.
Mr Samson:	Inspector, it must be clear that my client is in a confused state of mind. I have attempted to explain to him about premediated murder but I am not sure he fully understands.
Smith:	I'm not simple. I know what it is. If you say that's what I did, then it's what I did.
Insp. H.:	What happened when Eli came home?
Smith:	He came into the kitchen. He asked what I'd done. I told him I'd shot Mum and Dad. He could see Dad on the floor and he went past me into the washhouse, to check on Mum, I suppose. To see if I'd done it, like I said. Then he came back and went past me again, not saying a word, and went out into the yard. I reckon it had given him a bit of a turn. Couldn't be helped.
Insp. H.:	What did you do next, Nathan?
Smith:	I went upstairs to wash. To wash off the blood on my hands and face. It was Dad's blood. It went everywhere. Shotgun blast does that.

Insp. H.:	What was your purpose in washing it off? Why did you want to wash it off?
Smith:	I wanted to look tidy when you lot came, the police.
Insp. H.:	And you just waited there in the house until the police came?
Smith:	Yes. I thought about going out and bringing in the cows with Eli. But I heard a woman's voice. She was talking to him out in the yard. I think it was Doreen Warble. She's a friend of my mother's and comes regular to buy her eggs. I didn't go out there because I didn't want to see her. She's a terrible old gossip.

The door of her office opened with a soft swish as it brushed the floor. Jess looked up, startled. She'd been so engrossed in her reading that she wouldn't have been surprised to see one of the players in the drama on the page before her, standing there.

But it was Ian Carter. He stood in the doorway, half in and half out of the room, his hand still resting on the door handle.

'Working late, Jess?'

She couldn't remember if he'd called her 'Jess' before. She was pretty sure it was the first time.

'Yes, sir, well, sort of. I was reading the file on the old Cricket Farm double murder.'

'Oh.' He hovered in the doorway. 'No point in burning the midnight oil over it. The day's long enough.'

'I'm just about to pack up,' Jess told him.

He still hovered, a picture of awkwardness. She had an inspired guess at what was in his mind. *If I was a man*, she thought, *he'd ask me now to go with him to have a pint somewhere, before going home. But because I'm a woman and because he doesn't know me that well, he feels he can't. Or perhaps he thinks I'm running home to someone. No such luck.*

'Right,' he said. 'Goodnight, then.'

'Goodnight, sir, see you tomorrow.'

She was alone again. She put away the file on the Cricket Farm murders and unhooked her jacket from where it hung. Time she went home, too. The job can get to you, she thought. Perhaps Carter's detached manner had been intentionally cultivated to deal with that. He was determined it wouldn't get to him.

Her mobile phone was buzzing like a frantic bee caught behind a glass pane. She'd forgotten she'd switched off the call tune. She fished it out hurriedly. 'Hello?'

It was Tom Palmer, doing what Carter had failed to do, ask her out for a drink that evening. 'And if you haven't eaten, neither have I.'

It wasn't the first time she and Tom had spent a quiet, friendly evening together. Tom had a problem and she understood it well. He had the sort of job that put other people off. He couldn't talk about what he did. That sort of gruesome detail was hardly table conversation and if he met up with someone who really did want to hear about autopsies, that person was to be regarded with caution. It restricted his circle of acquaintances. If he shook hands with someone, that person wondered just what Tom had been cutting up that day. If he shared a steak meal, other diners watched him carve his portion with fascination.

'There was this woman,' Tom once told her. 'She sat next to me at a dinner party and asked what I did. So I told her. She asked me, fair enough, why I'd chosen that field. I told her, because I like doing it. It interests me. She didn't speak another word to me for the rest of the evening. She didn't even look at me. After dinner, she sat on the other side of the room. I was like Dr Frankenstein as far as she was concerned!'

So, from time to time, Tom liked to go out for a drink for an hour or two with a companion who knew what he did and didn't give it a second thought. Jess had often found telling someone you were a CID officer had a similar dampening effect on a budding conversation. She sometimes thought, when she and Tom sat over their drinks, that they were like a couple of compatriot exiles in a foreign land.

But it beat sitting alone in front of the TV with a bowl of pasta or a takeaway chicken fried rice.

'Fine,' she told him. 'Where? If you've got no objection, I'd like to try a place called the Hart. It's near Cricket Farm.'

'Is this work?' asked Tom's suspicious voice.

'No, just curiosity.'

The Hart hadn't travelled the route upmarket taken by the Foot to the Ground, but it was a similar stone building.

It had settled down on its medieval foundations and opened its doors now, as it had always done, to the hungry and thirsty. Like the Foot to the Ground it was still a popular place to eat. But its menu was less ambitious, with a heavy reliance on chips. Over the centuries it had catered to travellers and drovers, farmers and their workers, weary passengers on the post coach, any and everyone in need. People no longer arrived on foot or on horseback; like Tom and Jess they arrived in cars.

Inside it was well-worn and had a lingering background odour of fried food and spilled beer. One corner was dom-inated by the flashing screen of a fruit machine, and another was occupied by an old man accompanied by an elderly, red-eyed spaniel, but the atmosphere was relaxed and it seemed to be doing good trade.

'Looks all right,' said Tom. Given the surroundings in which he worked, he appreciated the day-to-day normality of fruit machines and aged dogs. He studied the menu card he'd picked up from the bar on their way to their table. 'Fish and chips, steak and chips, double bacon-burger and chips, chicken and chips. Oh, lasagne . . . with chips.'

'Actually,' whispered Jess, 'I'm afraid we'll just have to have a drink and move on somewhere else for food. See that couple?'

She indicated a spot on the far side of the room where Penny Gower and Andrew Ferris sat by the window.

'Yup. Who are they?'

'The girl runs a riding stable and the guy helps her out. I've interviewed them both in the course of present enquiries.'

Jess grimaced as she produced this phrase. 'The girl saw a suspect vehicle, told her friend, he rang the owner of the farm who went there, found the body and called us in.'

'Sounds like "This is the House That Jack Built"!' observed Tom.

'Well, anyway, I don't suppose they'll be too happy when they see me. They might think I'm, well, trailing them. You understand, don't you, Tom? You don't mind moving on?'

'Sure I understand. You want to get away from work. Not sit here eating chips and staring at it!'

They drank up and rose to leave, edging their way across the now crowded bar room. But Penny had spotted them. She whispered to Andrew who turned round, looking surprised.

'Have to say hello!' muttered Jess. She went over to their table.

'Well, good evening, Inspector!' Ferris greeted her. 'What brings you out here? If it's not official again, that is?'

'No, a friend and I just dropped in for a drink. We're not staying.'

'Put off by the menu?' asked Ferris with a grin.

'It's a bit heavy on the calories,' admitted Jess. 'But we didn't mean to stay and eat, anyway.'

'We haven't driven you away, have we?' asked Penny, more percipient.

'Goodness, no!' Jess lied blithely.

'Right,' she said to Tom when they got outside. 'You choose the next place! I might have guessed that, being so close to the stables, Penny might be there.'

To herself she thought, if Penny hadn't told me that there was no romantic connection between her and Ferris, I'd have thought otherwise. Why does it worry her, I wonder?

They drove five miles down the road and found themselves at an almost identical old pub, this time called the Black Dog.

'All right?' asked Tom, as they climbed out of his car. 'Not put off by the name?'

'Should I be?'

'Blacks dogs are associated in some legends with witchcraft or the devil.'

'Spare me; I can do without the paranormal. The so-called "normal" is weird enough.' She glanced round as they went through the door. 'All clear. So long as Eli Smith doesn't wander in for his evening pint!'

Fortunately, this didn't happen.

'What made you curious to see the Hart? This place has almost the same menu.' Tom had scanned the new menu card. 'Only it does chilli and chips as well.'

'I'll stick to the vegetarian option, I think, cannelloni with spinach and ricotta. Why did I want to see the Hart?' Jess had the grace to look mildly embarrassed. 'It was where Doreen Warble went twenty-seven years ago to report the previous murder at Cricket. It was the nearest telephone. She couldn't use the phone at Cricket.'

'What previous murder and who on earth is, was, Doreen Warble?'

Jess summed up the tragedy of the Smiths as briefly as possible. 'I was reading transcripts of the interviews from that inquiry this evening. It put the name of the Hart in my head.'

'So, a murderous sort of spot, Cricket Farm? Do you really want the veggie option? I'll fight my way to the bar and order.'

'I don't know what part, if any, the previous murders have to do with the present case,' she told him when he came back.

'What does the new boss think?' Tom asked unexpectedly.

'I don't really know,' Jess admitted. 'He's not the sort who tells you what's on his mind.'

'Think you'll get on all right with him?'

'I certainly hope so but it's early days. So far, I don't see why we shouldn't be able to work together just fine.' She paused. 'You get called outside the area, Tom. Have you ever come across a Superintendent Markby?'

Tom frowned. 'Yes, once. He's over at Cheriton, isn't he? I did come across him when I was standing in for James Fuller.'

'Markby was brilliant to work for,' said Jess. 'But the funny thing is, Carter asked me why I moved here. He mentioned Markby but he was very, well, enigmatic about it all.'

'Perhaps they've got a history,' Tom said. 'Watch your step. Oh, blimey, is that the cannelloni? It's industrial strength!'

Penny and Andrew remained at the wobbly circular oak table where Jess had seen them. They'd collected their drinks at the bar and delivered their orders and were awaiting their food: chicken, salad and chips for Penny and steak, chips and side salad for Andrew. To keep themselves going until this fare arrived, they were sharing a plate of nachos, a delicacy Palmer had missed on the menu. Now the place had filled up, the hum of chatter had grown louder. It was even starting to drown out the piped music which provided another difference between the Hart and the Foot to the Ground. The latter's clientèle didn't like their conversation disturbed by 'wallpaper music'. The Hart's clientèle was, on the whole, younger, and accepted the tinny background tones as normal. Most of them, without the thud of distant pop music, would have felt bereft.

'What do you suppose the fuzz was doing here?' he asked, raising his pint glass to his lips.

'Inspector Campbell can go out for a drink with a friend, like you and me, I suppose. I don't know who the man was. He didn't look too much like a policeman.'

'Still don't know why she had to come all the way out here.'

'She was out this way earlier,' Penny told him. 'She came to see me at the stables again.'

Andrew took a long swig of his beer. 'Oh? Likes it round here, does she? Saw the Hart and thought, that's the place for me. I must go there. What did she want at the stables?'

'To show us a photograph. Eli was with me. He got rather upset and I do hope the inspector understands his point of view.'

Ferris set down the pint glass on the oak surface, already marked with countless rings formed by damp glasses over the years. 'What photograph was this, then?'

'A group one, showing the staff of one of the pubs round here, the Foot to the Ground. Do you know it?'

'I know of it,' he said. 'Dearest pint for miles around, so I hear. Prices set high to keep out the riff-raff.'

'Well, it seems the dead girl has been identified and she worked there. Her name was Eva Zelená.'

'The police are on the ball!' Andrew sounded surprised. 'What did they hope to gain from showing you and Eli the photograph?'

'Just to find out if we recognised anyone in it. I didn't, of course. Eli recognised the dead girl and then got very touchy when the inspector wanted to know if he was sure. I suppose they have to ask. They want to know if anyone in the photo has ever been seen around Cricket. That takes in the stables, I suppose, as we're so near. They'll probably ask Lindsey and Selina, even you! Selina won't mind. I think she was chatting pretty freely to that woman inspector the first time she came to the stables, when you were there. I watched them from the door.'

'Chatting freely about what?' Andrew frowned. 'What does old Ma Foscott know about anything except nags?'

'Oh, Lord knows. I wouldn't mind betting she was telling the police all about Eli's family. Selina is a local, you know. Her family has lived here for yonks. I really hope the police aren't going to badger poor old Eli. It's not his fault someone left a body in one of his barns. But there's the history of the place which is unfortunate, to say the least. Do you think the police will suspect Eli? It would be awful, Andrew. Eli wouldn't hurt a fly and anyway, he wouldn't report it to the police if he'd left someone for dead in his barn, would he?'

He leaned across the table and patted her hand. 'Don't worry about Eli. He's more than capable of taking care of himself. I don't suppose for a minute that the police will suspect him of anything. Moving clapped-out fridges round the country hasn't become illegal, has it?'

Penny frowned. 'You have to take them to special places to dispose of them, don't you? Because of CF gases and all the rest of it.'

'If the cops are investigating murder, I don't think they'll be worried what Eli does with his old fridges. Incidentally, I don't know why you're so sorry for the old monster. He probably makes a fortune out of his scrap. There's definitely money in it. There's a worldwide metal shortage at the moment; thieves pinch it from everywhere, church roofs, town square war memorials, you name it.'

'Eli's not a thief!' Penny was shocked. 'I don't think he's got any lead roofing or valuable bronze figures up there at the farm. At least I've never seen any; just stacks and stacks of clapped-out freezer cabinets and cookers. He doesn't seem to do anything with them but let them rust. Besides, I don't think money means anything to Eli.'

She leaned across the table, her hair falling forward to frame her earnest face. 'They opened up the farmhouse, you know, unbarred the door and went in, tramping all over the place. That has upset Eli dreadfully. It's been closed up since that awful business of his brother going bonkers and shooting their parents.'

'Did they now?' Andrew raised his eyebrows and pulled a

face. 'I wish I'd been there. I'd love to see inside that spooky old place. Is it still open? We could sneak up there and take a look.'

'You might. I wouldn't, not if you paid me.' Penny shivered. 'Anyway, it's not still open. Eli was up there this afternoon with load of planks, boarding it all up again. I could hear him from the stables, hammering away up there.'

'I bet the cops don't know he's done that. They might call that tampering with a crime scene. But what the heck, I don't suppose there was anything in there but mice.' Andrew leaned his forearms on the table and rested on them, bringing his face closer to hers. 'I didn't bring us out for the evening to talk about Eli, you know, or the body that turned up in his cowshed.'

'Apologies. I don't suppose you did. But it's hard to talk about anything but the murder, isn't it? You can't ignore something like that, not when it's happened on your doorstep. I expect half the people in this pub are discussing it.'

'Then it's probably doubled the trade and is the reason our food is so long arriving. The landlord mightn't mind but I do. I want to talk about us.' He saw incipient alarm on his companion's face and went on hastily, 'Listen, please, Penny! I've had a letter from Karen. She's not coming back.'

'Not coming back?' she stared at him, bewildered. 'From the cruise?'

'No, no, she's coming back from *that* to the UK, at least for the time being. But not to *me*.' He shrugged.

'Oh, Andrew . . .' Impulsively Penny put her hand over his. 'I am so sorry.'

He seized it. 'Don't be *sorry*! I'm not. I told you, the marriage has been on the rocks for ages, over and done. It just needed one of us to say so, and now Karen has, thank goodness. To tell you the full story, I gather she's met some elderly American widower on this cruise. Now she's all set to cut her links with me and set up with this bloke in the States. Good luck to her, to both of them. This evening out, Penny, is by way of a celebration.'

She snatched her hand away from his. 'You ought not to say that. It's a sad occasion. Any marriage failing is sad. You can't just accept it, like that! What about counselling?'

'Give me a break, Penny! We've gone way past the counselling stage. Anyway, she's met someone else, don't you see?'

'But your house, the furniture you bought together . . .'

'Karen suggests we communicate henceforth through our respective solicitors. She's got some chap in a London firm, probably a divorce specialist. I'll have to make do with the local man I've always used. Anyway, what's it to me? We can sell the house and the furniture, for all I care, and split the money down the middle. She has said that's all she wants. It's her idea, too. Financially she's got her own career and now she's also got her sugar daddy. We've always had separate bank accounts and she's no intention, she says, of raiding mine.'

'You'll still have to meet. She'll have to come back. What about her personal belongings?'

'She suggests we arrange a mutually convenient time, when I'm not there, for her to come to the house and take her stuff.'

'She might take half of yours as well,' argued Penny. 'You can't just stand back and let her help herself, Andy!'

'I shouldn't think she'll make off with my golf clubs or my collection of Toby jugs. She always hated those. I don't see her taking a pair of scissors to my best suit. She doesn't care enough about me for that! If you're worried about it, I'll move anything I value out of the house before she gets there. If she takes too long coming to pick up her things, I might put them in store. Then she needn't come to the house. But I suppose she will; just to make sure I haven't kept anything back. Oh, what the hell, the solicitors can sort that out between them. But don't you see what it means to us? I'm free – or I will be very soon. We can get married.'

'No!' Penny burst out so loudly the people at the next table glanced across. 'No,' she repeated in loud whisper.

He was staring at her in amazement. 'Well, I wasn't sure how you'd react to the news but I didn't think you'd be horrified!'

'I'm not, I mean, I am, that is, after all I was saying this afternoon, how we were just friends . . .'

She broke off, turned a bright guilty red and clapped her hand over her mouth. But the damage was done.

'Saying to whom? To Eli? To ruddy Inspector Campbell?' Ferris's own face flushed and he began to look seriously annoyed. 'What's going on, Pen? I thought you'd been discussing some photo with the cops, not us. I take it that's what you do mean? You've been talking to Campbell about us? Why? What's it to her? She's supposed to be investigating

194

the stiff in Eli's cowshed. I don't know why she was snooping here tonight, or why she was hanging round the stables with her photo album of deceased barmaids. I certainly don't know why you've decided to confide in her, especially about something so private and between *us*.'

'Don't get mad at me, Andy, please!' She leaned earnestly towards him.

'I'm not angry with *you*!' He drew a deep breath and made a visible attempt to calm down. 'But I'd like to know what the hell that inspector is playing at, asking about you and me. It's none of her bloody business and when I see her again, I'll tell her so.'

'No, you mustn't! It wasn't like that. She didn't ask me anything about you, believe me. It was me, I wanted to explain to her. I didn't want her to get the wrong end of the stick. She didn't want to listen at first but I insisted. I stressed we were just very good friends . . .' Penny's face fell. 'But now it seems I was the one misreading the situation. I feel such a fool. Oh, Andy, I am pleased you feel that the situation between you and Karen is being resolved. But I have always tried to make it clear to you that we can't be more than pals. Karen has her tour guide job and it didn't help your marriage. I've got the stables. I spend all day every day there. What kind of marriage would that be? You'd be out of the frying pan and into the fire if you and I married. Lindsey's husband makes unkind remarks about her spending so much time with the horses, even though he's away a lot on business, or he says it's business. I think Lindsey is getting suspicions he's got a lady friend in London. She, Lindsey, has been trying to establish where all the money is, just in case. That makes her sound mercenary and she isn't, really, not in normal circumstances. But Mark's got all the cash; she hasn't a bean of her own and she doesn't trust him an inch. If she does divorce him, well, she's not letting him off the hook! That's why you should take your split from Karen much more seriously. People get awfully money-grabbing when it comes to divorce.'

'I don't have any hidden assets,' Ferris said promptly. 'That's why I don't give a damn. Harper now, well, I wouldn't put it past him to have money stashed in offshore accounts. If Lindsey divorces him, she'll take him to the cleaners. But I'm not his accountant, so I don't care. You're doing it again, Penny, worrying about other people.'

'No, I'm not. I'm talking about us. You work from home. Every morning I'd disappear and not return until the evening, weekends included. It would be the same situation as you've been in with Karen.'

'No, it wouldn't!' he argued. 'Karen and I had other differences. Really, we had absolutely nothing in common. But you and I do. I'd still come down to the stables and help out. I know you've got to spend most of your time there. Although between us we could afford to employ a full-time groom . . .'

'You see? You're already looking for a way round the problem. A way for me to spend more time with you, somewhere else, and doing something other than look after horses.'

He began to look annoyed again. 'Look here, what are you going to do for the rest of your life, apart from care for the nags? What kind of quality of life do you want? Do you mean to live in that ramshackle cottage you rent from Eli *for ever*?'

Penny flushed. 'I'm glad to have it. It means I can be near the stables. Looking after animals isn't like any other job! I have to be there, on the spot. Don't disparage it. It's what I want to do and what I'm happy doing. I told Inspector Campbell that.'

'You can't give them your whole life!' he exploded. 'And since you're so keen to bare your soul to Campbell, does it occur to you, you might have been franker with me? Don't say you had no idea how I feel. You must have.'

A short silence fell. Andrew looked down at his hands.

'I can't explain it, Andy, I'm sorry,' Penny said. 'I wish I could. I never meant to mislead you. I – I really cherish what we have. Our friendship means a lot to me. It works, or I thought it was working, and I don't want to gamble changing it for something that might not work. I was in a relationship before, in London. It broke down, as yours and Karen's has broken down. It would be wrong for you to rush into another relationship right away. I know it isn't right for me. So at the moment, and for the foreseeable future, I am prepared to give the stables my life. I'm happy, Andy, and I'm afraid of losing that happiness.'

'Not afraid of losing me, though?' He looked up into her face.

'I don't want to *lose* you, Andy,' she said wretchedly. 'Perhaps I am being unfair. But I can't marry you.'

'Then I won't mention it again,' he said stiffly. 'Would you like another drink?'

197

A shadow fell across their table and they both looked up. An unknown woman stood there, heavily made up and clad in skintight jeans and a Lurex top. Her mascara-ed eyes fixed Penny avidly.

'Here,' she said by way of greeting. 'Don't you run the stables? You're right next to the farm where the girl was found dead! You must have had the police all over the place. Did you see anything? Did you hear any screams?'

Ferris gave a bark of laughter.

'Do you know, Penny? You're a celebrity! You'll be able to sell your story to the tabloids soon. Only leave me out of it next time, won't you?'

Chapter 11

'Well?' asked Phil Morton. 'Which piece of news do you want first?'

He was replacing the phone on its rest as Jess entered the room. His appearance was rumpled. That wasn't unusual but he looked more dishevelled than normal today. Jess knew he was working hard on this murder. Morton was always reliable, despite the litany of grumbling that accompanied everything he did. This time, however, she suspected he was taking a personal interest in the case and was therefore prepared to go the extra mile. Whatever the reason behind his diligence, she meant to let Ian Carter know how much time and effort Morton was investing. But it was a week now since the discovery of the body, and time was slipping away from them. From now on, witness memories would fade; other events would crowd the murder from public consciousness. They badly needed a break.

'I take it this is good news, Phil? We're making progress?'

'Oh, we're making progress, all right. Of course, it depends how you look at it, how good you think it is. On the phone just now,' Morton nodded at the silent instrument, 'was a solicitor by the name of Fairbrother.'

'Should I know him? Is he local?'

'You'll get the chance to meet him if we want to interview David Jones again. It seems that young David's family is very concerned that our questions might upset the boy and bring on another bout of his nervous trouble. So, if we want to talk to him again, Mr Fairbrother would like to be present.'

Jess pulled out a chair from the next-door desk, currently tenantless while DS Nugent hauled his golf trolley round the fairways of southern Portugal.

'Let me get this straight, Phil. Fairbrother rang us at whose request? David Jones's or his father's?'

'I think it must be his father's, but I couldn't be sure. Fairbrother was a little evasive about that.' Morton himself looked cautious.

'You can bet he was,' Jess said grimly. 'David Jones is an adult. He is, of course, entitled to have his solicitor with him if we question him. Though why he thinks he should need him is curious! But it would be *his* choice. His father can't request it on his behalf. If he were underage, it would be different. A minor has to have an interested adult with him. But he's at least in his middle twenties, although admittedly he looks younger.'

'He didn't exactly say it was old man Jones who asked him to phone us,' Morton told her. 'But he didn't say it was David's idea, either. He did say they had a statement from the family doctor attesting that the young man's mental state is fragile.'

'Good grief!' exploded Jess. 'What are they trying to do? Pin it on David? The family rushes to get a medical statement saying their son's unstable. They don't want him questioned without the family watchdog present. Don't they realise that both those things serve to point the finger at him? I'm surprised Barney Jones, who is a barrister, has handled things so badly.'

'It might not be him,' said Morton doubtfully.

Jess clicked her fingers in triumph. 'Got it, Phil! It's *not* Barney who has got on to Fairbrother and the doctor. It's *Mrs* Jones, David's mother. Selina Foscott warned me she intended to talk to Julia Jones. She did – and this is the result. I bet, when her husband finds out what his wife's done, he'll hit the roof!'

'As yet,' Morton went on, pulling a notepad towards him, 'we have no grounds to bring in young David for questioning. I rang the garage where the forensic team are stripping down the pub's van. So far they've found no sign of either blood or body fluids, or any incriminating object. Nor does the interior appear to have been cleaned recently. They have retrieved some long strands of hair, of a colour matching Eva's, from the headrest of the passenger seat.'

Jess gave an impatient hiss. 'That's not going to do us much good, even if we can identify it as Eva's hair. Why shouldn't it be in the van belonging to the pub where she worked? All Jones will need to say is that he gave her several lifts into Cheltenham or elsewhere. It would probably be true. Westcott said the two girls were always cadging lifts. What we need is evidence that Eva's *dead body* was in it.'

'Nor is Jones the only one to drive it,' Morton pointed out. 'Westcott drives it. He must have taken Eva into town in it umpteen times. So does Mrs Westcott. She's very good about asking the girls if they want a lift, so Milada says.'

'Milada?' Jess raised an eyebrow.

'Yes, Milada!' Morton flushed. 'Her last name gets me flummoxed. It's easier to call her by her first name.'

'The point is, what does she call you?'

Morton grew even redder. 'She calls me "Sergeant". If you heard the way she says it, you'd think she was the superintendent here and not Carter!'

'Good,' said Jess unkindly. 'Just remember, if you fancy getting up close and personal, to wait until all this is over. At present Milada is a valuable witness.'

'Don't tell me my job!' snapped Phil, adding icily, 'Inspector, ma'am!'

'Don't get on your high horse, Phil. I'm not telling you your job which you do very well, as we both know. I'm not interfering unduly in your private life. But we've got a new superintendent here and you being discovered canoodling with a witness is just what we don't need.'

Morton's anger faded to be replaced by his usual doleful expression. 'A chance would be a fine thing. Don't worry, I won't be stupid. Anyhow, about the pub van, if you're interested. The handyman who's off sick also drives it. His name is Robert, known as "Bert", Lawson.'

'Ah!' Jess brightened. 'A possible?'

Morton took a clear malicious pleasure in being able to disappoint her. 'No, the bloke's got a slipped disc. He hasn't been able to move for the past ten days. I've seen him and he looked genuine to me. He's hobbling round at home getting under his wife's feet and she's pretty fed up about it. He also gave Westcott a note from his doctor, explaining why he wasn't at work.'

'What about Westcott?' Jess asked thoughtfully. 'Did you speak to him when you went out to the pub, as well as to his wife?'

'I spoke to both of them. His missus's name is Bronwen and she's Welsh, you won't be surprised to hear. She's also the cook. The waitresses help out in the kitchen, before the restaurant clientèle turn up. They chop up vegetables and keep an eye on the stove, that sort of thing. Once there are paying punters sitting at the tables then it's their business to get out there and take orders and ferry the food back and forth. Bronwen Westcott seems to have been fond of both girls. She's very upset about Eva being dead.'

'Being dead or being murdered?'

'Both!' said Phil promptly. 'She says she means to make sure nothing bad happens to Milada.'

'Do you think she might be feeling guilty? Because something bad did happen to Eva?'

Morton showed an unexpected awareness of psychology. 'People always do feel guilty after a death. If it's someone near to you, you feel you ought to have been able to prevent it. Bronwen Westcott says now she wishes she'd taken more trouble to find out where Eva went in her free time. But both girls were adults and, as she says, she's their employer, not their guardian angel.'

'Hm, how about the regulars? Did you get to talk to any of them?'

Morton smiled. 'Westcott didn't like the idea of that. I was tactful, or tried to be. I went out into the bar and bought a tomato juice and mingled. I intended to introduce the subject of the missing barmaid casually, but I was stymied.'

'Oh, how?' Jess raised her eyebrows.

'Because Harper turned up. He immediately started going on about the police wasting their efforts and the ratepayers' money. "Who knows what the damn girl did in her free time?" he said. Charming fellow.'

'Ah,' Jess said, 'Mark Harper.'

'He reckons we're hounding him. If we show up again, he'll be off to make an official complaint,' Morton informed her. 'Anyway, he seemed to take the feeling of the meeting with him. After he'd weighed in, no one wanted to talk to me.'

'Blast Harper!' said Jess crossly. 'I'm not taking my eye off him. Perhaps he persuaded his "old friend" in London to give him that alibi.'

'All his drinking cronies sang the same tune. Yes, they were regulars. No, they didn't take much notice of the girls who worked there. The girls were always foreign and one was much like another, they couldn't tell them apart. No, they hadn't noticed one was missing. Well, old Jake did mention something but they couldn't remember exactly what. All were very shocked to hear she'd been murdered. Rural areas not safe these days . . . Police slow to act . . . Government not interested in the countryside . . . You can imagine the rest of it.'

'They're in denial,' said Jess crossly. 'By choice, that is. They don't want to know anything!'

Phil rubbed his chin against his clasped hands. 'As for Westcott himself fooling around with his waitresses, I think he'd find it difficult to do it without his wife spotting something. They all work together under the one roof. The two girls lived there up in the attic where Milada still is. It makes her sad to see Eva's empty bed but she isn't scared of spooks. She's the practical sort. The Westcotts live in an annexe at the far end of the building. You could argue it gave opportunity to Westcott if he fancied one of them; on the other hand, there must be very little privacy. We know Eva's boyfriend with the silver car went to great lengths not to be seen at the pub.'

Morton gave a little snort. 'I talked to both Westcotts in their annexe. It's just a couple of tiny rooms. You couldn't swing the proverbial cat. But, as Mrs Westcott pointed out to me, they're hardly ever there, so it doesn't matter if it's small. They work all hours.'

'It didn't sound to you as if she was going out of her way to make it clear her husband wasn't misbehaving because he didn't have either the time or the opportunity?'

Morton opened his mouth to reply but at that second the telephone on his desk gave a shrill cry. He grabbed the receiver and put it to his ear.

'What?' He swivelled in his chair to face Jess and held up his thumb in a signal of triumph. 'Right, thanks. Tell me again . . .' He seized a pen with his free hand and scribbled on his notepad. 'Cheers.'

He slammed down the receiver and actually allowed himself a grin. 'Got him!'

'Who? David Jones? Mark Harper?'

'No, better than either of them. We've got Mr Silver Mercedes! Traffic finally got through checking all the film in the various speed cameras. Those that had film in them, that is. And there he is at twenty minutes past four on Friday last, burning rubber on the Cheltenham road. He had so much on his mind he mustn't have realised the camera had flashed! They've traced the registration. It belongs to a Lucas Burton and here's his address.' He pushed the notepad towards Jess.

'Right!' said Jess excitedly. 'Then let's you and I pay a call on Mr Lucas Burton and see what he's got to say for himself.'

The rain had begun to fall in a persistent drizzle. Jess and Phil Morton stood together damply on the doorstep of Burton's Cheltenham house and waited. The trees lining the pavement edge were turning mellow shades of ochre and russet as autumn crept in. All the houses were well kept. Some might have been turned into flats but, if so, the tenants were doubtless jointly obliged to keep the buildings in good repair. There was no peeling stucco. The railings were freshly lacquered black. Some cars were parked alongside the kerb, theirs included, but there was a limit on the time and if the residents had vehicles of their own, they must garage them elsewhere. Burton's silver Mercedes would be one such.

'Nice place,' observed Morton, staring up at the façade. 'What with Harper at Lower Lanbury House and now this, I feel I'm rubbing shoulders with the super rich! He must be worth a bit, this Burton bloke. I wonder what he does for a living? He's not a policeman, that's for sure.'

'Someone's coming,' warned Jess.

In answer to the summons of the doorbell, footsteps could be heard approaching on the other side of the lacquered front door. It opened on a chain and the central section of a face was revealed, peering through the gap. It was enough to identify the owner as female.

Jess held up her ID so that the suspicious eyes studying them through the crack could read it. 'Inspector Campbell and DS Morton. We'd like to speak to Mr Burton.'

'Not at home,' said a voice promptly through the crack.

'Can you say when he will be home?'

'Didn't leave a note,' the voice informed them.

Jess frowned. Beside her Morton muttered, 'Do you think he's done a runner?'

'Are you Mrs Burton?' asked Jess, although she thought it unlikely.

A sardonic snort reached them. 'No, I'm not. There isn't one. He lives here on his own.'

Conversation through the gap wasn't easy. 'Perhaps,' Jess suggested, 'you could open the door properly and we could have a word with you?'

'If you like,' said the woman, 'not that I can tell you anything about him. I only clean up after him.'

The door was pushed to, a chain rattled, and the door reopened to reveal a stout individual in a blue button-through overall worn over baggy jeans. Her feet were shod in bright pink plastic clogs. She was in her mid-fifties, had dyed auburn hair trimmed into a youthful and unsuitable spiky cut, and sported large gold hoop earrings.

'Do you want to come in?' she enquired.

Jess hid her relief. Yes, they did want to come in and take a look round. But they had no warrant and in the absence of Burton himself would not have been able to gain entry without invitation.

The woman's next words explained her apparent hospitality. 'Only if I stand here gossiping with you in an open doorway, the rain will come in and spoil the parquet.'

'Oh, right,' said Jess. She and Morton hastened inside and the door was promptly shut.

'I have to polish it!' said the woman resentfully.

'We understand. Your name is . . . ?'

'Sandra Pardy. *Mrs* Sandra Pardy. I've cleaned for Mr Burton for the past five years.'

'Nice house to work in,' observed Morton, waving a hand to indicate the hallway in which they stood.

'It's got too many stairs,' said Mrs Pardy. 'And the ceilings are too high. I don't like getting up ladders. You have to get up a ladder if you want to get the cobwebs down from up there on those cornices. I've told Mr Burton, I don't like climbing up high. I get vertigo.'

'Yeah . . .' murmured Morton, looking at Mrs Pardy as though he recognised a fellow expert in the art of complaining. 'I bet you do.'

'My knees are not what they were,' continued Mrs Pardy. 'And damp weather like today doesn't do them any good at all. What was it you wanted to ask me?'

'You say that your employer, Mr Burton, didn't leave a note? Does that mean, you think he's gone away? Does he usually leave a note?'

'He leaves notes all over the place,' said Mrs Pardy. 'Do you want to come into the kitchen? Only I was just going to make my cup of tea.'

They followed her down the hallway, wondering at its blue and pale yellow decor and crisp white cornices, until they found themselves in a large, very well-appointed kitchen. Every surface gleamed. The place looked like one of those mock-up kitchen unit displays in furniture stores. Was this, wondered Jess, because Mrs Pardy was a very good cleaner? Or was it because very little cooking went on here?

'Do you cook for Mr Burton?' she asked, as she and Morton settled themselves at a pine table, unscarred and clear of any clutter except for a folded copy of a tabloid paper.

'No, no one does. *He* don't.' Mrs Pardy clicked on the electric kettle. 'I'd offer you a biscuit, but my chocolate digestives have disappeared. I reckon he ate them. He don't usually eat a biscuit. But I know I had a fresh packet up there.' She pointed at a cupboard above their heads. 'Unopened. I was saving it. It's gone but I found the wrapper in the wastepaper bin in his study. Monday morning, that was. I didn't see him. He'd gone out early. Didn't leave none of his notes.'

'Where does he eat, then?' asked Morton.

'Goes out somewhere, or has someone bring it round, home delivery. I generally find all the little silver cartons in the trash. Sometimes I come in and the kitchen fair stinks of curry. He likes Indian food and Chinese. Sometimes he gets in a pizza. But mostly, he goes out. He's got plenty of money. He can afford to.'

Jess reflected ruefully that Burton's eating pattern much mirrored her own. She didn't cook, either, not to speak of. Her kitchen bin was generally filled with aluminium trays and pizza boxes, her cupboards with cook-in sauces. But unlike Burton, she couldn't afford to eat out much.

'You come in every day?' asked Morton, frowning. 'What do you—'

Jess managed to kick his ankle beneath the table. It wouldn't do to antagonise Mrs Pardy by suggesting her job was a sinecure.

'I come in on Monday, Wednesday and Friday,' the cleaner was saying, as she poured the tea into mugs. 'Do you take sugar? I don't work weekends.'

'Blimey . . .' murmured Morton with a touch of envy.

'When did you last see Mr Burton?'

The cleaner came to join them at the table and presented them with a mug of tea each. She sat down heavily and pushed her newspaper to one side. 'A week, it must be. Yes, last Friday it was. I came in early as I usually do, nine o'clock. He was just finishing his breakfast. He'd had cornflakes and some coffee. I did ask if he wanted toast. I do sometimes make him a bit of toast, although cooking's not really part of my job.'

Phil Morton's face was a picture.

'He said, no, he was going out to lunch. Then he did go out, about ten o'clock. That's the last I've seen of him. People keep ringing up, wanting to speak to him, just like you are. I tell them what I've told you. I don't know where he's gone. I did ring his other place, in case he'd gone there, just to ask him what I was to tell people. But there was no answer. Well, there was a machine answering but that was no good. I've never got along with those machines so I didn't leave a message. After all, it wasn't up to me to get in touch with him, was it? It's up to him to get in touch with me, that's how I see it.'

'Other place?' asked Morton quickly, taking out his note-book.

Mrs Pardy eyed the notebook. 'Do you want the address? It's a flat in London somewhere. He uses it when he goes up on business.' She reached for a capacious handbag perched on the windowsill by her chair and rummaged in its depths. 'Here –' she said as she handed a note to Morton. 'The telephone number's on there as well. He gave it to me ages ago when he was away for a whole fortnight, so I could forward his letters and ring him if anyone called here. Can't remember as anyone did. I may have sent on a couple of letters. It was about a year ago.'

Morton took the slip of paper and raised his brows, before putting it in his pocket.

'Are you sure Mr Burton hasn't been back here this week, perhaps while you weren't around?' asked Jess.

Mrs Pardy shook her auburn spikes and the hoop earrings

swung. 'Bed not slept in. Bathroom not wet. Towels not moved. No food trays in the rubbish. Post not picked up where it fell through the letter box.'

The cleaner leaned towards them with a grim expression. 'If he don't get in touch, or turn up, I'm downing tools. I'm not slaving away here looking after the place if I'm not going to get my money at the end of the week. It's the only reason I came in today. I thought he might turn up because on a Friday he pays me.'

'Did he pay you last Friday?'

'Oh yes, because he was here, like I told you. He pays me Friday morning because usually he goes out after that and I go home at three o'clock. He paid me Friday last and then he went out. But this week it looks as if I've worked the three days for nothing!'

She sat back and folded her arms.

Jess and Morton exchanged glances. Lucas Burton had last been seen properly a whole week ago, on the morning of the day that had seen the discovery of the body. He had paid his cleaner her usual weekly wages and left the house. Everything had seemed normal. What had happened later to change all that? Evidence suggested he had been, for a reason not yet known, at Cricket Farm and left in a panic. Penny Gower had spotted him hiding in his Mercedes car halfway down the hill between the farm and the stables. Selina Foscott had narrowly missed a collision with his Mercedes and the car had been picked up on the speed camera, all on the Friday afternoon. These were the last recorded sightings of the man. Since then only a discarded chocolate biscuit wrapper indicated Burton had ever returned to his house. Normally a regular leaver of notes for the cleaner, he hadn't left one.

Phil Morton drained his mug and asked the logical next question.

'Where does he garage his car?'

'What about this flat in London, though?' asked Morton as they walked the short distance to Burton's rented garage. 'If he hasn't done a runner, he might be there.'

'Let me have me that phone number.'

Morton passed the slip of paper given them by the cleaner and Jess took out her mobile and rang the London number.

'No luck.' She dropped the phone back in her bag. 'We'll get on to the Met and ask them to send a man round and check the flat out. We'll concentrate on this garage and hope it tells us something. If the car's gone, we know he's driven off somewhere. If it's there, where is he?'

The garage was in a row of windowless lock-ups and secured by a steel up-and-over door. Morton rattled at the catch.

'Locked. If it was a house, we could find a way in, or break in, but this? We'd need to pick this lock.'

'Lucas Burton has now been reported missing by his cleaner,' Jess said firmly. 'We believe he was at Cricket Farm only a few hours before a body was discovered there. We have good reason to believe he is in a distressed state of mind. Get a locksmith.'

* * *

213

'There you go,' said the locksmith, a little later. 'You should be able to open it now.'

Morton stepped forward and swung the door up. The interior of the garage was revealed and they savoured a moment of triumph as the large silver Mercedes came into view. But almost at once a powerful, sickly-sweet odour swept out and enveloped them.

'Faugh!' gasped the locksmith, stepping back. He gave way to a fit of coughing.

They had found Lucas Burton. But he wouldn't be talking to them, or to anyone else, ever again.

Chapter 12

'Here we are again,' said Tom Palmer, squeezing past the Mercedes to look down at the huddled form in the far corner of the garage. 'My, my, someone bashed his head in. You don't need me to tell you that. Very nasty.' He raised a hand to scratch his mop of black curls and stared at the body with concern on his face.

'We do need your report, Tom, as soon as possible,' Jess requested. 'Can you do the PM soon?'

'Well, tomorrow morning will be the earliest.'

'That means me, I suppose,' said Phil Morton lugubriously. 'Morgue duty again.'

'The SOCO team is in there now,' Jess reported much later that day to Ian Carter. 'At least a garage is a fairly small area. They'll be going over the car too, of course. There is some blood around the position of the dead man's head but no obvious disturbance. Burton seems to have been one of those people who keep their garages fanatically clean. There's no dust on the floor or on any of the tools on the rack. The team leader thinks the chances of a good fingerprint or footprint are slight. The car had recently been cleaned. So far we haven't turned up a murder weapon.

'Burton seems to have been working there and, from the articles around him, he had been busy polishing out a scratch on the wing mirror. Possibly he did the damage at Cricket Farm where we found the scraping of paint. The lab will be able to tell us if it's the sort used by Mercedes. It looks as if he liked tinkering with the car. There is one empty hook on the rack where a tool could have been removed. There's no tool left lying about in the garage that could easily have hung there, so possibly one is missing and it's the murder weapon. A spanner, perhaps? Tom Palmer thinks it could be something like that. If so, if the murderer grabbed it and struck Burton when he turned his back, then the murderer had the presence of mind to take the weapon with him. By now it could be anywhere. In a river or lake? In the middle of bushes out of town in the countryside?

'The cleaner's testimony suggests, and Dr Palmer's initial judgement is, that he was killed either very late on Friday, the day the body was discovered, or more likely the following day, Saturday. She didn't see him on Monday when she was at the house at nine in the morning and has had no communication from him since. It seems reasonable to assume he scraped the car at the farm. When he realised it, his first action was to make good the damage. He was interrupted while working on it by the arrival of his killer. But did he expect the call? How did the killer know where the garage was? It's not attached to the house. It's about three streets away. He turned his back on the killer. So we can also assume it was someone he knew.'

Carter had listened to this summary in silence and now nodded. 'Has the body been officially identified?'

'Mrs Pardy the cleaner has identified it as her employer. I felt bad about asking her to look at him, but as it turned out, I needn't have worried. She didn't turn a hair. "Oh, that's him, all right," she said. Then, if you please, she asked if she should get in touch with his solicitors about getting her week's wages from the estate.'

'Do we know who his solicitors are?'

Jess shook her head. 'Mrs Pardy asks we let her know as soon as we find out. That woman is the most self-centred person I've ever met! She had a cushy job with Burton and he was just about the ideal employer. You'd think she'd express some decent regret at his death. But not a word – just, what about her money?'

'He could be the ideal employer and still not inspire any affection or liking,' Carter said quietly.

There was an odd hiatus in their conversation. Jess went on hurriedly, 'I was just about to go over to his house and take a good look round it. Try and find out whom he did business with, and who his solicitor might be. Mrs Pardy has given me her keys. Oh, no keys of any kind have been found on the body. So another assumption is that the murderer has both house keys and car keys. He must have the key to the up-and-over door of the garage, because he locked it behind him when he left. There was also no mobile phone or BlackBerry in Burton's jacket. If Burton had one, the killer had made off with those, too. He was a very thorough

217

murderer. Eva Zelená's killer was also efficient at removing all personal items like phone, purse and jewellery.'

Carter narrowed his gaze and Jess was uncomfortably aware of the stare of his hazel-green eyes. 'But the cleaner says there is no sign of anyone having been in the house? I'm thinking that, if the murderer took the house keys, he might have meant to use them. Maybe there is something incriminating there, or the murderer might think there is.' He raised his eyebrows and waited.

Jess realised she was expected to play devil's advocate and did so.

'He might also be too worried about being seen to risk going there. The house is on a busy thoroughfare. It has no front garden, just a railing about a metre from the front wall. There may be no rear access. It's something I have to check. But anyone would have to walk up to the front door and let himself in in full view of the street and the neighbours.'

Carter leaned back in his chair. 'How thorough do you think that cleaner is?'

Jess smiled. 'Frankly, she's had virtually no work to do. She tidies the kitchen and bathroom, probably the bedroom. Those are the rooms in daily use. The other rooms, well, she doesn't have to do more than put a vacuum cleaner over the carpets.'

'We know,' Carter pointed out, 'that Burton didn't share the house and the murderer may well have known it, too. So, he would know that once the cleaner left, he wouldn't be disturbed. If he were tidy about his search and concentrated on, say, the study, then Mrs – what's it – Pardy? Mrs Pardy might not realise anyone had been there.' He stood up and came round the desk. 'We'll both check the place out.'

They stood in the street before Lucas Burton's house, as Jess had already done once that day with Phil Morton. It seemed an age ago, not eight hours. Unlike Phil, Carter made no comment as he stared up at the façade. As for Jess, the frontage was already familiar to her and mindful of her own words to the superintendent about the interest of neighbours, she found her gaze sliding sideways, up and down the pavement.

A chill evening breeze had sprung up and the light was fast fading. One or two leaves rattled along the paving stones, rolling over and over in orange and red cartwheels. A woman hurried past, gripping her coat together over her chest with one clenched hand. She didn't look their way, but she must have been aware of them. From the opposite direction a man came strolling along with a small, fat white dog, on their evening promenade, getting in the exercise before it got properly dark; an elderly man and clearly a resident, he had seen them and he didn't hide his interest. There were no Neighbourhood Watch posters in the windows in this street, but Jess was sure the residents operated an informal system of their own. Or possibly, after she and Morton left earlier, Mrs Pardy had spread the word of their visit. The street knew the police had been and now they were back again. From a door further down a young man in a leather jacket sprang into the street. The door slammed. He walked briskly to a car parked by the kerb, got into it and drove off. Just coincidence, perhaps, or also, just possibly, he'd spotted them from his window and didn't want to be at home if the police came knocking on doors and asking questions.

Whatever it was, she and Carter were too obvious, loitering here. There was a palpable quality to the darkness gathering around them and the street lighting would be on soon.

'Sir?' Jess murmured.

Her voice seemed to jolt Carter from whatever reverie he'd sunk into. 'What? Oh, yes. Got the cleaner's key there?'

She unlocked the door and let them in.

Walking into Burton's elegant house a second time felt odder than it had the first. At least on that occasion, Jess reflected, the cleaner had invited her and Morton in. This time she and Carter entered alone and uninvited. The house felt cold and unwelcoming without even Mrs Pardy's grudging presence and her cups of tea. Its blue and yellow perfection closed out any interloper. Carter paused by the hall telephone to examine the console table on which it stood. The top was of marquetry, the design one of swirls and flowers and fruit. It was beautiful and no doubt expensive and very old. The modern telephone on it looked awkward and out of place, just as they must do standing in the hall. Jess glanced up towards the first-floor landing, almost as if she expected to see someone there, watching them from above. But it was eerily silent and suddenly she didn't envy Mrs Pardy her easy job. To spend several hours here, in this empty perfection, three times a week, the silence only broken by a distant slam of a car door or muted roar of an engine, that was plain spooky.

Cricket Farm had been spooky, too, yet there could be no greater contrast between this and Cricket, a house she and the superintendent had also entered uninvited. The atmosphere at Cricket had been one of misery and toil, above all of agricultural poverty. It might not have been a happy home but it had been a home. Burton's place spoke of money but absolutely nothing else.

As they moved from room to room the feeling that they were unwanted and that there was something inherently wrong about the whole place grew on Jess. It was elegant, gracious and all too perfect. This wasn't due to the housekeeping skills of Sandra Pardy. It was due to the personality of its dead owner.

At last she had to speak. 'It's – it's like a stage set.'

Carter turned his head towards her, his expression mildly surprised and enquiring.

'It's as if Burton decided on the impression he wanted to make and set about presenting this house so that it gave it. Perhaps he was like that as a person, too.'

Carter made no reply and seemed to be waiting for her to expand her theme. She hastened on, 'Somehow it's not real. When we went into the house at Cricket Farm, it had been shut up for nearly thirty years and yet, even so, there was a feeling real people had lived there, with emotions and worries. It told us a lot about them and their lives. This tells us nothing about Lucas Burton except that he had a lot of money and operated as a loner.'

'My feeling exactly,' Carter said unexpectedly. 'The interesting thing will be to learn how he made his money. I think

221

we can take it he was at Cricket Farm last Friday afternoon. But we don't know why he went there. We are assuming it was because of Eva Zelená, perhaps to hide her body. Perhaps she accompanied him alive and he killed her there. If she was ever in that Mercedes, alive or dead, she'll have left some trace. But if he killed Eva, then who killed him?'

He shook his head. 'We could also be haring off down a false trail. Some other business took Burton to Cricket that day. He found a body and panicked. His murder could be unrelated, the result of falling out with a business associate. We don't know if we have one linked investigation here or two quite separate ones.' He heaved an irritated sigh.

By the time they reached the study the failing daylight obliged them to turn on the electric substitute. Now anyone who looked this way would know they were here. If the murderer had been here, he would not have been able to switch on the light, drawing attention. He had either to come in daylight: risky, or at night with a torch.

Jess looked about her. Superficially, at least, the study was as tidy as the rest of the house. The screen of an open laptop computer on the desk turned its blank face to them; like the hall telephone, a jarring note of modernity in the carefully harmonised antique whole. Carter went to it.

'The IT specialists will have to look at this.'

Jess joined him at the desk and, first slipping on thin plastic gloves, tried the centre drawer. There was a lock-plate in it, although no key, and she was expecting it to be secured. But it slid out easily.

'I would have thought,' she said, 'that he would have locked away anything personal because he was out of the house much of the time, and Mrs Pardy had free rein to go snooping if she was inclined.'

'Or the murderer has the desk key, along with all the other keys he took from the body,' Carter said. He came to stand by her and look down into the drawer. The contents – letters, bills, scribbled notes – were jumbled together in an untidy heap. 'This doesn't look like the way our man would keep his private documents, even in a drawer,' the superintendent added. He pointed downward and indicated a bulldog clip. 'What's the betting some of these papers were originally held together with this?'

Jess looked round the room. On one wall a watercolour seascape hung slightly askew. Carter, following her gaze, crossed to it and lifted it down with gloved hands. There was nothing behind it on the wall, and nothing attached to the back of the picture. He replaced it.

'That one's crooked, too,' said Jess, pointing at a companion seascape on the other side of the room.

Carter checked that one, too, without finding anything. 'That bookcase is out of position,' he observed, turning back to the room and pointing at a pretty glass-fronted set of shelves. 'It must have stood flat against the wall, now it's at an angle.'

'Mrs Pardy with her vacuum cleaner?' suggested Jess.

He walked over to it, stooped and stared at it, then shook his head. 'Someone's been here,' he said, 'but not the cleaner. He's had the books out, and although he's put them back, he hurried over it. Look, volumes one and two of *The Count of Monte Cristo* here together – and volume three on the next shelf down. *Peter the Whaler* upside down! Early twentieth-century English editions as read by Edwardian schoolboys . . . do you think our man was a reader of the classics? Or did he buy these books in some second-hand bookshop for decorative purposes, to match the bookcase?'

Carter straightened up and turned back, brushing dust from his hands.

'Whoever our searcher is, he's tidy and methodical by nature but on this occasion, rushed. I'd say he's a thinker. He's far too clever to tip the contents of that drawer all over the carpet and leave the mess to announce his visit – or pull these books out and leave them in a heap. But, because he was in a hurry, he tossed the papers back in the drawer and pushed it carelessly shut, forgetting to lock it again. He put back all the books, but didn't have time to make sure they were in order.'

Feeling she should say something and that, somehow, she was still expected to present some argument against his reasoning, Jess observed, 'Isn't there still a possibility the cleaner made a search the moment Phil Morton and I left? She might have looked round for money or some small valuable object to slip in her pocket. She knew, once we'd been, her employer wasn't going to walk in again. She's worried about her week's wages. She would probably argue she was entitled to compensation.'

His reply was prompt. 'She wouldn't be interested in personal papers or the contents of a bookcase. She'd help herself to some little trinket; a snuffbox or something she could take to an antique shop and claim her auntie left her. For my money it's the killer, using the keys he took from the body. We're too late. He's searched and taken away anything that might have led to him. He left things outwardly as he found them, but for minor details. He didn't take the computer, perhaps because it would be missed, signalling his visit. Or he's tried to wipe its memory? Well, that's easier tried than done.'

'He was looking for a wall-safe,' Jess said quietly, pointing at the crooked seascape.

'Yes, but did he find it? If it's here, we have to find it, too.'

But they found nothing.

'We'll get it dusted for fingerprints tomorrow,' Carter said with a sigh. 'But whatever the results they'll be meaningless until we get a suspect. Send DCs Stubbs and Bennison over here to box up the contents of the desk drawers and any other private papers, the laptop too, for further examination.'

They both stood for a moment in the hall, looking around them. Then by mutual consent they turned and silently left the house to hug its secrets to its cold, private bosom.

It was late when Jess heeled the door of her flat shut behind her. Small, stuffy and dusty, it was real and it was her home and she fancied it was pleased to see her back. The flat wasn't a mausoleum like Cricket Farm or even, in its own way, like Burton's place. She took out the enlarged group photograph of the Foot to the Ground's staff and dropped her little green rucksack on the floor. Then she propped up the photo carefully alongside the family photograph of herself, her brother and parents, and stood back to study it.

'Two family pictures,' she murmured. Westcott and his staff did form a family of sorts. How could they not? They spent their days together. The girls had slept under the same roof as the Westcotts. In the photo, the Westcotts inevitably acted the parental role; the older handyman, Bert, that of some elderly uncle. And the three youngsters? David Jones had his own real parents nearby. Had the Westcotts felt in any way that they stood *in loco parentis* to the girls? No, not according to what Bronwen Westcott had told Phil Morton. She had been an employer, she'd been at pains to point out, not a guardian angel. But now she felt guilty of some omission of trust.

Family pictures told the observer a lot. Was that why Eli had removed all the photographs from Cricket Farm, though he'd left everything else?

Jess peered more closely at the group. Eva Zelená and David Jones stood next to one another. Had the photographer arranged them like that? Was it chance? Or had David man-oeuvred himself into that position? He was leaning slightly towards Eva, whereas she stood straight, looking directly at the camera. His stance was both protective and proprietorial. He was associating himself with her. But Eva, in this line-up, somehow stood alone.

Jess knew she'd have to go back to the Foot to the Ground and talk to David Jones again.

Chapter 13

Cricket Farm had a visitor. It was late, just the moment before day turns abruptly into night. The horizon was rimmed by only the faintest red glow, marking the sinking of the sun. The moon had emerged like an invalid from the sickroom, pale and lacking luminosity or substance, but still emitting enough light to enable anyone to pick his way across the yard.

But the visitor avoided the open space. He moved slowly around the perimeter, sheltering in the lengthening shadows. In this way he reached the open-fronted cowshed and slipped inside. Here it was really dark but he had his bearings. The layout of the barn was imprinted in his brain. Above his head the corrugated-iron sheeting of the roof rattled and creaked in the stiff breeze. It was cold up here on top of the hill. It must always be cold, even in summer. In winter it must be icy. This thought ran through his mind as he moved slowly but confidently around the interior, putting out a hand from time to time to make contact with the wooden barrier of a stall, until he came back to the entrance where he stood for a long time, just inside, where the body had been discovered. Eventually he stooped and touched the ground, his fingers brushing against mud and straw.

He stood up and moved back into the yard. The moon had cast off its unhealthy pallor and was a vital, glowing ball, ruling the earth beneath. Small fluttering dark shapes swooped and dived across its surface. The bats had emerged from the attic of the house. The shadows around the yard were draped like sable velvet curtains either side of a stage. The open ground between was bathed in the moon's silvery light. Between gaps in the boards, the glass in the upper windows of the house glittered – and a point of light moved behind them. The man, who had been in the barn, frowned. He was not the only visitor to the farm that night.

Someone was over there inside the apparently barred house. The watcher in the yard withdrew into the shadow of the heap of scrap metal to wait.

The telltale light disappeared occasionally and then re-appeared unexpectedly in a different place. The person in the house was moving from room to room, but it wasn't always possible to predict his progress from the yard. The intruder wasn't being cautious. He thought he was alone and un-observed. But where one window was more successfully boarded up than another, the glow of his torch would be shielded and then it was guesswork where it would next appear.

After ten minutes or so the pinpoint of light vanished altogether, and moments later the watcher's ear caught a faint distant noise. It seemed to be coming from the back of the house. Thump! Someone had struck a blow against, probably, a wood surface. Thump! Another one. The watcher allowed himself a brief smile as he identified the activity.

The visitor to the house had gained entry by removing the plank freshly nailed across the back door. He was now replacing it, making it look to a casual observer as if no one had broken in.

Footsteps crunched towards him. From the side of the house a dark figure emerged and walked across the open yard. In the moonlight it was no more than a silhouette; no features could be made out. It appeared tall, gangling and awkward, the moonlight and shadows distorting its frame. Its clothing was baggy and concealing of sex. The anonymous figure left the farm and turned right. About five minutes later the watcher by the scrap metal heap heard the sound of a car engine starting up. The vehicle had been parked over the brow of the hill on the far side. He heard it drive away.

Now it was safe for him to leave, too. Cricket Farm was left to the bats and other creatures of the night.

'A Sergeant Gary Collins of the Met is on the phone,' said DC Bennison, poking her head, braids swinging, into Jess's office on Monday morning. 'Will you speak to him?'

'Sure, put him through.' Nothing new had emerged over the weekend and Jess's private prayer that something – anything – might turn up at the beginning of the new week would seem to have been answered. She grabbed for the phone as Bennison, braids still bouncing around as if possessed of a life of their own, disappeared.

'Gary Collins here,' said a voice in her ear, 'that you, Inspector Campbell? Right, well, I thought you'd like to know:

we went over to that address you sent us, the flat in Docklands. Expensive pad. Perhaps if I win the lottery, I might buy a place over there with the city boys.'

'You managed to get a look inside it?' Jess asked impatiently, wondering if she was speaking to the Metropolitan Police's equivalent of Phil Morton, chip on shoulder firmly in place.

'We had a bit of luck there. At first I thought we were up against it. The caretaker's a miserable old git, real jobsworth, name of Cyril Sprang,' continued Collins, the memory of his encounter with the guardian of the block of flats flooding back. 'He defends the place like national security was at stake. First of all, he didn't want us to go up to the flat. It's on the third floor. Then he insisted on coming with us and we all stood outside Burton's door arguing the toss. Mr Burton wasn't there, reckoned Sprang, and we ought to come back later. Forget it, we told him, we're here and we want to see inside the flat. Oh well, we had to wait for Mr Burton to be in residence or we had to bring a proper accredited representative of Mr Burton's with a key. I had to tell him there was no chance of that: the owner had died. I didn't say how but I made it clear the flat was now part of official enquiries.

'That gave Sprang a bit of a turn. We had to stand there and listen while he went into another flap. Then, all at once, he admitted *he* had a key. It seems a few weeks earlier there'd been some problem with the plumbing. Burton himself couldn't be there to let the plumber in so he'd given Sprang his spare key with strict instructions not to let it into anyone else's hands. Sprang had let the plumber in and stood over him all the time he was working there. That must have cheered up the plumber no end!

'"So, right, a key, let's have it!" we said. But oh, no, never! Burton had handed over the key to Sprang like a blooming sacred trust. None of the other porters were to have it, no one. That included us, apparently. We're police officers, we pointed out. So he told us to go away and come back with a search warrant. "I've got no authority and neither have you!" he said, silly old basket. I didn't feel like dragging my corns off to get a warrant so I told him bluntly, if I had to, I'd break in. You should have seen his face! Anyhow, it did the trick. He went off and got the key and we got in eventually. It didn't look as if anyone else had been there in a while. Sprang said it was three weeks since Burton had been there, at the time of the plumbing emergency, when he left the key. Sprang knew he hadn't been back because he'd have come to find the caretaker and retrieve his spare key. The colleague with me and I, we took a good look round but we didn't conduct a proper search. I reckoned you'd want to come up here and do that. But I did note down the one message on the answerphone, some geezer asking Burton to ring back and giving a mobile number. Got a pencil handy?'

'Yes,' said Jess, pulling a notepad towards her. 'Did he say what his call was about?'

'No, just asked that Burton call him as soon as possible. The call was made on Monday morning last week at eleven thirty.'

But by then, Burton was probably dead. Jess shivered, struck by the arbitrariness of mortality. *The best-laid plans . . .*

'The number belongs to a bloke called Archie Armstrong.' Collins gave the number. 'He lives up north,' Collins concluded his information.

Recalled to the present, Jess asked cautiously, having been caught out before, 'When you say "up north", do you mean north London?'

'Yeah, where else?' Collins sounded puzzled.

Like Yorkshire, chum, or anywhere north of the Watford Gap! But Collins, secure in his London insularity, probably gave such far-flung areas of the country little thought.

'Just checking,' she said. 'Thank you, Sergeant.'

Collins had done an efficient job. She was grateful. It had saved her time.

'Want me to do anything else?' Collins asked.

'Not at the moment,' she told him. 'I'll come up to London tomorrow and look over that flat myself. You say the caretaker will be there?'

'Either him or some other bloke just like him. Mention my name,' added Collins with an unexpected chuckle. 'But we've got the key here at the station, if you want to drop by first. I told old Sprang I had to seal the flat because of the nature of enquiries. When he saw I was taking the key away he nearly had a fit. I signed a receipt for him. But when you turn up, you'll get an earful, just as we did. You'd think it was the key to the Crown Jewels.'

Jess found herself smiling. 'Will do. I hope I'll find some

of Burton's neighbours at home. We're trying to build up a picture of the man. I also want to talk to Archie Armstrong.'

Collins was chuckling again when Jess put down the phone. She studied the scrap of paper with the bare information of Armstrong's mobile number. Collins was right. Whoever he was and whatever his business with the late Lucas Burton, Archie Armstrong wouldn't be happy to see the police arriving on his doorstep. She reached for the phone again.

A man's voice in her ear briefly said, 'Hi!'

She identified herself and the next words were spoken warily.

'Inspector Campbell? Sorry, may I ask where you got this number?'

'It's just an enquiry,' Jess said, ignoring the question.

She heard an irritable 'Tsk!' It was followed with, 'Well, what can I do for you?'

'I'm sorry to bother you,' Jess soothed him. 'I understand you're acquainted with a Mr Lucas Burton?'

'Burton?' A pause for thinking time. 'Oh, well, yes, in a manner of speaking. We've done a little business together in the past. It's all in order and above board. You can check it out.'

'You left a message on his answerphone in his London flat last week, on Monday morning.'

'So that's where you got my mobile number!' The voice at the other end hardened. 'What's going on? Is Burton involved in something? It's nothing to do with me if he is. How did you come to be listening to his answer machine?'

'I'm sorry to tell you that Mr Burton has died.'

Shocked silence.

'We are trying to trace people who knew him. He appears to have been a very private man. We know of no next of kin and business acquaintances are the next obvious area of search.'

'Now, just a minute,' Armstrong protested. 'When you say he's died – how did he die and when?'

'He died on Monday, the day you phoned his flat.'

'In London? He died here in London?' the voice was growing agitated.

'No, in Gloucestershire.'

She heard his sigh of relief.

'I never go to the West Country,' Armstrong said. 'I go down to the South Coast occasionally. I've got a little boat down there. I only ever met Lucas here in town and that only a couple of times.'

'But you wanted him to ring you,' Jess pointed out. Armstrong must be cursing the fact that he'd left a message on that answerphone.

'I was just touching base,' Armstrong said unconvincingly. 'Business contacts, you know. I like to keep them up to date. Honestly, I knew Lucas Burton purely in a professional capacity, and I don't know how I can help you. I never heard him speak about his family. Well, poor chap, naturally I'm sorry to hear he's kicked the bucket. Surprised, too. He seemed pretty fit.' Doubt entered his voice again. 'How did he die? Heart or something?'

'Can I come and talk to you, Mr Armstrong? I'd like to come tomorrow, Tuesday. I'm sorry if that interferes with your work schedule. It's a little late for me to set off to see you this afternoon.'

'That's all right.' Armstrong sounded conciliatory. He'd had time to get over his initial shock and now he was the concerned citizen, anxious to do his duty and help the police. He'd accepted Jess wasn't going to be put off by his feeble protests. 'I can work from home while I'm waiting for you.'

'Then I'll come to your home address. We can meet elsewhere if you prefer.'

But Armstrong wouldn't want her turning up at his office or anywhere where his business associates might see her.

'No, no,' came Armstrong's hasty assurance. 'That will be all right. My partner is away from home on a business trip to New York, so I'm all on my own here. Come to the house. You won't be in uniform, will you?'

Archie Armstrong lived in another old house, probably built only a little later than Burton's one in Cheltenham. But whereas Burton had owned his property outright, this house was subdivided into flats. That didn't mean they came cheaper. Jess pressed the appropriate bell on the list by the front door. The intercom crackled and when she identified herself, the disembodied voice told her to come up to the top floor. The street door was buzzed open. Jess toiled up a steep narrow staircase passing other white-painted doors. It was oppressively still and quiet. The other residents must all be at work. To own a flat here would cost a lot of money. No one here was strapped for cash.

Armstrong was waiting for her on the landing.

'Inspector?' He thrust out his hand. 'Good journey up from Gloucestershire?'

'Yes, thanks,' Jess said, shaking his hand briefly.

'Good, good, come on in!'

She suspected he had been rehearsing all this. Don't go down to the street and let her in – too eager. Wait on the landing – shows thoughtfulness. Shake her hand and ask about her journey – break the ice. In other words, make a good first impression as a regular normal nice guy.

Everything about his appearance suggested that Armstrong worked on giving this impression full time, cultivating the bonhomie. He was of middle height, youngish but probably not quite as young as the first impression conveyed, and fit-looking. She suspected he went sailing at weekends. He probably also belonged to a gym. He had close cut fair hair and a reddish complexion, and wore chinos and a pale blue shirt. For all his general air of good health, he was getting a little paunchy. His wristwatch looked expensive.

He ushered her past him through the door. It opened into a large open space and she realised that this really was the 'top' floor. The flat had been created from the one-time garrets. It ran across the width of the house and its ceiling was like a Dutch barn in shape with long windows nearly down to the floor. The area where they fetched up was sparsely furnished with two long white leather sofas and a glass coffee table. There was an oriental rug on the well-polished floor and a painting by some modern artist she couldn't identify on the peach-coloured wall. On another wall hung a flat-screen television. The dining area was in a recess behind them, glass table and stainless steel chairs. The table was laid as if for a formal dinner party, but not – Jess deduced – because Armstrong planned entertaining that evening. The table was always set out like this, with mathematical spacing between place settings, crisp red napkins and a rose in a specimen vase in the middle. It was all part of 'the look'. Unfortunately, the words that came to Jess's mind were 'goldfish bowl'. If Armstrong hadn't mentioned having a partner, she'd have thought he lived here alone.

'I can offer you some tea or coffee,' he said.

'Please don't go to that trouble,' Jess said. 'It's not necessary. I do appreciate your seeing me.' She seated herself on one of the white leather sofas.

'Oh, well, if it's an official inquiry, naturally I want to help. Although as I mentioned when we spoke on the phone, I don't see how I can.'

Now she was seated, Armstrong appeared happier and settled back on the facing sofa where he delivered another rehearsed speech.

'I'm sorry to hear about Lucas, not that I knew him well, as I think I also indicated to you on the phone. He was a pretty open, ordinary, straightforward sort of guy. I never had any reason to suspect him of anything that wasn't entirely above board. I wouldn't have done business with him if I had. I think you'll find most people will say the same of him. You didn't say how he died. Oh, I say!'

This exclamation was because Jess had produced a small tape recorder.

'Is this to be recorded. Is that necessary?' His relaxed manner had vanished.

'It's purely routine, Mr Armstrong. It's either that or I have to take notes. Do you object?'

'Um, no, well, of course not.' Armstrong eyed the little tape recorder as if it might jump off the glass coffee table and bite him.

'His death's the subject of our enquiries, I'm afraid, and there's not a lot I can tell you.' Jess smiled.

'But you're treating it as suspicious?' Armstrong appeared fascinated by the tape recorder, staring at it fixedly.

'Yes. He was found dead on Monday last.'

'At home? I believe he had a house in Cheltenham. He mentioned it to me once.'

'He was found in his garage.'

Armstrong leaned forward. 'Ohmigod! He didn't top himself, did he? Engine running, pipe from the exhaust, sealed car job?'

'No, he didn't kill himself.' Jess decided the time had come to take charge of the conversation. 'You say you didn't know Burton well, but you do appear to have met him on several occasions. Were these always business meetings? Could you be more specific as to what kind of business?'

Armstrong grew wary. 'Ye-es . . . Some friends and I – and Burton – formed a small company investing in property for renting out. My only contact with Burton was through that.

He had many other interests, I'm sure, but I have no knowledge of them. I wasn't – am not involved in those.'

Armstrong paused. 'I can't give you any actual details of our property portfolio, of course, without consulting my co-investors.'

'I don't need that today,' Jess said to his obvious relief. 'But I may do so later. What I'd like to know is, were you planning some new venture? Is that why you left the message asking him to contact you?'

'Oh, no, no, I was just touching base, as I think I told you.'

Jess wasn't inclined to believe this hasty denial, but she realised that if some new enterprise was planned it would be at an early stage and neither Armstrong nor his companions would want any wind of it getting out. He'd have to talk to them first; and she was sure that the minute she left the building, that was just what he'd be doing.

'In view of all this,' she said, 'perhaps you could be a little more frank regarding Lucas Burton? So far, forgive me, you've said all the right things but all of them pretty general in tone. I understand that you trusted him, or you wouldn't have done business with him. But your personal opinion would be of interest to us. After all, what you've described was rather more than a simple passing acquaintance. You must have socialised with him, got chatting over the dinner table. Had a glass or two or wine, perhaps, and relaxed?'

Armstrong studied her for a moment. 'If you were a newspaper reporter I'd ask that anything I said would be treated as "off the record", but I recognise you aren't. Lucas is dead. He isn't going to sue me. I suppose I can be frank. OK, some people thought him a slick operator. My associates and I always found him pretty straight as far as our own business interests went. We're a legitimate outfit. We keep our noses clean! We wouldn't have included Lucas if we'd thought he would be a problem. But, undeniably, he was very useful to have on board; one of those guys who always know what's going on but who, like journalists, never name their sources. Do you know what I mean?'

Yeah, I know them, thought Jess sourly. *They're wheeler-dealers. They always 'know a man'. What other businesses did Burton have his fingers in, I wonder? This one is eager to be seen as above board and open to scrutiny. But I wonder if all the others are . . .*

'He was pleasant enough,' Armstrong was saying, 'he could even be charming. He wasn't married and his girlfriends were always lookers. Never seemed to turn up with the same one twice, though. He didn't want to be tied down, I guess. Underneath it, he was pretty tough. If you ask me, and this is just my own impression, he'd come up from rough origins. There was a sort of edge to him, you know what I mean? He liked to act smooth. It didn't ring true. Nevertheless, I quite liked the man. Neither I, nor anyone I know, ever had a problem working with him. If we had,' his voice hardened, 'we'd have cut him loose, believe me.'

And perhaps somebody did cut him loose? thought Jess, remembering the body sprawled on the garage floor alongside the gleaming expensive car. *This group of investors never had a problem with him, but possibly someone else did?*

Armstrong leaned back against the soft leather of the sofa. 'He had a lucky touch. But he was a man of mystery, if you like.'

'Thank you,' Jess said and switched off the tape recorder. 'That was very helpful, Mr Armstrong.'

Armstrong visibly relaxed now the little machine had stopped whirring. 'I shall have to tell my colleagues about your visit, you do understand that? Lucas's death has left a gap and there are financial implications. His estate will have to be settled. It'll impinge on our affairs and us. Do you know who his heirs are?'

Jess frowned. 'No idea. I do understand you'll need to contact those involved in business matters with you and the late Mr Burton. But I'd be grateful if you didn't chat about it too freely. Work on a "need to know" basis.'

'Like the police do?' Armstrong smiled.

'Discretion is always advisable,' Jess said primly. 'Can you give me a list of the names of your business partners? Contact phone numbers, too? I'll need to talk to them.'

'Er, yes, I suppose so. Yes, of course you will. You don't just want to talk to me. This is going to be quite a shock to them. I've seen nothing in the papers about his death and they can't have, or they'd have let me know.'

'We shall be releasing his name to the press this week.'

'Poor old Lucas. Who'd have thought it? I can see him now, sitting on that sofa there where you are, a glass of whisky in his hand. We – well – the more I think about it, the more of a headache this is going to be for us. You do mean he was murdered, don't you? Good Lord, who'd do it? Why?' Armstrong blanched. 'We're none of *us* suspects, are we?'

Cyril Sprang was, in his own way, as reticent as Archie Armstrong and as anxious to make the right initial impression.

'Mr Burton was a very decent sort of chap,' he said, eyeing Jess up and down critically through thick-lensed spectacles.

Jess couldn't be classed as a 'decent sort of chap'. Even these days there were people who didn't quite approve of women police officers, certainly not in senior ranks. Mr Sprang was clearly one of them. He had held Jess's ID at arm's length and studied it for a full minute before returning it to her. It was as if, she thought half annoyed and half amused, he suspected she might have forged it.

Sprang himself was of middle age and middle height and generally 'middle' in all ways. Middling grey hair, middling complexion. Jess had eventually been allowed grudgingly into his lair. Here Sprang lurked keeping a watchful eye on the comings and goings at the block of flats created from a one-time Thamesside warehouse. He knew the residents to be wealthy, very private people and he made sure they got the privacy they required. They, in return, were no doubt generous with their Christmas and other tips.

'I've had a copper here already,' he said sourly, 'from the Met. I suppose now you want to go in there.'

'Sergeant Collins came to see the flat. I've spoken to him.'

'Then you'll know he took the key away. I'm responsible for those keys, you know. Has he given it to you?'

'Yes, I've got it.'

'Well, he'd got no business passing it on to someone else. He'd got no authority. *I* shouldn't have let him have it, by rights, because he'd got no authority to get it off me. But he was threatening damage. Break in? Over my dead body you do, I told him. But there were two of them, coppers, so I had to hand it over. I reckon there's a breach of civil liberties in there somewhere. Anyway, he went up and had a look. Why do you need to go up there again?'

'That's police business, Mr Sprang. We are enquiring into the circumstances of Burton's death.'

'Dodgy, are they? These circumstances?' Sprang asked and a gleam entered his eyes, both magnified and distorted by the thick lenses.

There was an opened tabloid paper on a ledge beneath the rack of keys. If there was sensational news to be gleaned from Jess's visit, he was inclined to be more helpful.

'I'm afraid so,' Jess told him. 'We suspect foul play. Early days, yet, of course.'

'Poor bloke,' said Sprang, sounding quite cheerful now that he knew for sure he was among the first to know something about a story that would probably soon appear in his newspaper. He'd be able to pass the news on to all the residents as one by one they returned home. He'd have the satisfaction of being able to cause a stir, not to say 'put the cat among the pigeons'. None of the other tenants would want to be drawn into a murder inquiry.

'You want me to come up with you? No trouble.' He rubbed his hands together with an unpleasant rasping noise.

'That's all right, Mr Sprang. I don't suppose I'll be very long.'

'Only I am responsible for the flat, for all of them when the owners aren't here.' The magnified eyes came nearer to Jess's face and she tried not to flinch. 'I'll need to know if you remove anything. Otherwise, someone might say it was down to me if anything went missing.'

'I'll give you a receipt, if I do remove anything.' She edged away.

Sprang was clearly disappointed but made a last attempt. 'I'll take you up there, show you the way.'

Jess opened her mouth to say he needn't bother but decided to let him win this one. She needed him on her side.

'Thank you, Mr Sprang.'

There was a lift but as the flat was on the first floor, Jess opted for the staircase.

'Did Mr Burton use the flat often?' she asked Sprang who climbed the stairs ahead of her.

'He came and went,' said Sprang over his shoulder. 'Say, a couple of times a month he'd be here. Sometimes he'd stay a week and go back to his other place at the weekend. Sometimes he'd come up for the weekend.'

'Did he have many visitors?'

Sprang didn't reply immediately to this. They had arrived

before the flat's entry door and he stood watching Jess manoeuvre the key in the lock and open it, before he answered.

'Not often. Not many people called to see him. He occasionally . . .' Sprang tailed off tantalisingly and peered past her into the flat. 'Mind if I come in with you and just cast an eye around? I won't touch anything.'

It was an exchange being offered. Sprang would gossip, but he had to be offered some inducement.

'Take a quick look round, by all means,' Jess said. 'But it would be best if you didn't touch anything. We may be finger-printing the place later.'

Sprang darted through the door and looked around him eagerly but wasn't rewarded with some extraordinary sight. No upturned furniture or ransacked drawers. Thank goodness, thought Jess, Collins didn't turn everything upside down on his visit.

Sprang masked his disappointment. 'Like I was saying, he was a single bloke, as I understood it. He never mentioned any wife and there wasn't any woman came regularly with him.'

'But he did sometimes bring lady friends here?'

Sprang didn't exactly leer, but a knowing expression crossed his face, made sinister by the light shining on the thick lenses. 'Oh yes, from time to time. Real stunners some of 'em. They looked like models, if you know what I mean.'

'Real models?'

'Well,' admitted Sprang, 'they were probably tarts but not the usual sort. They all had class.'

'Escort agency girls?'

Sprang hesitated and Jess went on, 'Don't tell me you've never seen any of *them* around here?'

'They're respectable people living here, you know!' Sprang hastened to defend the honour of his clients. He might be ready to dish the dirt on the deceased Lucas, but not on any living tenants.

'You're asking me about *Mr Burton*,' the caretaker said now firmly, letting her know it. 'I think he – he had like a circle of women friends. He didn't bring the same one every time, but I did occasionally see one I'd seen before, if you know what I mean?'

I do, thought Jess. Burton had an address book registering the names of his lady friends, the 'little black book' of tradition. But we didn't find it in his Cheltenham house. I wonder if it's here?

'Well, thank you, Mr Sprang,' she said aloud. 'I'll just take a look round and call back in to see you on my way out.'

Sprang accepted his dismissal.

Now she was alone, Jess slipped on a pair of thin rubber gloves and began a methodical search. She quickly decided Burton had deliberately kept nothing sensitive at the London flat. He knew Sprang had a key and he himself was away for long periods.

There was certainly no address book. Carter was sure the murderer had made use of Burton's keys to search the Cheltenham house before she and Carter had got there. Had that been what he'd been looking for? Armstrong had told her

Burton was a 'man of mystery', a man with inside contacts that he didn't divulge to his co-investors. In that case, Burton's address book had probably held, in addition to the phone numbers of his girlfriends, the phone numbers and e-mail addresses of his shadowy contacts to be tapped for insider knowledge. It had probably been a system resembling the not unknown semi-official arrangement under which individual 'grasses' passed their information on to specific CID detectives.

Was it this 'black book' that the murderer had searched for in Cheltenham, and had he found it? And had he searched here, too, in this flat, just as careful to try and leave no trace of his presence?

Jess toiled up and down the staircase in a trawl of the other flats, but her efforts yielded nothing. Those residents who were at home professed ignorance.

'Can't say I knew the guy. I must have passed him occasionally in the entrance or shared the lift with him, I suppose. But if I did, I didn't know his name. Most of us here work in the City and frankly, we don't socialise with one another.'

So much for top-of-the-range living. Jess thought her little flat in Cheltenham far more preferable. At least she knew who lived downstairs.

Sprang jumped out of his den when she reappeared and waited eagerly, spectacle lenses glinting.

She had to disappoint him. 'We'll be coming back with a proper search team. In the meantime, the flat will have to remain sealed. Tell me, apart from women visitors, did other people, men, come to see him here?'

'Hardly ever,' said Sprang grumpily.

'If I could ask you a slightly different question. Have you noticed any strangers around recently? Any visitors you didn't recognise? How difficult would it be for someone to get past your office unobserved? What happens when you're not on duty?'

'There's nobody gets past me!' snapped Sprang. 'I'm head caretaker but I got some help, yes. Mickey Fisher does the night shift usually. Nobody gets past him, neither. Then there's the relief man, Jason Potts. He's on the ball, as well. I won't have anyone on my team that's a slacker. And the company don't like it, either.'

'Company?'

'Runs the security.'

Perhaps, thought Jess, Gary Collins might be prepared to do another favour, go round and have a word with the security company, seek out the two junior porters and have a word with them. He might track down some of the residents she'd missed and talk to them, too. Collins seemed an affable sort, but in fairness the Met had a full load of its own cases to solve and Collins might feel he'd spent enough time on Jess's problems. Morton might like a day out in London.

Sprang drew himself up to full height and assumed the demeanour of a commander-in-chief.

'If you lose that key, there will be trouble, I can tell you. I'm responsible for these flats, not you and not that sergeant from the Met.'

Chapter 14

Her plan to revisit the Foot to the Ground and seek out David Jones had been relegated to the back burner due to the weekend and her trip to London the previous day. But it immediately put itself into the foreground on Wednesday morning.

Jess had pressed the button on the keyring that operated the remote locking system and been rewarded by the car lights flashing an acknowledgment. Her plan was to go straight to see Ian Carter and let him know how she'd got on in London. But as she set off towards the building she heard herself hailed. Looking round, she saw a young man in motorcycle leathers hastening towards her, his helmet tucked under his arm in the way the decapitated ghost of Anne Boleyn was said to carry its head.

'Inspector! Have you got a minute? I really need to talk to you. It's urgent.'

Jones had come to her. He panted to a halt in front of her.

'Sure,' she said. 'Do you want to come inside?' She indicated the building. He did look very agitated. Now what had happened?

Jones cast the concrete block of headquarters a hunted look and she wondered if the word 'inside' suggested imminent arrest in his mind.

'We'd be more comfortable than out here,' she added. 'And I could probably rustle up some coffee.'

He still hovered uncertainly. 'I haven't come to make a statement. I just want to set the record straight. I can speak for myself, you know. I don't need other people speaking for me!' His voice grew louder, more stressed, and threatened to crack.

As she should have guessed it might be, this visit was prompted by the actions of Mr Fairbrother, the solicitor, and his phone call to Phil Morgan. David Jones had learned what had happened, probably from his mother, and was predictably frantic at the unfavourable light in which they'd unwittingly cast him.

'Fair enough but we might as well sit down while you do.' She kept her tone easy, hoping to calm him down. He was very flushed. His eyes glittered. When she'd spoken to him before, at the Foot to the Ground, his face had been almost deadpan. The flashes of animation had been no more than that, flickering across his countenance. Now every muscle seemed to twitch, as if he crackled with electricity, standing there. She half expected blue lights to play around the helmet under his arm.

She took the lead, setting off purposefully towards the building. The crunching of motorcycle boots on the gravel behind her told her he followed.

A little later Jones sat hunched in a chair, his hands clasped round a mug of coffee. The helmet lay forlornly on the floor beside him. If her invitation had been intended to relax him, it hadn't worked. He still looked a bundle of nerves.

No wonder, Jess thought sympathetically, his family worried about him and had got on to the solicitor.

'Old Fairbrother phoned you, didn't he? It was nothing to do with me.' Jones's first words confirmed her suspicions. His eyes gleamed with anger, but not directed at her.

'Yes, he phoned us,' Jess said noncommittally.

Jones twitched and the coffee in the mug splashed out.

'Mind!' Jess warned. 'It's not the best coffee in the world, but it is hot.'

Jones leaned forward and put the mug on the interview room's scratched desk. 'It was my mum; it was her idea. She's pally with a woman called Foscott.'

'Selina Foscott?'

'Yes, you went to see her, apparently, and showed her that photo from the leaflet Jake had printed up, to advertise the restaurant. Mum panicked because she's afraid of me having a relapse, going off my head again.'

'You had a nervous breakdown, didn't you? That's hardly to be classed as going off your head,' Jess objected.

'I was ill!' Jones said crisply. 'You don't know the sort of things I did when I was going through all that. I put my family and friends through it, too. I painted my bedroom black.'

'What's unusual about a bit of home decorating?' returned Jess, trying not to look surprised. 'It's very handy. Black might be a depressing colour. I don't know I'd have chosen it.'

'No, no!' he said irritably. 'I painted all of it black, wall, ceiling, furniture. I dyed my bed linen black.' He paused reflectively. 'Actually, that didn't work very well. It all came out a funny colour.'

'Were your parents embarrassed by your breakdown?'

It might have been thought that this very personal conversation would make the young man more agitated. But as they spoke, Jess noticed a lessening of tension on his part. It was easier for him to talk about his recent illness than to pretend it was all in the past and had no relevance to here and now.

He's treating me like a psychiatrist, she thought wryly. *Pity I haven't a sofa he can lie on.*

'Yes, they were embarrassed. It sounds a harsh thing to say about them but it's true. I don't mean they weren't supportive. They did everything they could but it's not an easy thing to deal with – having someone sit round all day, weeping and generally talking wildly and doing odd things.' He looked Jess squarely in the eye. 'I am all right now.'

'Yes, I can see that.'

He shrugged. 'They're afraid, Mum and Dad both, but Mum particularly, that I'll do it all again. You can't blame her entirely. Mrs Foscott had wound her up. She's the most bloody tactless woman in the universe, did you know that?'

'You mean Selina Foscott?'

'Of course I mean Selina. I don't mean my mother! Dad's away at the moment. He went off first to some international conference in Strasbourg. Since he's been back, he's been in London, staying at his club. He's got a tricky trial coming up. So Mum took it on herself, after Selina showed her that picture and filled her ears with an image of doom, to ring up

Fairbrother and get him to call you. I think he did try and dissuade her but she was in a flap, so in the end he did. Of course when my dad heard about it he hit the roof. I thought the telephone would combust. She was just trying to protect my nerves. But Dad said it made them look as if they were trying to prevent me being questioned. In other words, as if I had something to hide regarding Eva's death. I don't. Dad was all for writing to you himself. But I said I had to handle it myself and anything they did would just add to the – the unfortunate impression made by Fairbrother's call. So Dad said, fine, just call on him if I got into a fix. So here I am.'

'I expect your mother's upset now – because she did the wrong thing.' Jess smiled.

'Yes.' Jones gave a wry smile in return. 'If this goes on much longer and you don't find Eva's killer, I think Mum's going to end up breaking down. There, I shouldn't have said that. But if you love someone, you worry about them, don't you?'

Jess thought of Simon in the fly-blown conditions of the refugee camp. 'Yes, you do.'

'I used to worry about Eva,' Jones said soberly. 'Because I was pretty keen on her, but I expect you sussed that out.'

'I thought you probably were. It's normal. She was a very pretty girl.'

'Yes, she was. She was beautiful. The photo didn't do her justice – and when you saw her dead, well, I expect she wasn't very pretty then, was she? As a medic, even a failed one, I've seen death.'

'No,' Jess said quietly. 'She wasn't very pretty then.'

'It takes away all personality,' Jones said, his gaze losing its concentration. He was going down memory lane. 'It leaves the human body just a husk. I think there must be a spirit – or something like a spirit – because something definitely leaves the body on death.'

Jess leaned forward and said softly, 'David . . .'

He blinked, jerked and his eyes refocused. 'Yes, well. Eva was very attractive and she was a nice person too, and I did fall for her. But she had a boyfriend.'

'Go on,' invited Jess, because he'd stopped again.

'Did Milada say anything to you about it?' Jones stared at her.

'She thought a man picked up Eva regularly on her free days, at the end of the lane. He never came to the Foot to the Ground, she said.'

'No, he didn't!' Jones burst out vehemently. 'And that's dodgy, don't you think? In all weathers she went down to the junction to wait for him. He never brought her back, even if it was pouring with rain. She always walked up to the pub from the main road where he dropped her.'

'Do you have any ideas why that was?'

'He didn't want to be seen,' Jones said simply. 'Milada and I talked about it once. Eva had come home very late, early hours of one morning. Milada told me that she'd had to go down and unbolt the door, after Eva called her on her mobile and woke her up. Eva had walked to the pub from the junction, down an unlit road, at three a.m.

What kind of a guy lets his date do that? Milada thinks he's married.'

'It's a possible explanation. There are others. Perhaps, as you suggest, he had lousy manners.' Jess paused. 'Did you ever try and find out who he was? Did you ever ask Eva?'

'I asked her once and she bit my head off, said it was none of my business. She was quite right, of course. So I didn't mention it again and left it to Milada. I thought, you know, girls chatting together. They shared a bedroom. She might tell Milada eventually, but Milada says she never did.'

Jones picked up his mug of cooling coffee. When he'd taken a few sips, he went on, 'I wish now I'd asked Bronwen Westcott to talk to Eva about this bloke. Bronwen wishes she had, too. She's on a big guilt trip now because she never tried to find out where Eva went in her free time. She says she was *in loco parentis*. I told her no, she wasn't, because Eva wasn't a child. But Bronwen says, Eva was all alone in this country and lived in their home. Not in their actual part of the pub, I mean, but under the same roof. So Bronwen and Jake now feel they were responsible for her, or should have been. Bronwen does, anyway.'

'Jake Westcott less so?'

'He's got a bit of a conscience about it, now that Bronwen is bending his ear so much. Left to himself, I don't suppose he'd see it that way. Jake's a businessman. He doesn't worry about his staff's private lives, only if they do their jobs. From my point of view, that's just fine. He's the one person who doesn't worry I'm going to flip again. I like Jake. He's a decent bloke.'

There was a moment or two of silence. Jones finished his coffee but didn't seem disposed to leave.

'Something else?' Jess prompted.

He flushed. 'It makes me look like a – a snoop and a bit of a voyeur.'

'David,' Jess told him earnestly, 'if people would only report the suspicious things they see, our lives as police officers would be much easier and a lot of crime could be prevented. All too often they don't want to be involved, or they fear they'll sound ridiculous or paranoid or, as you describe it, like snoopers. So they ignore the bruises on a woman's face, the terrified look of a child when the mother's new boyfriend comes into sight, children playing too near railway tracks. I know that sometimes a concerned member of the public does report something odd and the authorities take no action and later there's a disaster. People are rightly angry when that happens. I'm sorry if that does occur from time to time. But it doesn't mean people shouldn't at least try.'

'All right,' David interrupted, 'although it was nothing like that. Eva wasn't scared. She didn't have any bruises. I had no reason to suspect anything was really wrong or that she was in any danger. I just thought the guy she was going out with was the wrong type and he didn't look after her.'

He shrugged. 'After Eva and I had this little spat about her boyfriend when she told me to shut up, I brooded over it for a while, as you might say. I'm not saying she wasn't right to tell me off, but it rankled. I'd only asked because I was concerned for her. I wasn't jealous. Well, all right, I was a bit jealous but I respected her right to pick the company she wanted to keep. I thought she'd be sensible. I'd seen her give Harper and his cronies the cold shoulder. She wasn't stupid.

'At any rate, the next time she had a free day, I slipped away and got down to the corner of the road before her. It helped that Jake wasn't around that morning, gone to see some supplier or other, so he wasn't there to notice I'd bunked off. I hid behind the hedge, real Peeping Tom stuff. After a while Eva came down to the corner. She had her pink coat on. I could see it through gaps in the twigs. She hung about there for nearly ten minutes and I got crosser and crosser. I thought, for Pete's sake, why didn't she just go back to the pub? Why did she let him do this to her? Keeping her waiting like that . . . I was just about to jump out and tell her so, and never mind how angry she was with me, when suddenly I heard a car. It came at a fair old speed, so he must have been late. He screeched to a stop. There was a slam of a door as Eva leaped in and they were off. By the time I stood up and craned my neck over the hedge, they were disappearing. I just glimpsed them, or to be honest I saw Eva's pink coat in the passenger seat, before he swept round the bend. I was ashamed afterwards. I was spying on her and it wasn't nice. She came back quite late that night, too, Milada said. Milada wasn't happy about it, either, you know. It disturbed her when she'd just dropped off to sleep.'

'But this could be very important!' Jess's excitement broke through her voice. 'A breakthrough! You saw him, David, and you're the only person who did!'

'I didn't see *him*, only the car. It was only a glimpse. It was a silvery colour. I didn't get the licence plate, not even part of it, I'm afraid,' Jones apologised.

'Silver?' Jess nearly bounced out of her chair. 'Was it a big car? Did you see enough to name the make?'

'I think it may have been a Citroën Saxo. A friend of mine had one. It looked very similar. About that size, anyway.'

'It couldn't possibly have been a Mercedes?'

He shook his head firmly. 'Definitely not a Merc. A much smaller car, like a Saxo, and not the right shape for a Merc.'

Damn. Two steps forward, one step back. 'Listen, David,' Jess said earnestly. 'I don't need you to make a statement about your mother's fears for you. But I do need you to make a statement about this car and how you came to see it. It could be a vital piece of evidence. I can't stress too much you are the only person who ever got that close to Eva's man friend, even if you didn't see him. Don't worry about the hiding behind the hedge and all the rest of it. Believe me, we hear weirder tales than that! Just put it all in a statement and sign it, would you? Because that's evidence we may need to use.'

'All right,' Jones said. 'I don't mind doing that. Even the lurking behind the hedge bit. You must think I'm self-obsessed. Or obsessed with Eva. But Eva's dead and, as you say, I did see the car. I suppose I should have told you about it at once, when you came to the pub. But I was ashamed of my behaviour. I'll make a statement.' He paused. 'I'm sorry I didn't tell you before. And I'm glad I've told you now.'

'So am I,' Jess informed him.

Jones looked momentarily relieved. He fiddled with the empty coffee mug still in his hands. 'Your brother,' he said unexpectedly, 'the one working out in the refugee camps, I suppose you don't hear from him often?'

She had made a mistake. She ought to have thought more carefully before telling a witness anything personal about herself. Especially one she'd never met before and who had shared the workplace with the victim. It made a link between them. It was dangerous, the sort of thing she, as a professional, had been warned about and against which she should have an automatic safeguard in place. Sometimes it helped enquiries to be friendly. But an officer never gave hostages and she had given one to Jones in telling him of her brother.

To be fair, so far he'd showed no sign of using this to manipulate her. But all that could just be about to change.

'Not often,' she said, sipping at the cold remains of her own coffee and keeping her tone neutral.

Jones frowned. 'How do your parents feel about that? Are they still alive, your parents?'

Getting nearer the bone. 'They're fine with it.'

Not true. Her father was stoical about it but that didn't mean he didn't care or worry. Her mother worried all the time. She, Simon's twin, worried.

'Why do you ask?' She put a question in her turn, seeking to redress the balance of the conversation. She sat behind the desk here. She was the investigator, the interrogator if need be. That young man there was the witness and a potential suspect. But even as she thought this, another thought tacked itself on unwished. *He must be in his middle or even late twenties but he hardly looks out of his teens.*

Jones had been ill and sometimes illness made an unexpected change to physical appearance, not just the expected loss of weight or of hair condition, but an actual ageing or conversely, in Jones's case, a stripping away of the years. He was only a few years younger than she was but she had to remind herself of the fact. He's not a boy. He's a man.

But Julia Jones didn't think of her son as a man. Her panicked call to the family solicitor had shown that.

Jones was watching her face and she had the uneasy feeling he could read her mind. I mustn't underestimate him! she reminded herself. As a doctor in training he was taught to read symptoms, to work out what the patient was hiding or was unaware of. Every little telltale thing: the twitch of a muscle, the texture of skin, the fidgeting hands, all told a story. There were parallels with her own training. Watching the witness and watching the patient were akin. She had been studying David Jones since they met in the car park. But he had been studying her, too. Her unease grew.

'I'm an only child,' he said now, his manner suddenly so much more relaxed that it struck Jess as a sudden change of room temperature might have done.

'You think that makes your mother more inclined to worry about you?'

'There's that,' he agreed. He spoke now almost as if he was talking of someone else, not himself. This had suddenly turned into a case conference. She and he were put on a par, colleagues discussing a difficult diagnosis. 'But really I think it's because if parents only have one nestling, that one chick has to fly high, when it fledges. All their hopes are bound up in one human being. That child has to do well, or they, as parents, have failed.'

'I wouldn't know about that!' Jess said crisply. Who sat in the chair opposite now? A nervous witness or Dr Freud?

'Yes, well, take it from me,' Jones said wryly. He stooped to pick up the helmet. 'I have to get back to the pub. I've got work to do and I'm sure you have, too.'

'I still need you to make a statement about seeing the car,' she reminded him. 'I'll take you along to see DC Stubbs and you can make it to him. It won't take long.'

'OK,' he said, amenable now. All the tension had gone out of him like air out of a tyre. The session on the psychiatrist's couch had been successful.

I wonder if I'm in the wrong job? thought Jess.

'We can't dismiss that young man as a suspect,' Carter said, when he'd listened to Jess's account of her interview with David Jones. 'He has a history of instability and, whatever he claims, he was obsessed by the girl. He says he hid behind the hedge to see who picked up Eva because he was worried about her. But that's a familiar stalker's excuse. "I didn't mean any harm to her or anyone else; I was acting in her best interests" – you've heard it before, so have I.'

'Ye-es,' agreed Jess doubtfully. 'Yet somehow, I can't see him harming Eva.'

'He may not have intended to. We'll keep him in view, anyway. How did you get along in London?'

Jess summarised her adventures. 'I don't know if Burton only invested in the property market. Things aren't looking so bright in that at the moment, are they? Or according to the newspapers I read.'

'If he invested at the right time, and he and his associates probably did, they won't have to worry too much, I shouldn't think,' Carter observed. 'But he certainly will have had other interests, have diversified. He was obviously a seriously wealthy man. We'll track his other deals down, though it may take time. He may have stepped on someone's toes.'

'Armstrong thought Burton had worked his way up in the world from humble beginnings. It could be someone from his past,' Jess pointed out. 'We still need to trace his next of kin. They will be able to tell us more about the man, where he came from, how he made his first serious money, that sort of thing. No one has come forward but he must have had someone, some family member.'

'Some people don't.' Carter hunched his shoulders. 'Immediate relatives have died and they've never been in touch with more distant ones. They're loners. Burton did, however, have a local solicitor. He got in touch with me yesterday while you were in London. He'd been trying to contact his client and finally went to the house. No luck there and so he tracked down the cleaner. She told him Burton was dead and the police were involved. He's anxious to talk to us, that is, to you. He says you've already met him.'

'I have?' asked Jess, startled.

'It seems you went to see his wife. His name is Foscott, Reginald Foscott. I've got his business card here, if you don't want to tackle him at home.' Carter picked up a tiny rectangle of white card and held it out to her.

'Who'd have believed it?' Jess wondered aloud, as she took it. 'Reggie Foscott!'

'Thought you'd be surprised,' said Carter, his expression enigmatic.

'Ah, Inspector Campbell, I believe we have met,' said Foscott, rising from behind his desk to stretch out a long lean hand.

Jess shook it. It crumpled in her grip, as if it were boneless, an impression Foscott himself gave on closer inspection. Before, in their brief encounter at his house, she'd only received an impression of a tall, thin, pale figure. Looking at Reggie now, Jess was irresistibly put in mind of Munch's painting 'The Scream'.

Foscott invited her courteously to 'please be seated'. Jess sat and found herself on one of those chairs with a misnamed back 'rest' that lodged across the sitter's spine at the most awkward and painful spot. She was forced to sit upright, well away from it. A Victorian teacher of deportment would have approved. Why was it, she wondered, that the Foscotts, whether at home or at work, were incapable of providing visitors with a comfortable seat?

'I appreciate your coming to see me,' intoned Foscott. 'A great pity we did not realise, when you called to see my wife, that your enquiries would include my client – late client, I should perhaps say – Lucas Burton. Although . . .' A strange expression crossed his bony features and Jess saw with a start that he was smiling. 'A solicitor's client is no less of a client because he is dead, hm?'

Reggie Foscott had cracked a joke. Oh, dear. Reggie humorous was more disconcerting that Reggie serious, Jess decided. However, it quickly became apparent that this attempt at graveyard humour was strictly temporary. He probably trotted out that joke every time he met the executors of wills in an attempt to put them at their ease.

To confirm this, he resumed his lugubrious expression and said briskly, 'Now, to business!'

Jess decided it was time to take charge. 'Thank you, too, for making time to see me, Mr Foscott, and for contacting the police in the first place. We have been having some difficulty in tracing a next of kin for Mr Burton. We're hoping you can help us there.'

Foscott steepled his long fingers. 'Ah . . . quite so. Alas, no, I can't help you there, at least not at the moment. In fact, I was rather hoping you might have some information about that for me.'

Jess found she was gaping at him and hastily pulled herself together. 'Mr Burton was a businessman with several profitable interests. We are assuming there is a will?'

'There *was* a will,' corrected Foscott. 'Now there isn't and that, you see, is the problem and why I am very anxious to contact any relatives. Or, indeed, anyone else who may feel they have a claim on the estate. Otherwise it will go to the Crown. It is, as you say, a considerable one. There are two valuable residential properties alone, collectable antiques and furniture, personal property, all to be taken into account before calculation of monies in bank accounts and investments et cetera. It will take some time to disentangle everything, find out where it all is and come to an agreement with the taxman. Some of it is likely to have been invested offshore.'

'No will?' Jess frowned. 'But there was previously a will, you say. What happened to it?'

'It was destroyed by me on my client's instructions. There was a good reason for that. Let me explain. Mr Burton was one of those very rich men with no one to leave his money to. He was unmarried, that is to say divorced, and had no children. He was not in touch with any relatives. He said he didn't have any; although, in my experience, there is nearly always someone. It may be a person the testator has never met or of whose existence he may be quite unaware, a distant cousin in Australia, for example. But nonetheless there is generally someone.'

Yes, Carter was wrong. People might believe themselves without family, but a hunt through the family tree might discover a shoal of unsuspected relatives. That might turn out to be Foscott's problem.

The strange expression crossed his face again. 'Sometimes we find the missing heir is the family black sheep, whose name was struck from the records and never spoken aloud again.

Families, Inspector Campbell, can always be relied upon to spring a surprise. Death, funerals, above all wills, they all bring the secrets to the surface.'

His foray into levity was over again. Foscott's features settled back into their normal sedate gloom and it really did seem to suit him much better. Jollity, Reggie, doesn't become you! thought Jess.

'Mr Burton explained to me that his marriage had been a youthful one and had lasted only eighteen months. He and his young bride had parted amicably and, over the years, been in touch sporadically. She had remarried and divorced again. Her name was Janice Grey. Grey was the name of her second husband and she'd retained it. I think he took her out to dinner now and again when he was in London. In a curious, rather touching sort of way, he seemed to feel some responsibility for her. So he named her as the sole beneficiary of his will. As I recall, his exact words were: "Janice might as well have it."'

Foscott sounded disapproving of his client's cavalier manner of disposing of a considerable estate.

'I suggested to him that he might name some residual beneficiary, should it become necessary. That is to say some charity, for example, or other institution that might benefit if Ms Grey predeceased him. Mr Burton expressed himself – ah – forcefully on the subject of charities. In short, he didn't wish to make such a clause. Ms Grey, he said, was three years younger than he was. I gather she was only sixteen at the time of the marriage and he, therefore, nineteen. Little wonder it didn't last long! "Janice," he said, "is fit and healthy. Tough as old boots." Not very gallant, perhaps, but an encouraging thought if one is naming a beneficiary.

'Sadly, robust of health she may have been, but six months ago Ms Grey lost her life in a car crash on the M25. Mr Burton came in to see me, very upset. The only time, I think I may say, that I ever saw him distressed. He instructed I destroy the will at once and gave me his copy of it, so that I could destroy that too.'

'So he had to think of a new beneficiary, after all,' Jess said thoughtfully.

'Quite. I pointed out to him that he should instruct me with a view to drawing up a new, replacement, will as soon as possible. I don't want to sound as though I was touting for business. But my understanding was that Mr Burton, having destroyed one will, did intend to replace it with another and that he would be instructing me in due course. As delicately as I could, I drew his attention to the, um, random nature of Fate. At the time of our conversation Mr Burton was forty-six years old. I took Ms Grey's death in a car accident as my example. "Don't rush me, Foscott!" was his reply. "Let me think about it. I'll get back to you." But he didn't.'

Foscott broke off his narrative at this point and sat back, awaiting Jess's reaction.

'You were trying to get in touch with him when you learned from his cleaner of his death,' Jess said. 'Or so I believe you gave Superintendent Carter to understand.'

Foscott inclined his head graciously. 'I was. I was getting

worried. When clients start to put things off, time loses its meaning for them. In this case, six months had already gone by and six months soon becomes a year and then two. The prospect of my client dying intestate would be a bureaucratic nightmare for someone. Unfortunately, it's happened. We handled other legal work for Mr Burton. This office has a department dealing with conveyancing. The clerk there handled the purchase of his Cheltenham house and we hold the deeds of the property here for safekeeping, together with some other documents of a personal and private nature. He didn't like to leave sensitive material lying around at home. We are bound to be involved in sorting out the confused situation that has arisen now.'

There was a moment or two during which both of them sat in silence. Jess was thinking, That's why we found no wall safe. Burton simply sealed up everything in an envelope and left it with his solicitor. It probably has *To be opened in the Event of my Death* written on it. Foscott was tapping his fingers together and looking bland.

'Lucas Burton,' Jess said at last, 'was forty-six years old. He hadn't made his money overnight. Isn't it possible that there might be some even earlier will, not drawn up by you? Perhaps a will drawn up in London, twenty or more years ago? It could be even one of those do-it-yourself efforts on a form you get from your bank.'

'We don't approve of those,' said Foscott, presumably speaking for his profession.

'But it might exist, lying around somewhere,' Jess insisted.

'As you destroyed the later will on his instructions, would that mean a hypothetical earlier one would now be valid?'

Foscott shuddered. 'It might well be, if it came to light. I was not unaware of this possibility, Inspector. I made a point of asking him, at the time I drew up the will in favour of Ms Grey, if there was any earlier will I should know about. I stressed that if so, it must be retrieved and destroyed. Earlier beneficiaries appearing clasping old wills and claiming inheritance aren't unknown in my world. They generally don't take kindly to being told there is a later will, cutting them out. I made a little joke at the time. I reminded Mr Burton that confusion over old wills provided the plot for numerous – ah – detective stories of the sort Agatha Christie wrote. He assured me there wasn't any such will.'

Oh, Reggie, you and your little jokes! thought Jess. How many times, I wonder, have you told the Agatha Christie one? 'Who were the executors of his will? The one you destroyed?' she asked aloud.

'His bank.'

'Well, we can't help you,' Jess said, 'not in that respect, at any rate. But we still hope you might be able to provide some information to help us. Mr Burton died violently. We are treating it as murder.'

'His name was in this morning's newspapers,' said Foscott disapprovingly. 'It confirmed what the cleaner had already told me. I assumed the delay in releasing details of his identity was due to the police seeking next of kin. That, Inspector, made us allies. I contacted Superintendent Carter at once.'

'Perhaps, then, someone, some relative, might read about it and come forward? We rather hope so.'

'I shouldn't be surprised,' said Foscott with asperity, 'if half a dozen do and all of them false. A very rich man dies. The circumstances are mysterious. Journalists always try to find a grieving widow or girlfriend or ex-girlfriend, preferably photogenic. If they establish, as they'll quickly do, he was a loner with no known next of kin, then it may well suggest to a few opportunists they try to make some claim. Also, in any case, we shall have to put advertisements in the press, requesting anyone believing they might be entitled to do so to come forward. If anyone does, we'll take great care to make sure they are genuine. You may rely on me for that.'

Foscott put his hand to his mouth and cleared his throat. 'There is a further problem.'

'Yes?' Jess waited with sinking heart.

'His name wasn't always Lucas Burton.'

'*What?*'

Foscott's eyes gleamed. She was sure he was enjoying this, despite the problem his client had left him.

'No, indeed. He was born Marvin Crapper. He changed the name by deed poll some years before he arrived in Cheltenham. By then he had started to make serious money and climb the ladder socially. For him, the purchase of his house here was symbolic. He felt it somehow established him. Perhaps he'd felt his original name gave the wrong image, in his new circumstances. He became Lucas Burton.'

Jess sat back and took a moment or two to mull over the

information. Reggie smiled at her benevolently while she did so.

So now they had to track down not only a Lucas Burton but a Marvin Crapper as well. Another thought occurred to her.

'He was certainly well off,' she said. 'The estate will take some sorting out. I've been in the house in Cheltenham and in his flat in London. The Cheltenham house is stuffed with antiques, as you mentioned. The Docklands flat contains modern stuff but it looks as if it cost a packet. There are some paintings there. I don't know about modern art, or any art, but I'm sure they're originals. The contents will have to be valued for probate, I suppose? I mean, everything he had, like his car. He drove an expensive car, didn't he?'

Foscott, still smiling, said, 'I fear I have no idea. No doubt it was an expensive one.'

Hah! No flies on Reggie Foscott! He'd recognised the drift of Jess's carefully worded innocuous question, and neatly headed her off. If Foscott had known Burton drove a silver Mercedes, then if Selina had told him of her near-miss experience with such a car on the day the body had been found at Cricket Farm, he might have wondered whether his client were involved. Jess imagined Selina would have described the incident to him, graphically.

But perhaps she was being unfair to Foscott. There was no reason why he should know what kind of car Burton drove.

Another thought struck her. 'A man like Burton, with that sort of income, must surely have an accountant to do his personal tax returns and so on?'

'As regards his business investments, there is a firm of tax lawyers in London whose address I can give you.' Foscott put his hand to his mouth and coughed discreetly. 'As regards his personal tax matters, yes, he did have a local man who worked all that out for him and kept his records.'

'A local man?' Jess heard the enthusiasm in her own voice. 'Then I can go and see him. Which firm is it?'

'It's not a large company. It's a one-man band, but one with a good reputation locally. Andrew Ferris. He works from an office at his home. I can give you that address, too.'

Foscott was quite a man for springing surprises. Mentally Jess found herself doing some nimble reshuffling of information to date. It was like one of those computer games where a click of a button sends coloured blocks tumbling into a new pattern.

'Inspector?' Foscott raised his eyebrows.

Foscott had noted that her concentration had momentarily shifted away from him. Jess rallied.

'Yes, please,' she said. 'I've been meaning to go and see Mr Ferris anyway. I want to show him the photograph I showed your wife,' she added hastily.

'Do you indeed?' said Foscott thoughtfully.

'I'd be obliged,' Jess said, getting to her feet and gathering up her backpack, 'if you didn't phone and let him know I'm on my way.'

Foscott flushed. 'It was not my intention.'

Chapter 15

The professional classes stick together, thought Jess grimly, as she left Foscott's office. They socialise, too. Despite my asking him not to say anything, I wouldn't put it past Reggie to bump into Andrew Ferris 'by chance' in the bar of the golf club or somewhere like that, and say something like, 'How did you get on with the police?' followed by, 'Oops! I wasn't supposed to mention that.'

All of which meant she should lose no time to going to see Ferris. This case was dragging on long enough. Phil Morton might turn up something in London today, but Jess wasn't counting on it.

'Tomorrow will be Thursday, when it will be the anniversary of Nathan Smith's crime.'

With a start she realised she'd spoken aloud. Of course they wanted to wrap up the investigation, but why should she feel it so important to have it settled before tomorrow? The date loomed oppressively over them. It worried Eli and it worried her. These two modern-day murders – of Eva and of Burton – seemed to demand they were settled before they collided with the anniversary of those two other murders, nearly thirty years before. Jess couldn't explain why this should seem so important but somehow it did.

Strictly speaking, anniversaries fell on dates. But Eli chose to remember the murder of his parents on the nearest Thursday to the calendar date of the event, because Thursday had been market day; and a market day had been selected by his brother for the deed. After all, what did a calendar date mean to a man who was not only illiterate but had grown up in a world governed by the seasons and the weather, not according to a numbered square on a sheet of paper?

Ferris lived outside town on an estate built some fifteen or twenty years earlier. The gardens had had time to settle and shrubs to grow. Some of the trees were already threatening to cause a problem with subsidence before too long. The brickwork had weathered and the pavements cracked. Nevertheless these had been pricey houses when new and their value had certainly increased. All were detached and some, like Andrew Ferris's, had double garages. The garage at his house attracted notice because the up-and-over double door was not quite closed and in front of it stood ranged a row of large cardboard boxes.

Jess got out of her car and approached the boxes curiously. One contained books and CDs, another female clothing. A third held a woman's shoe collection, an expensive one, Jimmy Choo and Manolo Blahnik designs among the jumble. Jess gazed down covetously at a shiny bright green pair of 'ballerinas'. The last box held kitchen equipment, mixers, blenders and a set of bright, almost unused steel pans.

A couple of glossy cookbooks had been tossed in on top. They looked as unused as the pans. Someone was moving out.

'Inspector?'

Jess jumped and turned, flushing guiltily at being found snooping. Andrew Ferris stood behind her, holding more clothing in his arms.

'Sorry,' she apologised. 'I came to see you about something and I was surprised to find all this . . .' She indicated the boxes. 'Are you moving?'

'No, I'm not. My wife is. We're getting a divorce. She's in London at the moment and we're communicating through our solicitors.'

Aha! In Andrew's case, the solicitor was probably Reggie Foscott. No wonder Foscott's eyes had betrayed his interest on hearing Jess was planning a visit here.

Ferris walked to the clothing box and dumped the garments in his arms casually into it. 'Karen's coming down at some point to collect her things. I'm trying to speed it all up by doing a bit of sorting. I hadn't realised she'd got so much. This –' he pointed at the clothing box – 'is just the start of it, one wardrobe. There's another cupboard in the spare room with all her skiwear, that sort of thing. She's a travel courier. She has clothes for every occasion, as I'm finding out!' He pulled a wry grin.

'Sorry about the marriage breakdown,' Jess said, feeling she ought to make some suitable remark.

'Don't be. It's been a long time coming but on the cards for ages. We should have called it quits a couple of years ago.

With Karen being away so much, it's meant we've been *de facto* separated for much of the time. I suppose that delayed having to make it legal. Anyway, come inside. I'm ready for a cup of coffee or even something stronger. But you're on duty, I suppose?' He raised an eyebrow.

'Yes. Coffee would be fine, thanks.'

She followed him into the house. The hallway was cluttered with items not yet moved out to the boxes: more books, guides to tour destinations by the look of them, more CDs, two framed watercolours of Italian scenes, a set of those Russian dolls that contain smaller dolls inside them and some ethnic-looking pottery.

'By the time I've finished and Karen's been down here to clear out anything I've missed, the house will be virtually empty,' Ferris said cheerfully. 'She doesn't want the furniture, fortunately, except for some items she inherited from her family, so I won't be sitting on orange crates. But it will look very bare.'

He climbed past the books and pushed open a door at the end of the hall, leading into the kitchen. Jess followed him.

In the kitchen, all the cupboard doors were open. Ferris indicated them. 'This is the tricky bit. Nearly all the stuff left in here came to us by way of wedding presents. So I've got to try and remember which came from my family and which came from Karen's lot. I'm sure Karen will know, anyway, so perhaps I'd better leave it until she comes. I wonder if she'll want the microwave?' He frowned at it. 'She bought that and she's entitled to it. But it's about the only thing in here I use. I'm not a cook.'

He was busying himself boiling a kettle and spooning coffee grounds into an upright jug as he spoke. 'Do you like it strong? I'm used to brewing it up thick enough to stand the spoon up in.'

'Not quite as strong as that, please!' Jess said hastily.

She swung her backpack from her shoulder and unzipped it with a view to finding the blown-up publicity photo from the Foot to the Ground. The green bag was full and it was awkward to root around in it with one hand while holding it with the other. Jess looked for a clear surface to put the rucksack on, but there wasn't one.

'What's the problem?' asked Ferris, seeing her dithering. 'Looking for somewhere to put down your bag? Try the lounge, it's tidier and we can sit in there comfortably.'

Jess picked her way past the books and watercolours and found the lounge. It was tidier by comparison, but hardly tidy. Many of the books outside must have been taken from the tall oak bookcase. It now had significant gaps in its rows and the remaining volumes had collapsed on one another. Others, perhaps of disputed ownership, had been left scattered or in unsteady towers on the carpet. Among them lay yet more CDs from another case. The only things untouched were several Toby jugs peering beerily at her through the glass doors of an otherwise emptied display cabinet. Either Karen didn't want those, or they belonged indisputably to her estranged husband. No wonder the Ferrises had put off the final moment of their parting of the ways. The time and trouble dividing up every single thing collected in several years of marriage was enough to make any heart fail.

There was plenty of confirmation that Andrew Ferris wasn't in any way domestically inclined. Not only did he not cook; he didn't dust. Jess could have written her name on an occasional table. Unlike Burton, he appeared not to have employed a cleaner. The division of property completed, she wondered how he would ever establish order again. She hoped he kept his clients' personal account records in better order.

'But,' she murmured to herself, 'I'm not one to talk.'

She had to admit she too was a stranger to housework. She comforted herself with the thought that she and Ferris weren't alone among those whose offices were kept in good order, but whose homes were tips.

Jess set the backpack on the sofa and finally managed to extricate the group photograph. She straightened up as Ferris entered with the coffee and as she did so a cushion was dislodged; behind it, rather crumpled, lay one of the publicity folders from the Foot to the Ground, identical to the one David Jones had given her and from which she'd taken the photograph held now in her hand.

She stared at it and then up at Ferris.

'What is it?' he asked. 'Sorry about the mess. I did say "tidier" and not "tidy".'

'Yes,' Jess said, 'it's not that. It's this.' She picked up the leaflet.

'Oh, that.' Ferris set down the coffee cups on a low glass-topped table. 'All the talk about that poor kid whose body turned up in Eli's cowshed put the name of that pub in the news. I've never gone there with Penny or with Karen, my soon to be ex-wife, come to that. I thought I'd check it out. Pen and I usually go to the Hart to eat, where you saw us when you came in with your friend. Well, word's got about of the business at Cricket. Not long after you left, last Thursday night, just as we'd settled down to eat, some ghastly bottle-blonde teetered up to our table and wanted to know if Penny had heard any screams, if you please!' Ferris pulled a face. 'So I thought, right, we're too well known there. The Foot to the Ground is reputed to be a bit pricey but perhaps its customers don't pester one another for gossip.'

And CID doesn't drop in for a pint, he might have said, but hadn't, thought Jess. Ferris sank into an armchair opposite her and stared thoughtfully into his coffee mug, as if not quite sure what kind of brew he'd made.

'When did you go to the Foot?' Jess asked, looking back to the leaflet.

'Sunday morning, this weekend just gone. Nice place. Penny might like it, I think.'

'Well,' Jess told him, 'that lessens the impact of this.' She held out her photograph to him. 'I brought it to see if you recognised anyone in it, noticed anyone like any of those people around Cricket Farm or anywhere else, in Cheltenham perhaps, in a restaurant or a pub. But you've already seen the photo; it's in that leaflet.'

'I know there's a picture of the pub and its staff in the leaflet,' Ferris said, taking the enlargement from her. 'But I didn't study it.

I was more interested in the prices on the sample menu. They were, I have to say, rather steep. But the food's supposed to be good and I, for one, am getting rather fed up with chips.'

'I wanted to show it to you earlier. I had rather hoped to find you at the stables on Wednesday morning but you weren't there, then other things turned up. I had to go up to London and this morning I've been to see Reggie Foscott. We are investigating another death, besides that of the girl found at Cricket Farm. Lucas Burton, a local businessman.' Jess waited to see how mention of Burton's name would be received.

'Ah,' said Ferris, looking rather embarrassed. 'I did wonder if I should have rung you first thing this morning. I saw in the paper that one of my clients appears to have met his maker. He was found in his garage, the rag said. Perhaps he found someone trying to steal his Merc. Lucas Burton, poor chap. Who'd have thought it? Reggie's handling the will, I suppose? He'll be in touch with me pretty soon, if he is. I'll give him a ring.'

'You know the Foscotts quite well,' Jess observed, 'one way and another. Selina's daughter keeps her pony at Berryhill stables.'

'I wouldn't say I knew them well. I know Reggie casually, odd civic occasion, drinks parties, that kind of thing. Occasionally our paths have crossed professionally. Now I'm headed for divorce, I suppose I'll be seeing a lot more of him. As for Selina, I'm pleased to say I've only ever encountered her at the stables. Reggie's OK,' added Ferris. 'His wife is a terrible old bat and word has it she rules him with a rod of iron.'

'Did you hear that she had a close encounter with a silver-grey Mercedes on leaving the stable yard on the Friday the body was found at the farm?'

He shook his head. 'No. Ah, you think it was the same car Penny spotted earlier?'

'We think it was Lucas Burton's car.'

There was a silence. 'Merry hell,' said Ferris.

'You obviously knew he had a Mercedes.'

'Yes, I knew. He came here in it. Look, I didn't think it was *his* car Penny saw! Why should I? His car wasn't the only Merc around and why on earth should Lucas go out to Cricket Farm? Oh . . .' He sat back and stared at her. 'You don't think . . . ? *Lucas?* Oh, come off it. If Lucas was playing around with a barmaid, he could have got rid of her without wringing her neck. He'd have paid her off. He was a professional bachelor, you know. That's how he described himself. Not a bad idea, perhaps. But, honestly, do you think Lucas is in the frame for this murder at Cricket?'

'We don't think anything, Mr Ferris,' Jess said firmly. 'We are still in the middle of enquiries. But Lucas Burton does seem to have been at the scene on the day in question and we had been hoping to question him. Now, obviously, we can't. Perhaps someone didn't want us to. Anything you can tell us about him would be helpful. He seems to have been an excessively private man.'

Ferris chewed at his lower lip and studied Jess for a moment. 'Sorry, I can't tell you a load of salacious detail about Lucas. I would if I could. Or, given he got himself murdered, I suppose

I could peddle my gossip to the tabloids, if I had any. That *is* a joke, by the way! He was my client and anything I know about him I'd treat as confidential. With the exception of the police, of course. I really would tell you anything I knew that I thought might help you, but it wasn't a personal friendship; it was a business relationship, pure and simple. I keep his tax papers but you'll have to get authority to look at those, won't you? I don't think I can just open them up for you. At least, not until I've discussed the legal position with Reggie. I'm not a lawyer; I'm a number-cruncher.'

'Well, actually, I haven't come about Burton today,' Jess told him, 'although anything you can remember about him will be useful. If you do think of anything, call me. I came about that photo.'

He sat back, the photo in his hands, and frowned at it. 'No, don't know any of them. Hang on, this young chap! I think he was at the pub on Sunday morning when I was there. He served me in the bar.'

'No one else? How about the girls?'

Ferris shook his head. 'Didn't see either of them, sure of it.'

'Thanks.' Jess took back the photo. 'We're releasing this to the press tomorrow and it will be in the papers, so perhaps we'll have some luck. Someone might have seen one of the girls.'

'Just a minute!' exclaimed Ferris. 'I'm being thick, aren't I? The dead girl worked at the Foot to the Ground, so one of them is her. Which one?' He reached for photo again.

Jess returned it to him. He studied it again and shook his

head. 'Still don't know her. Pretty kid, though. If she took Lucas's eye, I wouldn't blame him.'

'Thank you for looking again,' said Jess politely, taking the photo back for a second time and returning it to the backpack. She took a sip or two of the coffee. 'Nice coffee but I'm afraid I can't stay to finish it. Thanks for your time. You'll want to get on with your packing.'

'Karen's packing,' he corrected her.

He stood on his front doorstep to wave her goodbye. Jess got into her car. She drove down the road and round the corner where she stopped again. For a moment or two she sat there, sunk in thought.

I'm being thick . . . Ferris had said to her not ten minutes earlier. But he wasn't thick. He was a pretty sharp type, and not averse to gently sticking the knife into the back of his late good client, Lucas Burton. *Oh, Lucas would've paid her off . . . but if she took his eye, I wouldn't blame him.* Ha! I know a diversionary technique when I hear it, Mr Ferris. You knew the dead girl had worked at the Foot to the Ground; that's now common knowledge. So when shown a picture of the staff – or when you saw in your own leaflet that there was a group snapshot – you must have realised the dead girl was among those shown.

'Which one?' he'd asked Jess, on taking the photo back for a second look. Jess hadn't replied to his question or pointed out Eva. Yet Ferris, without the information, had still replied, 'I don't know her.'

That might have been no more than a slip of the tongue.

He might have meant, he didn't know either girl. But that wasn't what he'd said. 'I don't know *her*.' He'd followed that with a comment of 'pretty kid'.

He knew which girl to look at.

Jess drummed her fingers on the steering wheel. Last Thursday night Ferris and Penny Gower went to eat at the Hart. Jess and Tom had seen them there. Earlier that day, Jess had shown Eli and Penny the enlarged photo. Penny must have told Ferris about her visit to the stables. He knew Jess was showing the photo around. So had Ferris gone to the Foot to the Ground on Sunday morning in order to get a copy of the leaflet and the photo it contained to study it himself? Out of curiosity? Or because the possibility of a good likeness of Eva Zelená in the hands of the police, a photo they would almost certainly release to the press, worried him? He'd picked a good time to visit the pub. Sunday would be a busy time at the Foot, probably there would be weekend visitors as well as locals, so Ferris wouldn't have stood out in the crowd as not being a regular.

Jess got out of her car and locked it up. She walked back to Ferris's house, approaching it cautiously in case he was outside by the boxes. But there was no sign of him. Still looking over her shoulder towards the house (and hoping no other neighbour was watching who might come running out to ask what she was doing), she sidled past the boxes to the half-opened garage door. An attempt to peer under it wasn't satisfactory. She pushed it up slowly, hoping the creak wouldn't be audible from the house.

Two cars were parked side by side within. One was Ferris's dark blue Passat. She'd seen that the first time she'd gone to the stables. The other was a small silver Citroën Saxo. It must belong to the absent Karen. Ferris was indeed by no means 'thick'. He'd been intelligent enough not to use his own car when taking out his Czech girlfriend, 'moonlighting' from his supposed relationship with Penny Gower. Instead he'd used his wife's car and by a stroke of luck the lovelorn David Jones had spotted it, with Eva in it. But David hadn't seen the driver, that morning he'd hidden behind the hedge, which had been a stroke of luck for Andrew Ferris. Otherwise, when David served him in the bar of the Foot to the Ground on Sunday, he might have recognised him. Although Ferris had been careful never to collect Eva from the pub or return her there, he had taken a risk in going there on Sunday. Of course, he didn't know about David observing his tryst with Eva. Still, it had been a gamble and he wouldn't have done it if he hadn't been worried. With reason – some newspaper reader might recognise Eva's picture and remember when and where they'd seen her, and with whom.

That was her last conscious thought. She felt a sudden sharp pain originating at the back of her head. Stars danced and then there was blackness.

She rose slowly through a black soup, swimming ever upward seeking the surface and light, but it eluded her. How much further could it be? The stars were still there but they were smaller and came in shoals like little silver fish, darting across her brain from one side to the other. She moved her head and heard herself exclaim in pain. She struggled to think coherently, issuing herself orders. Take it easy, Jess. Try again slowly. That's better.

Now she dared to open her eyes and to her horror it was still dark. Was she in a box? In a cave? No, she was in a darkened room, a bedroom, lying flat on her back on a double bed. The room smelled very bad, musty and damp. It was a sort of graveyard smell. She turned her head again to one side – careful, now! The pain had stabbed viciously in response. Something was rotting very close to her nostrils. She must sit up. She must get away from this awful smell. She must make sure she *could* sit up. She had to establish she was uninjured and also not tied up. She had to find out just where she *was*.

She pushed herself upright to a seated position using both arms, and her hands, as she pressed downwards, sank into something soft, very cold and damp. Light came into the room through chinks in windows that appeared to be boarded up. Her eyes were adjusting to the gloom but now she could make out furniture. Not Ferris's house; that was for sure.

Suddenly she knew where she was: in the main bedroom at Cricket Farm. She lay on the bed last occupied by the slaughtered Smith parents and probably on the same bedding, last warmed by their doomed bodies and now rotting.

Despite her throbbing head, she couldn't get away from the bed fast enough. She swung her legs to the floor, still exclaiming in pain, and tried to stand up. But her legs buckled, a blinding white light flashed through her head, and she sank back to sit on the edge of the bed, on the mouldering satin eiderdown, her feet on the floor.

Give yourself time, Jess! she instructed herself. Count up to ten. Right, that's better. How had she got here? Andrew Ferris had brought her. She'd been so busy looking at Karen's silver car, she'd failed to hear his approach. Was this how he'd killed Burton? Burton had died in his garage, where he'd been repairing the scratch on his car. Had Ferris crept up, spanner in hand? But, if so, he'd hit Burton an awful lot harder than he'd hit Jess. Why kill his client? Almost certainly something to do with Burton having been at the farm and finding the body. But why had Burton been at Cricket Farm?

Sort that one out later, Jess continued her lecture to herself. Your mind isn't up to dealing with more than one thing at a time right now. I don't know why he killed Burton, but he didn't mean to kill me. He just wanted to get me out of the way. So he's dumped me at Cricket Farm. Why here? What was his purpose? To buy time in which to escape? We'll find him. He must have known I'd come round and raise the alarm.

Raise the alarm . . . Jess looked around for her backpack but it was nowhere to be seen. It held her mobile phone and its loss meant she couldn't call for help. She would have to get out of here first and find a phone. If she went down the hill to the stables, Penny might be there and she'd have a mobile.

But he'd overlooked her wristwatch. She still wore that. Jess tried to read the time on the dial but the light was too poor. She got to her feet and managed this time to stay upright.

She stumbled to the window and held her wrist up to the light filtering through the gaps in the boards. Five o'clock.

Five o'clock! Had she been here unconscious for half the day? She had to get out of here. Jess turned towards the door and froze.

She wasn't alone. There was someone in the room with her. Ferris? Her heart leaped in alarm. Had he come back for her already? No, not Ferris. Her companion, whoever he was, was shorter. Ferris stood over six feet. Eli? The figure standing by the door was much his build, stocky and wearing shabby clothes. Yes, Eli, of course! Who else? He'd come to check on his property and, finding her unexpectedly stretched out on his late parents' bed, was wondering what on earth she was doing there, indeed in his house. He'd probably got as much of a shock as she had. But the needed help was at hand.

'Eli?' Jess called eagerly.

The man didn't answer and then she realised that it wasn't Eli after all. It was a man she'd never seen before, resembling Eli but rather younger. He had an odd sort of smirk on his face and what appeared to be a rope trailing over his shoulder. The phrase 'blood ran cold' had never seemed anything but a literary fancy to her before. But that was exactly how she felt now, chilled to the marrow.

'Who are you?' she demanded, trying to keep her voice steady but hearing a tremulous quiver in it despite her efforts.

Receiving no answer, her training kicked in. She decided to take action and walked as firmly towards him as she could.

'I am a police officer!' she said more sternly, thinking how foolish it sounded. She fumbled in her jacket pocket for her ID but it had gone. Ferris had removed it in his thorough way, as he removed all his victims' small portable possessions. She couldn't prove it if challenged.

In the event, she had no need. No request came. The shadowy figure's response to her claim was extraordinary: he simply faded away.

This wasn't possible. Her heart was thumping painfully. She'd seen him, for goodness' sake! Jess blinked, tried to shake her head and quickly thought better of it. She edged closer and stretched out her hand to where he had stood. It brushed the old dressing gown hanging on the coat hook on the back of the door, disturbing ancient dust that rose up and tickled her nostrils. Now she saw that the tasselled silk cord serving as a belt was looped up somehow over the collar. That was what had appeared as a rope.

A mixture of emotions rushed over her: relief, embarrassment, even an impulse to laugh.

'You really have been affected by that bang on the head, Jess!' she told herself aloud. And spending too much time poring over the transcripts of statements made by Nathan and Eli and Doreen Warble. Imagining this old dressing gown was a person, was Nathan Smith, for pity's sake! What next?

Her priority must be to get out of the house before Ferris returned. There was no time to loiter here seeing things.

Jess let herself out of the bedroom and made her way cautiously downstairs. She couldn't be sure Ferris wasn't somewhere nearby, still couldn't explain why he'd brought her here. Her first guess, in the bedroom, had been that he wanted to give himself time. It was an unsatisfactory explanation, not logical. To run? They'd track him down, sooner or later. He must know that. Or to do something else? What? All his careful plans had been thrown into disarray when Jess saw his wife's car. He probably wasn't thinking straight any longer. He was panicking and a complete loose cannon.

But neither was she able to order her thoughts. She could pose the questions but not grasp any answers. Her head ached and there was a persistent buzz in her ears. Ferris might be losing his grip but she, Jess, mustn't; and she was afraid she was doing just that. No, she *must* think logically and that meant get out of here immediately.

But getting out of the place proved more difficult than she'd imagined. The windows downstairs were better barred than those upstairs. The front door was well secured. She went into the kitchen and rattled at the back door but that had been locked too. The washhouse! Jess darted in there, avoiding the sight of the old copper in case she should start imagining the bloody body of Millie Smith propped against it. She didn't trust the recent blow to the head not to play more tricks on her.

She gave the handle of the washhouse door a savage jerk. The catch gave way and it flew open inward so that she stumbled back. But exit was still barred by three stout wide wooden planks hammered horizontally across the opening. To crawl under them wasn't possible; the gap was too narrow. She had to knock out at least a couple.

Jess went back into the kitchen and looked for something suitable to use as a battering ram. There was a heavy, cast-iron pan on the stove with a pair of handles fixed to the rim. She took it out to the washhouse and, grasping a handle in either hand and holding the pan in front of her, ran at the middle plank. She collided with it with a deafening crash but although it shuddered, it stayed fast. Ferris, or someone, had made a good job of it, making sure she wouldn't escape easily. Jess took another run at it and this time was rewarded by a snapping sound. Nails had been loosened sufficiently to allow one end of the plank to be pushed outward.

She had readied herself to take another run at it when she heard a voice, outside.

'Who is it? Who's in there?'

It was a male voice. Ferris? Oh, damn! No, he wouldn't be asking who was in here, Jess reasoned. He knew. And the voice sounded worried, as well it might. Its owner wouldn't be expecting anyone to be inside this old house.

'Inspector Campbell!' she shouted.

'Inspector?' Not surprisingly the voice was even more startled, and now sounded familiar. 'What are you doing in there?'

'Never mind that! Get me out!' howled Jess.

'Hold on!'

She heard footsteps retreating and then coming back.

'I've got an iron bar. I'll lever off the planks. Stay clear in case they splinter!' ordered the voice.

Jess retreated to the kitchen end of the washhouse. She could hear him labouring at the task, grunting and muttering to himself. Then there was a loud crack and the central plank fell to the ground. The one above followed.

David Jones peered into the washhouse. His face was flushed with his efforts but his eyes still betrayed the shock he'd had on hearing her. 'Can you climb over the bottom plank?'

'Yes! Give me your hand,' Jess panted.

With his help, she scrambled out.

'Have you got a phone?' she gasped.

'My mobile, yes, hang on . . .' He produced the phone.

'Is it on? I need to ring for back up!' Moments later Jess spoke urgently into the mobile, 'Phil? It's me, Jess Campbell. Pick up Andrew Ferris and be as quick as you can. He's our man. And send a squad car out to Cricket Farm to collect me. I'll explain later!'

She pushed the mobile back into Jones's hand. 'Thanks.'

'How did you get in there?' He pointed at the house behind them. Then he scowled. 'What did you mean, "Pick up Ferris, he's our man!" – did he kill Eva?'

'If I can prove it,' Jess said. 'He knocked me out and shut me up in the house there. Thanks for coming to my rescue. What are *you* doing here, by the way?'

He flushed. 'I've been up here a couple of times, in my free time, just looking round. I – I feel close to Eva here.' He shrugged. 'Perhaps that's just because this is such a spooky place.'

'Yes,' Jess agreed soberly. 'It is a very spooky place.'

The breeze had veered round sharply as she was speaking and a new odour filled her nostrils. At first she'd dismissed it as a lingering smell from the interior of the house. But this was quite different. She sniffed.

Jones had noticed it, too. 'Something's burning!' Then he flung up a hand to point. 'Look!'

From above the woods screening the stables lower down the hill, a plume of smoke curled into the air and was followed by a fountain of red sparks as if someone had lit a giant firework.

'The stables are on fire!' Jess exclaimed.

Chapter 16

'We have to get down there! Have you any transport?' Jess demanded. 'How did you get here?'

'On my motorbike!' Jones was already running towards the entry into the farmyard. 'But I haven't got a spare helmet for you.'

'Can't be helped!' she told him. 'It's an emergency. Just get us down to the bottom of the hill.'

The motorcycle coughed into life and, with Jess clinging on tightly, roared down the hill towards Berryhill stables.

They skidded to a halt at the end of the lane that turned off the road and led to the stables. Now they could hear the snap of the fire and the terrified whinnying of the horses.

'Call the fire brigade and the police!' Jess ordered as she scrambled from the pillion seat. But Jones was already shouting into his mobile.

She ran into the yard and took rapid stock of the situation. The fire had been started in a pile of straw and licked along the base of the row of loose boxes on the left-hand side of the yard. Although a good deal of smoke was thickening above the roof and the dry wooden walls crackled and sent up more sparks, there was still time, Jess reckoned, for prompt action to get the horses out. The problem was that the animals were panicking and she had no experience of dealing with frightened horses plunging around, all hooves and teeth.

Jones, however, proved unexpectedly competent. 'Get the paddock gate open!' he ordered. 'We'll let them out and drive them down that way.'

Just then they heard a new noise. From inside the end loose box, the one used by Penny as her office and tack room, came muffled shouts followed by a furious hammering at the closed door from inside.

'Is anyone out there? I can't get out! Please, if anyone's there . . .' The voice rose in a despairing shriek.

'It's Penny!' Jess ran towards the door.

She found that not only had both halves been shut from outside using the hooks on the doors designed to drop into rings screwed into the wooden frames for that purpose. The lower half-door had also been secured by a braced pitchfork.

Jess kicked the pitchfork aside and scrabbled at the hooks. 'It's all right, Penny! It's Jess Campbell. We'll get you out!'

The lower half of the door flew open and Penny staggered out doubled up. She clawed at Jess to steady herself. Jess seized her and hauled her upright.

'It's OK!' she managed to say before smoke filled her lungs with the next breath and reduced her to coughing, her eyes watering and unable to help Penny further.

'It's not!' croaked Penny. 'It's not OK! There's a gas canister!' She pointed behind her. 'A gas canister in there. If the fire reaches it, it will explode!'

Mud, Muck and Dead Things

The loose box next to the tack room shook beneath the onslaught of maddened hooves.

'Solo!' Penny ran towards it. 'I have to let him out!'

'Penny! If there's a gas canister, it could go at any moment!'

But Penny's thoughts were only for the horses. Jones had come running back from the opened paddock gate. He began at the other end of the line of boxes, opening the doors. Jess lent a hand, praying that the gas canister didn't blow. They managed to get all the doors opened, but Solo refused to come out. They could see him inside, turning this way and that, continuing to try and kick his way out, throwing himself around ever more wildly and cannoning off the smouldering walls of the loose box like an equine pinball. The other horses plunged wildly around the yard. Jones was shouting hoarsely and waving his arms like a windmill in an attempt to drive them towards the open paddock gate. Most turned that way but Sultan seemed determined to make a break for the open road.

'Solo!' cried Penny. 'He's only got one good eye and he's confused!'

'You can't go in there!' Jess grasped Penny's arm to hold her back. 'He can't see you properly and he's out of his wits with fear. He'll kick you to pieces.'

'Give me your jacket!' Penny demanded. 'Quick!'

Jess pulled off her jacket and Penny grabbed it from her. She ran towards the loose box and disappeared inside. Jess could hear her as she called to the frightened animal, trying to soothe him by the sound of her voice. Then Penny reappeared, hauling at the horse. Solo came into view suddenly, his head covered with Jess's jacket. Sensing he was no longer confined, he shot forward, sending Penny sprawling into the mud. The jacket flew off and Solo bolted away, by some miracle galloping towards the paddock.

Just then they heard the sound of the approaching fire engine.

'Get away from the building!' Jess ordered. 'Get down to the paddock and help Jones with the horses.'

She herself ran towards the entry to the yard and flagged down the engine as it swept into view.

'Gas canister!' she howled at the top of her voice, pointing at the burning building. She knew that, of all hazards, gas canisters were particularly feared by firemen.

'Right! You get back!' one of the firemen yelled.

At that moment a small convoy of police cars swept into the lane and drew up behind the fire engine.

Jess ran towards the leading one and, as she reached it, Carter scrambled out with his driver, Bennison. Behind her the loose boxes were all now well alight and there was no hope of saving them. The flames leaped high into the air and even the wood they hadn't yet reached was scorched and smouldering dangerously.

'This is arson!' Jess shouted at him above the roar of the fire, the hiss of water and crack of splitting wood. 'And attempted murder. Someone barricaded Penny Gower in the tack room! I got her out.'

'Any idea who?' shouted Carter.

'At a guess, Andrew Ferris. Don't ask me why. I thought he was in love with her!'

Penny had somehow made her way back across the yard and appeared at their sides. Her face was blackened with smoke and flying ash and streaked with tears. Her arms flailed in distress as if she wanted to grasp at some vanished object.

'How could he do it!' she wailed. 'How could Andy do this to me!'

'You're sure it was Ferris?' Jess caught at her arm again. 'Penny, did you see or hear him?'

'Of course I did! He just appeared in the tack room without warning. He was yelling at me. He shouted something about if I wanted to spend the rest of my life with the horses, and without him, he'd bloody well arrange for me to do it. Then he gave me a socking punch in the face that sent me sprawling back and locked me inside.' Penny stared at them wildly. 'He tried to kill me, Jess! Andy tried to kill me!' She broke into sobs.

'Plenty of murders have been committed by people crossed in love,' remarked Carter in that enigmatic way Jess might have found intriguing had other things not diverted her attention from what he was saying.

The headache that had lurked in her skull since she came to in the bedroom at Cricket Farm now returned to the fore with a vengeance. It sent lightning flashes of diamond white across her vision. Nausea rose in her throat. The world swayed around her. She was aware that someone had grasped her shoulders. Carter's voice (she could no longer make out his form) sounded in her ear.

'In the car. Mind your head! We're taking you to A and E.'

She was being bundled into the police car with someone's hand on her head to prevent her cracking it on the door frame, just like an arrested felon.

In the background she heard a female voice saying, 'Right away, sir!'

She thought muzzily, 'Bennison . . .' and wanted to say the name aloud but never knew whether she managed to do so or not.

Chapter 17

Carter proved adamant in the face of Jess's impassioned plea to be allowed, at least, to sit in on the interview with Andrew Ferris. They'd picked him up easily. They had gone to his house and found him there, still methodically sorting through his wife's belongings. He'd offered no resistance.

'You are not even supposed to be in the building, you're on sick leave,' Carter said now firmly. 'You have concussion.'

'I *had* concussion. Now I'm fine. Now I haven't even got a headache! The back of my head is a bit sore, that's all. And this is *my* case!' Jess all but danced about in her frustration. 'I want to conduct the interview!'

'You are also a victim of a serious assault on a police officer by the accused. We'll charge him with that, along with anything else we find against him. You can't interview him and it would be unwise and inappropriate for you even to sit in when it happens.'

'Not sit in? But—'

'Inspector!' Carter said sharply. 'I am making allowances, but I expect my officers of all ranks to behave in all circumstances in a professional way.'

'Yes, *sir* . . .' Jess managed through gritted teeth.

She then stormed off to her office and allowed herself a prolonged, childish and thoroughly satisfactory sulk.

He was right, of course. He knew he was right. She knew he was right. He knew she knew etc.

It didn't help.

Fortunately, a distraction arrived at that moment in the form of a message saying Penny Gower was downstairs, asking for her.

'Hi,' said Jess, when she saw the small, slightly scruffy figure standing disconsolately by Joe Hegarty's desk. She noticed Penny sported a fine blue bruise on her forehead. 'How are you?' Jess indicated the bruise.

'All right, I think,' said Penny. 'This . . .' She touched the bruise gently. 'Is just a souvenir. Every time I look in a mirror and see it, I remember how Andy told me he loved me. I'll never believe any man ever again. I just stopped by to check how things are going on and to ask how you are.'

'Also fine.' There was an awkward pause. 'Do you fancy a coffee?' Jess asked on the spur of the moment. 'Not one of ours. I'm not being inhospitable. The coffee is better at a little café just down the road.'

'I suppose,' Penny said, when they were established with a coffee each at a corner table, 'you can't discuss the case, not with me.'

'Not really, and it's somewhat out of my hands now, since I am also a victim of an assault. We could form a small exclusive club, I suppose. Women attacked by Andrew Ferris.' Jess grimaced.

'One of them is dead,' said Penny flatly.

'Right. To be fair, he didn't want to kill me, he just wanted to keep me quiet and out of the way while he tried to kill you. I don't know why he left me in that house.' Jess shrugged. 'Perhaps he jibbed at killing a police officer. But you, Penny, you had a narrow escape. I'm not pretending otherwise. The stables fared badly, too. Thank heavens you're alive and well, apart from a bruise, and the horses were all got out OK. It's not the end of the world. Look, what I'm trying to say is, don't let a really bad experience sour your life. Take your time getting over it, by all means. But, well, life goes on and you will meet someone else.'

'Meeting someone else is the last thing on my mind,' Penny told her frankly with a grimace. 'Like I said, after Andrew I don't think I'll ever trust another man and I couldn't live with a man I didn't trust, like Lindsey.'

'Mark Harper?'

'Yes, they've had some sort of bust-up. Lindsey found out he had a mistress in London and she was all set to divorce him. But Harper panicked and talked her round, promising to be a good chap from now on. Ha! Divorce would've cost him a fortune, but it's more than that. He needs Lindsey socially, you see. Lindsey's from a local family of down-at-heel gentlemen farmers. Everyone – I mean all the local gentry and People Who Matter – round here know her and knew her parents. That's the circle Harper wants to move in; and to do it, he needs Lindsey. He couldn't just buy his way in.'

'I see,' said Jess.

Selina Foscott, Lindsey Harper, Eli Smith: they were locals and it mattered. Not social standing or whether you had money; whether your family reputation was blameless or whether you had a double murderer as a relative; but belonging here because of links going back generations, and because your forebears lay buried in the quiet country church-yards around the county. Everyone else was tolerated until he or she made a mistake. She herself would do well to remember that.

In some ways, she thought, Lucas Burton and Mark Harper were alike. Both had wanted to create an image. But Burton had essentially been a loner, fearing that on too close acquaintance people would suspect his origins. Harper had wanted to join the interrelated and interconnected county set. He'd gambled on making the right sort of marriage. Now he was discovering that he needed his wife more than she needed him. Burton had perhaps been shrewder.

Penny was still talking. 'I'm not nursing a broken heart. I wasn't in love with Andrew, I told you that. I just thought he was my friend, a very good friend. At the time I told you it, I honestly hadn't realised he was imagining himself in love with me. Oh, he used to *say* he loved me, but always in a joking way and I always called him to order. It was a sort of *game*, or so I thought. More fool me.'

She sipped her coffee. 'I can't believe how stupid I was. You know, I was really sympathetic about his marriage breaking up. I tried to support him at what I thought was a difficult time. You can't imagine how that bugs me now! I was so damn *sorry* for him. I thought he was getting a raw deal. I was worried that he didn't seem to care what his wife took from the house. It was because I nagged him about it that he was sorting out her stuff when you went to see him.'

'There was certainly a lot of sorting to do,' observed Jess. 'I think he was a bit surprised when he realised how much she had.'

'Oh, yes, he was. If she didn't come and collect it soon, he was planning to put it all in store. But the only thing on *my* mind, when he first told me about his divorce, was the concern that Karen would rip him off. I didn't for one moment consider the divorce might mean he and I would be free to get together. Married, for crying out loud! And then he locked me in the tack room and tried to incinerate me! *And* the horses! Poor dumb brutes, what had they done to him? He liked horses. He was good with them! I feel as though, as though I never knew him at all.'

Realising her raised voice was attracting some interested glances to their table she leaned across it and whispered, 'Do you know, Jess? I think being betrayed by a friend is worse than being betrayed by a spurned suitor. If you've turned a guy down he might, I suppose, go off his rocker with frustration and try and bump you off. But friendship is supposed to be something you can *rely* on.'

There really was no answer to this. 'How about the stables?' Jess asked. It seemed a safer subject. 'Have you been able to start the repairs?'

Penny looked, if anything, glummer. 'I don't think I'll be able to carry on. The insurance people are being difficult. They found out I kept that gas canister in the tack room. All right, I know I shouldn't have done. Funny thing, it was Andrew who always wanted me to move it out. Then there's Solo. He's eating his head off and costing me money but I can't hire him out as a riding horse. I'm hoping to get some sort of temporary shelter rigged up before winter, but I'll have to reduce the livery fees and as to rebuilding the stables . . .'

She fixed Jess with a bright angry gaze. 'Life's a bugger!' she said fiercely.

Jess picked up her coffee cup and held it high. 'I'll drink to that,' she said.

In the interview room, Ferris sat with his solicitor, Reginald Foscott. Phil Morton sat by the door looking on mistrustfully as Carter took a seat at the table. The usual preliminaries of time, and names of those present were established for the benefit of the recording. Ferris listened impassively. He might have been there purely as audience. Foscott flicked an invisible speck from his sleeve, folded his hands and tilted his head slightly to one side like an attentive hound.

'We have a witness,' Carter began, 'who saw the victim, Eva Zelená, getting into a car described as silver grey, probably a Citroën Saxo, at the end of the lane leading to the Foot to the Ground pub and restaurant where she worked. We have retrieved a car of that description from your garage and subjected it to forensic examination. We took it apart, Mr Ferris. The forensic team found clear traces of body fluids in the boot and DNA analysis has identified them as coming from Eva Zelená. We also found human hair inside the car, which has been established as from the head of Eva Zelená, and a smear of blood, which is yours. An attempt had been made to clean the vehicle, both the interior and in the boot, but it's not easy, believe me, to clean away that sort of evidence.' Carter permitted himself a bleak smile. 'It takes more than a vacuum cleaner and a bottle of fabric shampoo. We have also recovered traces of mud from the underside of the chassis corresponding to the mud in the yard at Cricket Farm.'

'If you say so,' said Ferris dismissively.

Reggie Foscott put his fist to his mouth and coughed.

Carter went on, 'This evidence shows that Eva was in the car when she was alive and that she travelled in the boot of the car when she was dead. We believe you moved the body to Cricket Farm where it was found, in the first instance, by Lucas Burton.'

Ferris had listened to all of this in the same detached way. He must have been expecting it. Foscott, however, stirred on his tubular chair so that the legs scraped on the floor.

'My client is prepared to make a statement regarding the young woman, Eva Zelená.'

'A confession?' Carter raised his eyebrows and looked at Ferris, who returned a sardonic half-smile in his first reaction of any kind.

'A statement,' repeated Foscott. 'It was not his intention to do the young woman any serious harm. He acted in self-defence.'

'Indeed? Well, then, Mr Ferris. Perhaps you'd tell us just what you did intend and how it came about that she died?' Carter asked. 'Did you dump her body at Cricket Farm? If so, why?'

'Her death was an accident,' Ferris told him, spacing the words out as if he expected Carter to write them down. He then paused as if he expected some comment but as the superintendent said nothing, was obliged to go on. 'You know that my wife and I are in the process of divorcing?'

'We understand that to be the case,' agreed Carter. 'Your wife, Karen Ferris, has explained this, and backs your claim.'

'Big of her,' said Ferris dismissively. 'We have been separated for some time, not officially, but for all practical purposes. I have also been friendly with Penny Gower for some time. Frankly, I had hoped our friendship might grow into something more. But that didn't seem to be happening and, well, I was frustrated, I suppose. I went off for a drink on my own one evening, at a pub called the Foot to the Ground. I picked it because it wasn't one Penny and I used, and there I met Eva.'

'Eva Zelená?' Carter said tonelessly, again for the benefit of the tape recorder.

'That's right. She seemed like a nice, friendly girl. I got talking to her. It was the classic situation of a slightly drunk and depressed man, pouring out his heart to a barmaid. I don't mean I told her all my troubles. I wasn't that drunk or that stupid. But I found it helpful, talking to her. I found myself asking her for a date. She said all right. I took her to the cinema and that was the beginning of it, such as it was. It was only ever a casual affair. It started as a lonely man flirting with a pretty girl. A thousand other men up and down the country were probably doing the same thing at the same moment. But for me, like every other relationship with women I've ever had, it went wrong.' Ferris's voice gained animation. Until then he had been speaking in a flat tone, reciting his rehearsed story.

Hearing the change in his client's voice, Foscott glanced at him and pursed his lips.

'Look.' Ferris threw out a hand and leaned towards Carter. By the door, Phil Morton tensed into alertness. 'You can't blame me for getting into a situation like that. I was being dumped by my wife and getting nowhere with Penny. How do you think I felt? How would you feel? I just wanted to be with a woman who was good company, didn't stink of horses like Penny, didn't communicate with me via a solicitor like Karen, and enjoyed sex. Surely you can understand that?'

'Just carry on telling us how you felt and what you did about it,' Carter replied, unmoved by this man-to-man appeal.

'What I did? I started dating Eva regularly. But it wasn't serious. In my mind, it remained a flirtation, a bit of relaxation. I looked on it as a sort of therapy, if you like. Eva did all right out of it. She liked having fun, dancing, going around with me. I was generous. I took her to decent restaurants. I took her to the theatre in Cheltenham and to clubs. Not that clubbing is my kind of thing. I'm getting a bit old for that teens and twenties scene, all flashing flights and deafening noise, but she liked it. We went to the cinema. It was all the usual stuff.'

'You weren't concerned,' Carter asked, 'that Ms Gower might find out about your liaison?'

'No! She hardly ever left the stables before evening and then she always wanted an early night because she had to get up at the crack of dawn the next day and go back down there, mucking out, feeding and grooming and all the rest of it. We'd grab a quick bite and a pint at the Hart and that was our social life. Penny had what she wanted, I tell you! I wasn't cheating on her in the usual way because what the hell was there to cheat on?' There was real pain in his voice.

'As for Eva.' Ferris shrugged. 'I thought I was giving her what she wanted. She didn't appear to want anything more. I thought that she saw our relationship the way I saw it. I never collected her from the pub on our days out because I didn't want anyone there getting the wrong idea about us. Eva never suggested I did pick her up where she lived or took her back to the door. That confirmed for me that she didn't want our names associated in other people's minds, any more than I did. It was not what you like to call a *liaison*, for crying out loud! I thought – I believed we had an *understanding*.'

Behind him, on his seat by the door, Morton's expression said, Oh, yes? You did, mate, she didn't. Aloud he said nothing.

Ferris hesitated. 'I was feeling very stressed at the time and perhaps not thinking very clearly. The divorce wasn't the only thing on my mind.' He paused.

'Yes?' Carter prompted. 'What was that, then?'

'I was worried about a client of mine, Lucas Burton.'

At this point Reggie Foscott said crisply, 'My client denies any responsibility for the death of Lucas Burton.'

'Why was Burton a worry to you?' Carter asking, ignoring Foscott and his interruption.

Ferris hesitated. 'It doesn't matter. It has no bearing on this.'

'We think it does,' said Carter. 'We have the records of mobile phone calls you made on the day before her body was found. You phoned Lucas Burton on the afternoon of Eva's death, that is to say, on Thursday, the afternoon of the day we believe she died. The next day her body was discovered at Cricket Farm. We'd like to know what that call was about.'

'Business,' said Ferris. 'I had a query about his accounts.'

'We had a long and interesting conversation with Mrs Karen Ferris,' Carter went on. 'She told us your acquaintance with Burton goes back many years, although you had only fairly recently become his accountant here. She said you knew him in London when you worked there some years ago. At that time he'd gone under a different name. There was some history between you because when you spoke of him you had looked and sounded very angry. She thought perhaps Burton had cheated you, so she was very surprised when you took him on as a client here, some years later. She asked you about it and you became angry and more or less told her to shut up. At the time she put that down to the deteriorating situation between the two of you. But now she isn't sure.'

'Mrs Karen Ferris must be regarded as hostile to my client,' said Foscott loudly. 'Anything she says must be weighed carefully against the impending divorce proceedings.'

'Thank you, Mr Foscott. Mr Ferris?'

'All right,' Andrew admitted. 'We do go back years. My first "proper job" was working in a small accountancy firm in south London. Its clients were all kinds of small traders, market stallholders. But it also had one or two bigger fish: perma-tanned guys in vicuna overcoats who ran clubs you wouldn't want your sister to set foot inside. All the business we took on was legit, mind you. But, well, the clients were a rum bunch. The firm doesn't exist any more, by the way.

'I wasn't earning much and London is expensive. I'd just got engaged to Karen, my wife. She – she always had ambitious tastes.' He scowled in memory. 'I had to save every penny. Lunchtimes I used to nip down to a pub on the corner of the road where the office was. It didn't offer cooked food but it did sandwiches, crisps, that sort of thing. It was the cheapest place to eat around there.

'I met a chap there. He was something of a regular.' Ferris gave a mirthless smile. 'He was a real wheeler-dealer, had the patter, always planning some moneymaking scheme. There were any number of guys like him around in those days, especially in that part of town. I quite liked listening to him, because he was amusing. He went out of his way to cultivate my acquaintance, but I wasn't so stupid that I didn't realise he had some purpose. I thought he was going to suggest I do some cut-price accounting for him, on the black. His name was Marvin Crapper.'

He paused and waited to see if this name got any reaction from Carter, who just nodded.

'Well, it turned out he had something quite different in mind. He was planning a "big deal". He wanted information, personal private information on the financial situation of a client of the firm. It was one of the bigger clients, the ones I told you about, who turned up at the office in a flash car with a muscleman minder in tow. I told Marvin, forget it! I'm like a priest, I said, I don't pass on anything. To tell you the truth, it wasn't just moral scruples. I didn't want my legs broken. But Marvin kept on. He offered me serious money. Nobody would know, he insisted. He'd never tell anyone, how could he? He had as much to lose as I did, probably more.'

Ferris shrugged. 'Well, Karen wanted us to buy a house or at the very least a flat. I needed my share of the deposit. I listened to Marvin. I should have avoided the pub and him, made it clear I wasn't going to play ball. But I didn't. I passed him the information he wanted. He paid me. I thought, stupidly, that would be the end of it. I changed my job, I moved to another part of London, Karen and I married. We came down here. I started up on my own. Everything was fine. Well, it wasn't, because Karen and I were drifting apart.

But aside from that, from a business point of view, things were turning out nicely.'

Ferris looked up at Carter. 'You know what they say about bad pennies. They always turn up? Marvin Crapper was a real bad penny. I should have known that wherever I was and whatever I was doing, and however much time passed, sooner or later he'd come rolling along my way. It took some time, but two years ago, he did just that.'

He gave a sad smile. 'He rang my doorbell. I opened the door and there he stood. It was as simple as that. I was surprised; of course I was, but not particularly by the fact he was *there*. That had always seemed inevitable, as I was saying. No, what really surprised me was that at first I didn't recognise him. Gone were the black leather jacket and the gold bling. Gone was the south London accent, too. This was a bloke in a sports jacket and handmade shoes, expensive wristwatch but otherwise no jewellery, speaking like a county gent. Goodbye, Marvin Crapper and hello, Lucas Burton! He changed his ruddy name! He'd changed everything.'

At this point Ferris laughed unexpectedly, the sound echoing around the small room and disconcerting the rest of them. Carter sat back in his chair. Phil Morton stood up and then sat down again. Reggie Foscott looked distinctly alarmed and leaned toward his client as if he would give him some advice.

Ferris waved his legal adviser away. 'All those schemes of his must have worked out because he'd made it big. Only, in some ways, he hadn't changed. He was still the same old Marvin Crapper underneath all that new gloss. He came in and sat down, quite at home. He spent some time telling me how well he'd done, showed me the wristwatch, wanted to tell me it was by Cartier. He told me about his big house in Cheltenham and his Docklands pad in London. He was scouting round for a holiday place in Florida with a pool. He'd had a place in Spain, Marbella, but it hadn't been big enough and he'd sold it at some vast profit. I sat and listened to him like a rabbit mesmerised by a stoat. He'd heard I was living and working in the area, he said. He'd been meaning to look me up. Oh, yes, I thought. I bet you were. He wanted someone to do his tax returns, he went on. Who better than his old mate, Andy Ferris?'

Ferris shook his head. 'I should have told him to shove off. I didn't. I couldn't. I was tied to him. It wasn't just that he knew there was one time when I'd behaved as badly as he did all the time. That one slip doesn't make me a crook! I didn't want to be associated with him. But he – he was like blasted Svengali. In the end I told him, "I'll do the returns but no dodgy schemes, Lucas!"'

'He gave me a big cheesy smile and patted my shoulder. "Oh, that sort of thing is all in the past, Andy! We're different men now, you and I. You've done well. I've done well." He'd done a hell of a lot better than me, I can tell you that.'

Ferris paused for a split second and then said thoughtfully, 'All the time he was talking, I couldn't take my eyes off his teeth. They flashed at me like something in a toothpaste commercial. He'd had those fixed, too.

'Well, he listened to my feeble protests. "Don't worry about it," he said. Some hopes! He must have thought I was stupid. All that patter was as fake as the capped smile. He'd got respectable over the years, all right, for outward show; but the leopard doesn't change its spots. Sooner or later, he'd have another dodge up his sleeve and try to pull me in. I didn't know how I'd cope if he came up with a new plan. I knew by the way he looked at me, grinned at me like a conspirator, that he didn't expect me to believe him. In his mind, we were going through the motions. He thought I was a soul mate. He thought *I was just like him!*'

At this point Ferris broke off and asked politely if there was any chance of a cup of tea?

The tea arrived, brought by Bennison, and they resumed. 'The day Eva died,' Ferris began carefully.

Foscott sat up straight. They were back on script, thought Carter sourly. Foscott didn't like all that about Burton because they hadn't rehearsed it. But they have worked out what Ferris is going to say about Eva. However, *I* call the shots here.

'I was very depressed and worried,' Ferris repeated. 'I wanted Burton out of my life and I'd decided I wanted Eva out of it too. I was afraid Penny would find out about us, even though I'd been so careful. So I took Eva out to lunch and told her I wanted to break up. I didn't tell her actually *at* lunch, in case there was any kind of argument and other people seated around us would notice. The trouble is, when you're in business like me, there mustn't be any scandal. I was still married even if my wife was off cruising with millionaires. Also, if you have a lot of clients your face gets known. You don't know who may recognise you. I always took Eva out of the area but I still didn't want to attract any unnecessary attention. So I told her in the car as we drove away from our lunch and I reckoned she was in a good mood and would be reasonable. She was a bit sleepy, too. We'd had a glass of wine.'

Ferris began to look and sound genuinely puzzled. 'I just didn't get her reaction. I couldn't understand it at all. She wasn't sleepy any more and the good mood went out of the window. She went mental! I had to pull over and we had a flaming row. Her English wasn't perfect but she knew enough to swear at me like a trooper. She told me she was going to contact my wife. I told her, go ahead. My wife doesn't give a damn if I've got girlfriends. She's got a sugar daddy of her own. But then Eva threatened to tell Penny about us. "I know about your other girlfriend!" she yelled at me. "The one who stinks of horses!" I'd never told her Penny's name or about the stables. But, well, perhaps I got careless one night . . .' Ferris shrugged.

'I tried to calm her down. The stupid little scrubber wouldn't shut up. She attacked me. She really did! She clenched her fists and pummelled me and she was surprisingly powerful. The blood smears of mine you found in that car came from a punch on the nose she gave me. I had to wrestle with her to protect myself. I grabbed her wrists and then I grabbed her shoulders and tried to shake some sense into her. And then . . .' Ferris made a gesture of resignation. 'Somehow my hands got round her neck and then, I don't know quite how, but she went very limp. I thought it was temporary. She'd fainted. But I couldn't revive her. I realised she was dead. It was – it was horrible.' He gazed at Carter desperately. 'I hadn't meant to kill her! I hadn't meant her any harm. Good lord, I'm a respectable businessman. I have a reputation to preserve! Why would I set out to murder her?'

Again he waited to see if Carter would react. Carter only nodded.

'Go on, Mr Ferris.'

'Well, I panicked at first, of course I did. Then I thought that if I could dump her body somewhere where it wouldn't be found for a while, there was no one who'd connect her with me. Perhaps I could bury her? I thought about all that unused land at Cricket. There were a few sheep in a couple of fields. Eli wandered round the property sometimes and Penny rode across it, but no one inspected every corner. But next I had an even better idea, a real brainwave, or so I believed. I could get rid of Eva's body and get Lucas Burton out of my life at one and the same time.

'Lucas wouldn't want the police around his place, asking him questions, digging up his past. He'd built himself a nice brand-new shiny life, no past history, nothing he'd want his new friends to know about.

'But people like Lucas are too damn clever for their own good. My old grandma used to say, "Be too sharp and you'll cut yourself!" Old Marvin, lurking there inside new Lucas, he was different. He couldn't resist a scam or the hint of one.

'I called him to say I had a business proposition. I wanted

to discuss it with him but not at my house. Nor did I want to meet him anywhere public. I knew the ideal spot, I told him, and described Cricket Farm. I said I'd meet him there at three thirty the next day. I knew he wouldn't able to resist it. I took Eva's body up there in the Citroën late that evening, nobody about but me and the bats flying round that Dracula's residence. I arranged it, the body, just inside the cowshed. I knew that when Lucas arrived, he'd take a look round, recce the lie of the land. He'd want to make sure no one else was hanging about up there. He'd stick his nose into the barn for sure, and he'd find Eva.

'Of course, there was a chance Eli might decide to go there during the following morning and he'd find Eva before Lucas did. If he did, well, too bad. My plan for getting rid of Lucas wouldn't have worked but I'd still have disposed of Eva. There's a history of murder at Cricket. Eli might not necessarily have gone straight to the cops. He might just take her out somewhere on his land and bury her himself. Eli was like Lucas in that he wouldn't want the police around, either. The old boy minds his own business and dislikes strangers. I wanted *Lucas* to find Eva first, because I knew he'd be in a blind sweat about it. He'd get out of there as fast as he could and the next thing he'd do would be to cut himself loose from me, because I'd suggested it as a meeting place. I could put him at the scene. You cops might think him a suspect.'

Ferris chuckled. 'And, do you know? It worked like a dream. He rang up minutes after he'd found Eva's body to tell me to abort the meeting. He was scared witless. Then he rang again in the evening to tell me our association was at an end. I put up a show of arguing; I don't know if it fooled him. It didn't matter. He was terrified and no way would he go to the police. You check out people who take you that kind of information, don't you? In case it's the killer, trying to be clever?' Ferris stared interrogatively at Carter.

Carter nodded and then said aloud, for the tape recorder's benefit, 'Yes.'

Ferris nodded. 'Well, then, you'd check out Lucas. You might find out about his change of name. For all I knew, he might even have some kind of criminal record. Anyway, there was a good chance you'd get curious about him. Murderers behave in weird ways, or so I've read. They return to the scene of the crime and you might think that was what old Lucas had done. No, he didn't want you checking him out.' Ferris gave a satisfied nod. 'Perfect . . . except that Penny, by a bit of bad luck, saw Lucas in his car, parked up near the farm, and she thought it looked suspicious. So I undertook to phone Eli and he jumped in that truck of his and rattled off to investigate. And, what do you know? He *did* call you. Surprising, really. But, so what? By then it didn't matter. I was clear and Lucas was in the frame.'

'What made you decide to contact him again the next morning?' Carter asked. 'Why did you go to see him at his garage?'

'I didn't,' Ferris said serenely. 'Why should I? I told you, I'd already got exactly what I wanted, Lucas running scared. I had nothing to do with his death. I didn't need him dead, just out of my life. Plenty of other people must have hated his guts. Who knows what funny business he was involved in? He must have had more enemies than he could count.'

Ferris leaned forward, the look in his eyes frankly mocking. 'You may have DNA evidence putting Eva in that car. You haven't got anything putting me in that garage and you won't get it.'

He sat back. 'I didn't kill him. Like it or lump it, believe it or not. If you do believe it, prove it.'

Foscott cleared his throat warningly.

'We'll do our best,' said Carter. 'We recovered a partial palm print from the Mercedes in the garage. The car had recently been cleaned and polished so that suggests the print was made immediately after that process had been completed. It didn't come from Burton, so it must have come from someone else who was there, a visitor. We've checked it against your prints, and we believe you were that visitor, Mr Ferris.'

Ferris sat up straight and for a second or two seemed nonplussed. Then he opened his mouth but, before he could speak, Foscott leaned towards his client and frowned.

Aloud Foscott addressed Carter. 'We were not informed of this before, and at this point in time my client has nothing to say about it.'

Carter took the rebuff calmly and moved on. 'Meanwhile there are other charges made against you: that you physically assaulted Inspector Jessica Campbell, causing her actual bodily harm, and that you kidnapped her and imprisoned her against her will at Cricket Farm. Also, that you imprisoned Penelope Gower and in an act of arson fired the stable block with intent to endanger Ms Gower's life.'

Ferris scowled at him. 'Bloody women,' he said, 'they're all the same. You can't trust them, any of them. Women got me into this mess. It was Karen wanting us to buy a property out of our financial bracket that made me listen to Crapper, all those years ago, and get entangled in his dodgy schemes. Then Karen dumped me. She did it slowly, by degrees, but I knew what she was up to. Penny dumped me. I sweated all hours down at those stables, shovelling muck, building fences, fixing anything that needed a hammer and nails. I did it for love and she knew it. But oh no, she wouldn't marry me! I was just the mug who worked for free. She used me in the same way she used old Eli. She told me she wanted to spend the rest of her life with those nags, so I thought, right! I'll arrange that for you, fix it like I fixed loose slates and broken fences after your kid—'

Ferris broke off to twist on his chair and glare at a startled Reggie Foscott. 'Your kid smashed through them for the umpteenth time! Penny could die amongst the horses, just like she wanted. As for your Inspector Campbell, she was snooping round. I'd already answered her questions. What the hell did she want to come back to the house for? Why did she have to go poking around in my garage? Just like Crapper – or Burton, as the stupid sod liked to call himself! Why did he have to seek me out? Why walk back into my life? Do you know?' He jabbed a forefinger at Carter whose watchful expression hadn't changed in the face of Ferris's tirade delivered inches away at the top of his voice.

Phil Morton, however, had left his seat by the door and moved closer, standing by the wall just behind Ferris. The accused man was aware of him and cast him a dismissive glance over his shoulder before turning back to Carter.

'Two women I loved, Karen and later Penny, wanted to walk out of my life. Yet I couldn't get rid of two other people, neither Eva when I tried to terminate a silly little fling, nor Burton, someone I wanted to stay out of my life for ever! There's no such thing as natural justice, do you know that? Life plays a series of dirty tricks. That's all it is, just one big sick joke.'

He fell silent abruptly, only the echo of his shouts hanging in the air of the suddenly quiet room. The anger slowly faded from his expression. There was a protesting creak from the frame of his chair as he leaned back and the backrest took his weight. He was sweating, pearls of moisture beaded his forehead, but otherwise something of his former detached manner had returned. It was as if a window that had been opened into his mind had suddenly been shut. Ferris was gazing at Carter as if the superintendent had been some kind of mildly interesting object in the scenery.

'None of it was my fault,' he said with the air of one who had solved a problem. 'If all of them had been reasonable, none of it would have happened.' He half stretched out a hand towards the superintendent, palm turned uppermost. 'Don't you see?'

Chapter 18

'He's a nutcase, in my opinion,' said Phil Morton later, to Jess. 'Whether or not a shrink would think so.' He sat in her office and for the past twenty minutes they had been rehashing the whole investigation.

'He's not mad enough to get off, as far as the law is concerned. He's a vicious killer and perfectly aware of what he's doing. Let's hope a jury decides that,' returned Jess firmly. 'And that a judge puts him away for as long as is possible. He's self-obsessed, is unable to take any responsibility for anything he does, and vindictive. Ferris is a very nasty piece of work.'

'Ah, but he bashed you on the bonce; and his defence lawyer will say that's coloured your view of him,' said Morton wisely. 'You know what these legal guys are like.'

'My view of Ferris is that he's a murderer! And what was his explanation for attacking me? I'd returned to his house; I was looking into his garage. He was forced into it. It was my fault. He's the worst sort, sees himself as a victim.'

'So do half the violent types in gaol now,' said Morton. He adopted a whining voice in mimicry. '"I wouldn't have stabbed the bloke if he hadn't tried to stop me nicking his mobile phone . . ."' He grimaced.

'Exactly, a psychopath.'

'That's what I said, he's a nutter. How are you feeling, by the way? Not that it isn't a pleasure to see you back at your desk, ma'am.' Morton gave a rare grin.

'I feel fine, thanks. Now then, we need a watertight case against him. He's clever and articulate and if we slip up, he'll wriggle out of both those murder charges.'

'Oh, he's a regular smarty-boots,' said Morton lugubriously.

Jess tilted her chair against the wall in the way she'd always been told not to do when she was small. She stared up at the ceiling where a loose strand of cobweb floated in the breeze from the half-opened window.

Loose strands, she thought. Is Ferris going to get off murdering Eva Zelená on a technicality because of something we've – I've – neglected?

She began to enumerate the points of the case in her head. Ferris admits she was in the car and they fought. He admits he put his hands round her neck and throttled her. The body fluids show he transported her in the boot of the Citroën and he doesn't deny it. The only thing that puzzles me is how he packed her in there. A Saxo doesn't have that much boot space. She was a small girl, though. What a pity the blood in the car turned out to be his. I suppose a defence lawyer will use that to point out that she really made a serious attack on his client, even if she was half his size. Ferris will stick to saying he was defending himself and it all got out of hand. We'll have to trust the jury, won't we? He wasn't defending himself; she was defending herself.

326

She drew blood when the poor kid got in a lucky punch on his nose.

Then there's the order in which he says things happened. First, he says, he killed Eva unintentionally. Only after that he decided to involve Burton in finding the body because he wanted Burton out of his life. But what if he had wanted to get rid of Burton first and foremost and decided to kill Eva – someone else he wanted rid of – to do it?

She tipped her chair forward to its correct position. Aloud she said, 'Anyway, he can't deny he did hit me on the head and shut me up in that house of horrors; nor that he imprisoned Penny Gower in her tack room and tried to set fire to it.'

'True,' said Morton more cheerfully before reverting to his natural gloom. 'But there's less to tie him to the death of Lucas Burton. He is still denying it. I wish we had found the weapon. I've a bad feeling about that. The partial palm print suggests Ferris was in the garage. But unfortunately it's incomplete. It's not enough.'

He scratched the back of his neck and looked reflective. 'You know, when Carter told him we'd found that print, Ferris looked pretty sick: surprised and worried. He's a very careful chap but he overlooked the fact that he might have touched the car.'

'His defence is that the print was made at some earlier time; when Burton was visiting him to discuss his accounts,' Jess pointed out. 'Ferris works from home, and generally goes outside to see his clients off. He must have touched Burton's car on the last such occasion – so he says. He also says when Burton later cleaned his car, he must have missed that patch. Andrew Ferris has an answer for everything.'

Morton snorted. 'Burton spent his time after the visit to Cricket Farm polishing the Mercedes to showroom perfection! It'd be a blooming miracle if he failed to wipe off an earlier palm print.'

'We can still expect a battle royal in court over the palm print.' Jess sighed. 'No one actually saw him at the garage, that's the problem, and he says he didn't even know where it was. Burton probably *did* have enemies, lots of them. Smooth operator like that, must have trodden on a lot of toes along the way.'

Morton eyed her. 'What does the superintendent reckon?'

'He's arguing Burton only had one enemy we know of hereabouts, Ferris. We know how much Ferris wanted to be free of him. Carter thinks, and so do I, that Ferris wasn't satisfied he'd got Burton off his back for good, even after his elaborate scheme, fixing to have Burton find the body. Burton had turned up in his life once already after being out of it for years, remember! Who was to say that after a while, when Burton had got over the fright of finding Eva, he wouldn't turn up again? Carter and I both think Ferris wanted to make sure of him.'

'Nice to know we're all agreed here,' said Morton enigmatically. 'Let's hope the Crown Prosecution Service is part of our merry party.'

The cobweb was still moving gracefully to and fro. Jess

could stick it no longer. She stood up and collected the rusty black umbrella that lived in the corner of the room for emergency use in unexpected rainstorms. It had occupied this office far longer than she had. Forgotten years before by an unknown owner, it was so shabby that anyone who took it home invariably brought it back. Watched with interest by Morton, she reached up and managed to hook the cobweb with the ferrule and drag it down.

'Got you!' she said. She pointed the ferrule at Morton, who raised his eyebrows.

'You know what would be nice, Phil? It would be nice to show Ferris was in Burton's house after the time we know Burton died. I'd bet a month's salary on Ferris going to the house; using keys he took off Burton's dead body, and searching it, removing everything that might indicate a link between him and Burton in the past.'

'My granny always told me,' Morton said sanctimoniously, 'never to bet money I couldn't afford to lose. We can't prove he was in the house. SOCO crawled all over it. Not a fingerprint. Not a DNA trace. Not one witness who saw him creeping in or out. No useful testimony from that weird woman who cleaned for him. She just said everything looked the same to her. Mind you, she must be the most unobservant woman in Gloucestershire.' He shook his head wonderingly. 'It still takes my breath away that she turned up three times a week to sit in Burton's kitchen and make herself cups of tea.'

'It's Ferris's modus operandi,' Jess persisted obstinately. 'He strips his victims of all personal items: phones, keys, credit cards and money, the lot. He took Eva's mobile phone and purse, plus her lipstick and any other make-up items she had on her.'

'Milada says,' Morton informed her, 'that Eva never went out without her mobile.'

'What nineteen year old does? But we haven't found anything in his possession, not a sausage. If we could locate just one item . . . What does he do with all these things? We've turned Ferris's house inside out and there's nothing there belonging either to Eva or to Burton. We persuaded Reggie Foscott to open the sealed package she left for safe-keeping with him, and it contains personal papers, mostly relating to Lucas's change of name. Nothing to do with Ferris.'

'He's got a stash somewhere,' opined Morton. 'He may have successfully disposed of the murder weapon, but he just didn't have time to destroy everything or hide so much.' He collected the umbrella Jess had left lying on her desk and tidily returned it to its corner home.

'You know,' he said diffidently, over his shoulder. 'Perhaps he doesn't. Doesn't destroy things, I mean. Perhaps he's a bit of a collector. He wants to keep personal items, like a lipstick or a mobile phone.'

'Toby jugs!' said Jess immediately. 'He collects them. There's a display cabinet full of the things in his house.' She recalled all the boxes of personal items standing in Ferris's drive and the heaped oddments lying around indoors, awaiting disposal.

'His wife was a real hoarder. You saw the masses of stuff she kept there when you went out to the house.'

'Oh, her,' said Phil, 'that's another weird one. She's a compulsive spender, if you ask me.'

'I did think,' Jess went on, 'he might have concealed his victim's possessions amongst Karen's stuff. But, as you know, we turned out every one of those crates and boxes, and all we found were enough shoes to make Imelda Marcos envious and a junk shop full of holiday souvenirs.'

She broke off and snapped her fingers. 'Storage units! Penny Gower told me Ferris said he might send his wife's stuff to store once he'd packed it up. Get on to it, Phil. Storage units, bank deposit boxes, anything of that nature.'

'Will do,' promised Morton.

Bennison appeared. 'Oh, there you are, ma'am, I've been looking for you. How are you feeling?'

'Thank you, Hayley, I'm very well. Is that all you wanted me for? To ask after my health?'

'Oh, no,' said Bennison brightly, 'There's a woman downstairs wanting to speak to you. She says she's Lucas Burton's auntie.'

Her name was Mrs Joy Gotobed. In a draw for one of the most unfortunate combinations of first names and surnames, thought Jess in deepest sympathy, Joy Gotobed had held the winning ticket. Perhaps she was resigned to it, and the avalanche of inevitable jokes, because she'd always been burdened with an unfortunate name.

331

'I was Joy Crapper,' she said. 'And Marvin – Lucas, he called himself later on – he was the son of my sister, Marilyn.'

Her appearance lent a subtle cruelty to her name. She was elderly and thin and poorly dressed in a rusty black suit. The skin on her workworn hands was loose and wrinkled, as if she wore a pair of overlarge gloves. Her wedding ring too was loose. She wore no engagement ring. Her teeth were false, too even, too white and not particularly well fitting. But there was something painfully honest and lacking pretence about her which commanded respect.

'I saw in my paper that he was dead.' Her hands twisted nervously in her lap. 'It said he'd been murdered. It gave me a really bad turn. He wasn't – I mean, I hadn't seen him for years – but he was flesh and blood and Marilyn's boy. I brought him up, you see. Me and my husband, together, that is. We had no kids of our own and Marilyn, well, she couldn't look after the baby. We never knew who his father was. Marilyn never said. Chances are, she didn't know herself.'

Mrs Gotobed looked down at her hands and becoming aware of their nervous action, clasped them tightly to control them. 'It's not a nice thing to say of your own sister,' she said. 'But it's true. Marilyn always liked a good time. She liked a few drinks, too. Next morning she never could remember where she'd been or who she'd been with . . . But she was a good-hearted sort. I was very fond of her.'

'She's dead now, I take it?' Jess asked as Mrs Gotobed faltered to a stop.

'Oh, yes, dear. She didn't make old bones. Well, with

her lifestyle, she wouldn't, would she? I think Marvin must have been about five when his mum died. But, like I said, Ronnie – that's my husband – and me, we were Marvin's parents. We brought him up. Ronnie, he's dead too, now. Died ten years ago. Asbestos, you know? That's what did for him and his lungs. He worked on demolition sites in the days before they knew how dangerous that stuff was and all the old buildings they were pulling down, well, they were full of it.'

Mrs Gotobed seemed to remember something and reached for her capacious plastic handbag. She rummaged in it and brought out two newspaper clippings. 'This one,' she said, holding it up for Jess to see, 'is the one in the paper about his being found dead. And this one . . .' She held up the other clipping. 'It's some lawyer, asking about next of kin. I phoned up his office and I came down from London today to go there and see him. He told me to bring documentation.' She spoke the last word carefully, wanting to get the unfamiliar term right. 'I brought everything I'd got. My marriage lines and Marvin's birth certificate and the certificate he got for his "O" levels and photos . . .' She was rummaging in the bag again. 'I've got Marilyn's death certificate. Her liver packed up. Well, it would do, wouldn't it?'

She turned her attention back to Jess. 'Only I thought, I ought to come and see you first. I wanted to ask if you knew yet who killed Marvin? I want you to catch him.'

'We want that, too, Mrs Gotobed,' said Jess. 'And we are doing our very best. When did you last see your nephew?'

Mrs Gotobed chose not to answer this directly. Jess sensed the question embarrassed her.

'It was a month or so before Ronnie died,' she said at last, staring past Jess towards the blank wall opposite.

'Ten years ago?'

Mrs Gotobed's thin cheeks flushed. 'We'd drifted apart, like you do. He married very young and it didn't work out and after that, we saw less and less of him.

'That last time I ran into him, it was coming up to Christmas and my friend said to me, "Come on, Joy, you need a break. Let's go and take in the shops. We don't have to buy anything, just look." I didn't really like going off and leaving Ronnie for more than an hour. He was very ill by then. But an old mate of his said he'd come and sit in with him. Ronnie liked that idea so off I went with my friend. We were walking down Oxford Street when who should I see coming straight towards us but Marvin. He was older, of course, and he'd put on a bit of weight and was dressed very smart, but it was Marvin all right.

'I called out to him, "Marvin! It's me, Auntie Joy." He looked as though you could have knocked him down with a feather. But he was very polite and asked after Uncle Ronnie. I told him, Ronnie wasn't too well. I didn't want to worry him with telling him just how bad it was. He said he was sorry to hear that. His name wasn't Marvin any more; it was Lucas, Lucas Burton. Well, I was the one who was surprised at that! I just said, well, that was very nice. What else could I say? He did look as though he'd done well for himself.

He was always full of ideas, ideas for making money, that is. But he was a bright boy, did well at school. I introduced my friend. We chatted a bit about the crowds and the Christmas lights in the streets. Then he took out his wallet and gave me fifty pounds. "You and your friend go and have yourselves a nice lunch," he said. He was sorry he couldn't come with us but he'd arranged to meet someone. So, off he went, and my friend and I went and had the lunch. I told Ronnie, when I got back, I'd seen Marvin and he was looking as though things were going all right for him. Ronnie was pleased, I think. Although, to be honest with you, by then Ronnie had sort of lost interest in everything.'

'Yes,' Jess said awkwardly, 'your nephew did do well.'

What could she say to this woman? Joy Gotobed née Crapper had worked hard all her life for little reward. It had been no picnic. She knew it was no use complaining about one's lot and so she didn't complain. Now, late in life, it looked as though she might be sole heir to a fortune. Did she have any idea how much nephew Marvin had been worth when he died? Probably not. Reggie Foscott would wait until he'd established her credentials before he gave her any idea. But if there really was no one else, then Joy Gotobed was now a very rich woman. What would she do with the money? It was too late to share her good fortune with Ronnie. It was hard to imagine her going on a world cruise or even going back to Oxford Street to buy in the shops, not merely to look. A habit of thrift would be built into her system.

Nor was she young. When she died, who then would inherit? She had no children.

Lucas Burton! Jess mentally addressed the dead man. This woman and her husband brought you up. They gave you a home when your feckless mother couldn't. She and her husband considered you their son. You couldn't even keep in touch. When you met her by chance you gave her fifty quid. *Fifty pounds!* You'd have spent more than that on a pair of shoes! You originally left your entire estate to your divorced wife and never mentioned to Foscott you had anyone else. You wiped them from your memory bank. You knew how poor they were. Couldn't you have done something for her and for your Uncle Ronnie during all those years? What was the *use* of all that damn money, Lucas? Some one should have reminded you: you can't take it with you.

'Got it!' said Phil Morton with satisfaction, putting down the phone. 'It's a private despository company. You know, the sort of place that will store anything you like for a price: your personal documents, your antiques, stuff you haven't got room for at home. They don't ask questions. There's plenty of stuff stored in those warehouses that the owners don't want anyone to know they've got. That's why whenever there's a break-in at one of them – as does happen from time to time although their security is pretty tight – you can't find out exactly what's missing. No one will tell you!'

Nor was it easy, as it turned out, to get access to Andrew Ferris's locked container, even brandishing a search warrant. The manager, a plump, worried-looking individual with a receding hairline who could have been any age from thirty to fifty, was clearly rendered even more unhappy by a visit from the police.

'We don't question clients as to precisely what they choose to deposit here, Inspector, that's not our business . . .' the manager said, gazing at Jess's warrant with something like horror. 'We only insist that there are no dangerous substances, flammable, explosive, a threat to our staff's health . . . We get them to sign a declaration to that effect. Health and Safety regulations are very strict these days. But we can't ask them what's *in* the boxes. Discretion, that's what they pay for, that and security. They trust us. Where would our business be without trust?'

'Do you know what my business is?' Jess retorted. 'Right now, it's murder.'

So they got access to it at last, and there, in an old black japanned box, they found it all: Eva's lipstick, her mobile, Burton's mobile, his little black address book . . . the lot. In a separate plastic rubbish sack they even found Jess's backpack with her mobile phone and her ID tossed in with the rest.

'Told you he was a collector,' said Morton smugly.

'If you ask me,' returned Jess, flourishing the address book, 'he was a potential blackmailer!'

Chapter 19

'I am glad you have arrested him,' said Milada.

Still basking in the rare light of Milada's approval, Phil Morton had been emboldened to ask her out. Suspecting that taking her to a pub would be too much of a busman's holiday for her, and also that she'd probably like to go out of the immediate area, he'd taken her to a flat race meeting at Bath. Milada had unexpectedly proved to have a keen eye for a winner.

'There, look!' She laid out the twenty-pound notes in a neat row before him. 'Now we can go somewhere and have a proper meal!'

Morton decided to overlook the implication that without Milada's winnings, he'd have taken her to the nearest pizza palace. 'We're going for a proper meal, anyway,' he said firmly. 'And put your winnings away. It's my treat.'

'You lost all your money,' Milada pointed out. 'No, no, we spend mine.'

The argument had been postponed. The bill hadn't yet arrived and they were still sitting at the table in the restaurant Milada had picked out. It was, Morton had realised with sinking heart as soon as they went in, an expensive one. But he'd asked her out and, call him old fashioned, he would pick up the bill.

'I think,' said Milada now, selecting one of the peppermint creams that had accompanied their coffee, 'I shall look for a new job.'

'Here in England, I hope,' said Morton. 'You're not going back home already?'

'No, I came for one year, maybe two. I stay. But I don't like it now at the Foot to the Ground. Mr Westcott grumbles because he says Eva's death was bad publicity. Photographers come and take pictures. It takes the business . . .' Milada took a deep breath and produced the new word in her vocabulary. 'Downmarket!'

'Business will pick up,' said Morton. 'Westcott needn't worry. No publicity is bad publicity, they say.'

'I don't stay, anyway. Mr Westcott is going to hire a waitress to replace Eva and she will share our room, the one Eva and I shared. Sharing with Eva was OK, but perhaps I don't get on well with a new girl. He hasn't got one yet,' she added, 'because of the bad publicity. No one wants to come.'

'If you go, he'll really be left in the lurch,' Morton pointed out. 'He won't have anyone.'

'Oh, I wait until he has a new girl working there. Then I shall go. David Jones, he's gone already.'

'He has?' Morton was startled.

'He has gone to Canada,' said Milada, selecting another chocolate.

'Blimey.'

'He will come back for trial. He is a witness, yes? He has uncle there, in Canada. He will study at Canadian university, perhaps. Not medicine, no, he's interested in archaeology now.' She shook her head. 'He is a strange one, that one. Eva didn't like him much.'

'You met Eva's parents, when they came over?' Morton asked.

'Oh, yes, they collected all her things. They wanted to talk to me about her. They asked if she was happy in England. They wanted to know how she met that man Ferris and why she liked him enough to go out with him. But I couldn't tell them about her, not much anyway. She never said anything to me and I didn't ask her. We only worked together.'

It seemed to Morton a sad little epitaph on a young life.

'I come down here,' said Eli, 'to see how you're managing, now you lost part of your stable block.'

He stood foursquare in front of the ruins of the former tack room and office and now shook his head dolefully.

'I'm having a bit of trouble with the insurance company,' admitted Penny. 'But I do hope they'll pay up. At the moment I can keep the horses in the field you so kindly let me use. But that means I'm not really offering proper livery services. Somehow or other, I'll have to get the money together to reconstruct the loose boxes that burned down.'

Eli rubbed his chin and surveyed the scene further. The acrid smell of charred wood still pervaded the air. Surprisingly, only half the row of loose boxes had been lost and the row on the other side of the yard hadn't been touched. But it was a desolate scene of blackened planks and puddles of water, a fine powdering of ash over everything.

'Puts people off,' said Penny sadly. 'They think their animals aren't safe here with me. A couple of owners are talking of taking their horses elsewhere.'

'What you need,' said Eli in a slow, deliberate way, with a cautious sideways glance at her, 'is proper brick-built stabling, and one of them all-weather exercise surfaces, cinders or the like. Maybe even put a roof over it, no sides, just a roof to keep the water off folk on a rainy day.'

Penny looked at him in surprise. 'My, you have thought it out, Eli.'

Eli reddened. 'Townies, they don't care for getting wet. A nice yard would bring folk in. They'd pay more, too.'

'Can't afford it, even if the insurance people pay up,' Penny told him briskly, after a momentary daydream of a splendid all-brick stable block with a cinder exercise yard, rows of happy horses poking their noses over their brand-new doors and even happier owners begging her to take in their animals; or ambitious parents bringing their offspring for riding lessons. 'The insurance will only replace like for like. To build in brick I'd have to find the extra money myself. Forget the cinder surface.'

Eli cleared his throat and rubbed his chin even more vigorously, his fingers rasping on the stubble of whiskers.

'I've been thinking,' he said. 'I got a lot of land. Government people keep coming down and snooping. I'm getting on. I'll have to get rid of some of it. Oh, I don't want to sell it *all*. I don't fancy seeing it disappear under a lot of them little brick boxes they call houses nowadays. But it's a lot to be thinking about and worrying over. So I'm minded to sell some of it. But then I'll need to invest the money I get for it in something else.'

More clearing of his throat and rubbing of his chin. 'I always liked horses. You got a nice little business here but what you need is capital. I got capital, or I will have when the land's sold. I've got a little bit now, put by. I'm not talking of taking over your little business and running it. You'd still do that. Do whatever you'd want. But I'd invest in it.' Eli paused and ventured a look at Penny. 'What do you think of that?'

Penny, rendered almost speechless, managed to gasp, 'Think? Eli, it would be wonderful!'

'Ah!' Eli brightened and his embarrassment faded, now that his suggestion hadn't been rejected. 'We'd see a lawyer feller and get it all done legal. So that when I drop off the twig, you get my share of the business. Me being a lot older than you,' he added in explanation.

'Haven't you got any other heirs, Eli?'

'No,' said Eli, 'unless you count my daft cousin Walter that lives down Newnham way, and he's not likely to outlive me. He's eighty-five already. There would be plenty of grazing left for the new business. You could keep that old one-eyed horse of yours out to grass for as long as you wanted. We – I mean you and me, if we were partners in the business – we could buy a couple of nice riding ponies, build up that side of it. I know a feller deals in horses.'

343

'Oh, Eli!' Penny flung her arms round him, or as far round his substantial girth as they would go. 'You're *wonderful!*'

Puce in the face, Eli mumbled for a moment or two and shuffled his feet. 'I'm getting fed up with the scrap business, anyway,' he said. 'Especially since another government feller came down the other day and began poking his nose into *that*! Wanted to see my receipts. I got them, mind, I keep them all in an old shoebox. I give that to him, after I tipped the cat out. She likes to sleep in it. He sat there all day sorting them out and muttering, "You need to keep proper accounts, Mr Smith." "Whaffor?" I asked him. "Anyway, I never took to schooling. I can't write and can't read. So how am I going to do it? You tell me." That shut him up. He got in his little car and drove off. Reckon he took a flea or two with him, out of that shoebox. The cat's got a few. I noticed the other day.

'I'm a countryman,' concluded Eli, 'I always was, always will be. Horses would suit me.'

'The arrangement would suit me fine, too, Eli,' Penny said.

'Right, then,' Eli declared, now it was settled. 'I'll tell them.'

'Tell the Inland Revenue?'

'What?' asked Eli, 'Oh, see what you mean, I'll tell them as well, I suppose. I was thinking of— just thinking.'

That evening Eli explained his new business project to his family. It was the first time they'd gathered since the recent anniversary. Somehow they'd got wind of the proposed changes to his life and sat waiting to hear about it. He couldn't keep anything from them.

'I'm going into the stabling business,' he announced. 'Livery and hiring out horses for townspeople to ride.'

His father looked even more disapproving than usual. But the old bugger never did like any new idea suggested by either of his sons.

'I know it's not farming,' said Eli defiantly, 'but I'm getting older, you know, and farming's changed.'

He *was* getting older and one day he'd be joining them. There was a thought: stuck with them all for eternity. Well, he was stuck with them anyway. But tonight there was an addition to their table company. As Eli had suspected she would, the girl he'd found in his cowshed had turned up, just like that. She'd pushed herself in between him and his brother in a way, thought Eli, that smacked of bad manners and want of tact.

The cat was skulking outside in the woodshed where she always went to hide. Eli was pretty sure that even after they'd all left, old Tibs would know a stranger had been there. He'd been bracing himself for the girl's appearance. But now she had arrived, you couldn't deny it presented something of a problem. He particularly didn't like her sitting so close.

His father didn't know what to make of her. He sat scowling away at the head of the table. His mother, oh my, she didn't care for the development at all. She sat glowering at the newcomer and hadn't shown much interest in Eli's future plans at all, not even enough to look disapproving of them. Even Nathan looked discomfited at finding the girl sitting next to him. His eyes were nearly popping out of his head.

He'd stopped fiddling with that silly rope halter and taken to smoothing back his hair instead.

As for the girl, she took no notice of any of them, ignored Nathan's patting of his hair, didn't seem to be listening to Eli talk about the stables. She just sat there, looking down her nose as if the kitchen wasn't good enough for her, not fancy enough, probably.

Her disdain annoyed Eli even more. The cause was probably that wallpaper with Chianti bottles on it. The snooty little madam didn't like that. Well, she'd have to learn to live with it. No, wait a bit, wrong word. She'd have to learn to be dead with it. If she thought herself a cut above them all, too bad. She'd chosen to turn up. He hadn't asked her along. Uninvited, that's what she was, even if not unexpected.

'You'll have to budge up a bit, Nat,' he said loudly to his brother, jerking his head meaningfully at the new arrival. 'It's getting very crowded in here.'